THE NEW ABJECT

First published in Great Britain in 2020 by Comma Press.

www.commapress.co.uk

A CIP catalogue record of this book is available from the British Library.

ISBN: 1905583591
ISBN-13: 9781905583591

The publisher gratefully acknowledges assistance from the Arts Council England.

Supported using public funding by
**ARTS COUNCIL
ENGLAND**

Printed and bound in Great Britain by Clays Ltd, Elcograf S.p.A.

The New Abject

Tales of Modern Unease

EDITED BY SARAH EYRE & RA PAGE

Contents

CONTENTS

Introduction

ALL OF US HAVE had bad dreams during the pandemic. One of mine takes place several years from now, when the world has finally recovered. For some reason I'm rooting through a box of old clutter when I come across one of my face masks from the dark times. It wasn't the most comfortable mask I owned, nor the safest, but it was the one I wore most often – dark burgundy, stylishly contoured, with an imposing black side-vent. It made me look badass, or so I thought, like a Hong Kong protestor back when face-coverings were still exotic. However cool I thought it looked at the time, though, in the dream the old mask horrifies me, like finding a dried umbilical cord in one of my mother's scrapbooks of pressed flowers. Stiff, lifeless, alien, its very appearance is a betrayal of the trust I once placed in it, wearing it so often that I forgot I had it on; so habitually that, for those people outside of my bubble who saw me, it was effectively my face.

The horror, disgust or recoil we experience when we are faced with what we have shed, let go, expelled, sloughed off – that is the fear of the abject. The philosopher Julia Kristeva developed a psychoanalytic theory to explain this revulsion in her book *Powers of Horror* (1980). She argued that the boundary between the self (I, the subject) and its environment (objects, things and other people) isn't always a cleanly defined border, that it can be disrupted by encounters with anything that was once part of us but has since been disowned, cast off or jettisoned. Encountering such abject objects horrifies us because, according to Kristeva, it reminds us of the much more seismic separation that took place at birth and in early childhood: the separation of the 'self' from the m/other. Experiences of abjection contain traces of this early traumatic separation – that of being ripped from a continuum, from a unity with the other, from that first 'home' from which we are permanently evicted.

Kristeva offers a scattered list of examples for the kinds of things which constitute the abject as we experience them in everyday life, those disgust-inducing 'border objects' which trouble the distinction between self and other. It is a list we can easily elaborate on: shed skin, cut or malted hair, nail clippings, faeces, urine, breast milk, menstrual blood, lost teeth, amniotic fluid, afterbirth, severed limbs, etc. All fairly gross and fairly straightforward. These were once in us, living parts of us, but we discarded them, and their reappearance repels us because it troubles the integrity of the self. Kristeva has a special place set aside in her own personal hell for milk, in particular the skin of milk, its separation into cream and the start of its decay – milk presumably being a stand-in for breast milk and infant feeding, a reminder of prior maternal dependency. The abject horrifies us not because of what it signifies but because of what it is. Kristeva uses the example of a wound compared to a flat-lining encephalogram to illustrate this point: a flat-lining ECG signifies death; a wound, cutting through the skin envelope of the self, puts us in the presence of death, slap bang in the theatre of it.[1] It disrupts the clean border between us and not-us, both reminding us of the 'great separation' and confronting us with our own ongoing and inescapable materiality. This lifeless, drying-up piece of scab – this was us. This is us.

Kristeva's development of this theory of the abject is perhaps restricted by its origins in psychoanalytic theory; in this field, there is limited space for cultural, historical, socio-economic or political considerations; everything is contained within the drama of personal psychological development; everything is traced back to the infant and its immediate relations. But there is another reading of the abject, a social abject to counterweight Kristeva's psychological rendering. Social abjection – as written about much earlier by the philosopher Georges Bataille in his essay 'Abjection and Miserable Forms' (1934) – comprises of such things or 'others' that the body politic casts off, rather than what the individual body does: things and people that society expels. Examples here range from obvious enemies of the state and social order, like traitors, spies, and criminals, through to those whose difference is felt (or constructed for political ends) as a threat to the integrity or identity of the body politic: social and political scapegoats or demographics collectively imagined as disgusting or abhorrent. To use the social theorist Imogen Tyler's words, abjection in Bataille's reading is 'the imperative force of sovereignty, a founding exclusion which constitutes a part of the population as moral outcasts: "represented from the outside with disgust as the dregs of the people, populace and gutter"'.[2]

Tyler's recent re-evaluation of this social abject in her book *Revolting Subjects* (2013), provides a persuasive occasion for putting this anthology together. Thanks to her work, we are now able to talk about what disgusts us, abjectly, across both the realms – the psychological and the social – and to examine how the pre-history of the self is entangled with the histories and practices of the body politic. It was with this dual understanding of abjection in place that Comma, in late 2019, set about inviting authors to respond to the abject with short stories that would explore new examples of it – much as we had with a previous anthology, *The New Uncanny*, updating Freud's own drop-down menu of irrational fears. Again, we had a suspicion that our current historical moment had new manifestations of the theory to offer. And we weren't disappointed.

The first six stories collected here – by Bernardine Bishop, Christine Poulson, Gaia Holmes, Lara Williams, Meave Haughey and Margaret Drabble – all ostensibly explore the corporeal, intimate abject that Kristeva alerted us to. We encounter excrement, teeth, hair, menstrual blood, picked-off moles, amniotic fluid, urine and nail clippings, with conflicting states of disgust, horror, fascination, occasional relish and even empowerment. Saleem Haddad's 'An Enfleshment of Desire' transitions us into a broader reading, intertwining both the intimate and public politics of abjection and desire, and reversing the direction of the subject/object boundary-blurring with an insertion, rather than an ejection. Matthew Holness, Sarah Schofield, Adam Marek and Karen Featherstone all offer stories that flip perspectives on the 'great separation', exploring the rejection, disconnection or abandonment of the child from the parent or society's point of view. Gerard Woodward considers social abjection in the light of a perceived invasion from outsiders, whilst Paul Theroux focuses on the materiality of the abject, in particular sex in the age of mail-order brides. Mike Nelson and Alan Beard dig deeper into this materiality and what happens when we become so separated from other people that we have only physical objects – random belongings, furniture or the walls around us – to relate to. Mark Haddon and Ramsey Campbell explore the abjection of one's own past from one's present, while David Constantine and Lucie McKnight Hardy consider the abjection of whole categories of people – refugees and the 'underclass' – in present day and future Britain, respectively.

Throughout these stories, there is an attempt to expand and complicate the often very singular (self- or ego-oriented) perspective on the abject provided by purely psychoanalytic readings. Instead the authors examine it from multiple perspectives: from the points of view of mothers, maternal subjects, women, queer subjects, working-class masculinity, class disgust and bourgeois revulsion. The presence or absence of mothers (or of mothering tendencies or connection) is often a recurring theme. In certain moments, such as in Karen Featherstone's and Ramsey Campbell's stories, the image of a neglected infant hints at how our (social) disgust for poverty takes root in the most intimate image, before propagating into a disgust for all those around it. To quote Bataille: 'Filth, snot and vermin are enough to render an infant vile. His personal nature is not responsible for it, only the negligence or helplessness of those raising him.'[3] Instead of soliciting simple sympathy, these images of extreme vulnerability somehow elicit a mix of physical disgust and moral outrage.

Some of the stories here were commissioned and written before the pandemic struck, some after, and one (Bernardine Bishop's) was written separately, years earlier, though never published. Many of those written pre-COVID, like McKnight Hardy's 'Wretched' or Constantine's 'Out of Blue', felt imbued with a sense that things in British life were already falling apart. In a post-truth, post-Brexit context, our mechanisms for maintaining social fabric and interaction – the value of evidence over opinion, the ability to encounter difference and dissent without being triggered – all seemed to be slipping through our grasp. We were already morbidly disconnected from others, siloed in our echo-chambers, addicted to the hollow, self-selected approval of our online bubbles, and unable to see the othering implicit in our own likes and smiley faces. Then, at a point where we couldn't be much weaker – by which I mean, when we couldn't have been more divided and isolated – we were hit again.

The virus arrived – like something only horror films had prepared us for – appearing to herald the final act in this nightmare of disconnection. Borders are now closed, walls appear to have been a good idea all along, economic isolationism seems a done deal. At a personal level, we find ourselves bricking up the last window in the cell we've built for ourselves, socially distancing from precisely those loved ones who could help us most (and who need us most): our parents and grandparents. As for that original 'other' we were so violently separated from in early childhood – our mothers – we can't even hold their hands anymore. If abjection has an endgame, this feels like it.

Our first responsibility to this double-blow, surely, is to acknowledge the horror. History shows we're all too capable, as a species, of completely ignoring atrocity when it happens, of closing ourselves off and pretending it's not there. The better reaction, surely, is to face it, to let it get to us. To scream.

There is another side to this horror, it should be noted. In psychoanalytic theory there always is: a flip side, a diametrically opposed twin. Kristeva's work owes much to that of Jacques Lacan's, and underpinning the horror of abjection is its subconscious opposite – not a desire exactly, but a generic blueprint for all desires, what Lacan called *objet petit a*. In short, this is a tiny remnant of the object that the subject once separated from, lying dormant in the subject (us), as a trace or outline of what we now lack and require to be whole again; an outline-absence into which all objects of our desire must fit (the 'a' stands for autre, the French for 'other').

Imagine the first time you watch Hitchcock's *Vertigo* you tune in halfway through, missing all the stuff about Madeleine Elster and how she thinks she's haunted by the ghost of

Carlotta Valdes, and her inevitable plummet from the tower. Instead you join the film just as Jimmy Stewart's character, Scottie, starts to follow a complete stranger on the street, a woman who turns out to be called Judy Barton. Over the next few scenes, Scottie offers an object lesson in the *objet petit a,* persuading Judy to dress like his pre-existing idea of perfection (Madeleine), even getting her to change her hair colour to fit the mould. In this truncated version of *Vertigo,* we, the audience, feel revulsion at the way Scottie butchers this woman's identity to meet his own design. That revulsion is an abject horror, a recognition of something in us all that's able to reduce what we desire into pure materiality: a grey suit, blonde hair, etc. However, what Scottie feels is the opposite of revulsion: love, the actualisation of his desire-blueprint, *objet petit a*.

Georges Bataille, talking about the social abject, argued something similar. As a society, we may be revolted by transgressors and outsiders, but secretly and subconsciously we collectively desire the other. In Bataille's thinking, taboo and transgression go hand-in-hand; one feeds off the other, is defined by it, and cannot exist apart from it. Taboos are what keep our behaviour in check, so by being dependent on them, we are dependent on the things that trigger them: transgression. This co-dependency, according to Bataille, amounts to a subconscious desire for that which revolts us.

Whether or not you buy into Kristeva's abject school of psychoanalysis, or Tyler and Bataille's sociological configuration of abjection, the fact is we do, as humans, have a damaging predilection for othering (and implicitly exoticising) anything or anyone that differs from us, even anything that is simply not us. These theories, and the stories written here in response to abjection, offer thought experiments for understanding how and why our egos are so injured by difference that, when we encounter it, we develop disgust-impulses towards it. Perhaps they also offer insight into why, with our increased isolation and retreat into online bubbles over recent years, our trigger-threshold for these impulses has been so drastically lowered. According to Bataille, writing in the 1930s under the spectre of rising fascism across Europe, society tends to adopt one of two approaches to the other: it either rejects it – expels, dismisses, or eradicates it (as the fascists did) – or it neutralises and then assimilates it. A political example of the latter might be Martin Luther King Jr. Only after his assassination did he start to be exalted within US society, and only then after being stripped of everything that was radical about him. Bataille, Tyler, intelligent horror writing generally, and these stories specifically, all argue for alternative ways of approaching the other: not to reject it, and not to neutralise it either, but to face it, as squarely and unflinchingly as we can. That is to say, ultimately, to get over it. As Margaret Drabble's narrator concludes, 'We are all disgusting, it's just that we have different ways of expressing it.'

Ra Page
Manchester, September 2020

Notes

1. *Powers of Horror: An Essay on Abjection* by Julia Kristeva, translated by Leon S. Roudiez (Columbia University Press, 1982), p3.
2. *Revolting Subjects: Social Abjection and Resistance in Neoliberal Britain*, by Imogen Tyler (Zed Books, 2013), p19.
3. 'Abjection and Miserable Forms' by Georges Bataille (1993 [1934]) in *More & Less 2*, edited by Sylvere Lotringer, translated by Y. Shafir, Los Angeles, CA: Semiotext(e), p10.

Stool

Bernardine Bishop

Two women, in houses half a mile from each other, were beginning a day. It was a Spring day, which each of them noticed with a lifted heart.

Joan was particularly glad, for it was the day of which she had hoped to dedicate the morning to a neighbour's window boxes. Joan had bumped into this neighbour, and the customary chat had revealed that the neighbour was too busy this year to do her front window boxes and tubs. Joan gladly offered to do them for her. Pleased and relieved, the neighbour volunteered to have a delivery from the garden centre ready for Joan. The delivery was to be ready for today, stacked, or preferably laid out, in front of the house.

The neighbour was pleased and relieved by Joan's offer, and, indeed, was already wondering what to leave on Joan's doorstep in a day or two as sufficient mark of gratitude; but she was not surprised. Joan was retired and active, and did things for people. It was usual to meet her with at least two dogs on leashes, dogs she was walking for neighbours too elderly to walk their own. She would otherwise be seen coming out of her house with a covered dish, soup for the lunch of someone no one else in the neighbourhood had yet realised was laid up. She could give excellent advice to those hesitating about going in for cabbages

1

and potatoes in their garden, and would happily take them through her own house to look at her vegetable area, the lettuces surrounded by broken eggshells rather than by Slugdeath. She was smiling, weather-beaten, busy and reliable. Sometimes on a day of desperation, a young mother might bethink herself of Joan as someone who might possibly be free to collect her child from school, and mind it for an hour. If she could, Joan would manage to be free. The front of her own house, although it was early, was already a cultivated riot of Spring flowers. It was the sort of front garden that even hurrying people stop for a moment to stare at, arrested by beauty, and, perhaps, memories. From her front window, if she was in, Joan watched them staring, and sometimes waved.

Hazel did not pass Joan's house on her way to the tube, so had not yet seen the new and burgeoning display. She knew Joan, of course, as everyone did. When Hazel had her operation, two years ago now, she had not wanted the neighbourhood to know about it. Word travels fast, and far. If Joan had got wind of it, the operation would have been outed indeed. The friends who brought soup to Hazel, and there were plenty, were not neighbours. Because she worked on TV, Hazel was slightly well known, though probably not as much so as she believed she was; and the notion of people thinking about her colostomy while she demonstrated how to recognise Chippendale filled her with horror. From her own point of view, she had accepted and come to terms with her colostomy, for what else can a sensible person do? She saw the stoma nurse every three months, and they discussed the stoma's state of health, and what to do about its frequent constipation. Now that she had the stoma, Hazel never thought of herself being constipated. It was the stoma. Her body did not belong to herself in the old way. But she made the best of the new situation, as she must, and had forged routines that minimised time and trouble. She had quickly gone back to full-time work, and this helped her to feel normal. She did not feel normal, and never would; but other people's view of her as normal distracted and comforted her. So she walked briskly to the tube, carrying her briefcase, pleased by the coming of Spring.

In the tube, Hazel was unaware that the day which had promised so well had clouded over, and when she got to her destination, distracted by the small piece of work she had been able to do on her journey, she did not even remember that the morning had started fine. For Joan it was different. The sun still shone while she inspected the plants that had been duly delivered, and disentangled them from each other. It was sunny while she delved into last year's soil and made decisions about what was dead and what deserved another chance. She had a large window box and two tubs to fill. She had brought gloves, a trowel, a fork, and secateurs. This was an activity she loved. Before the sunshine disappeared, flowery contents for one of the tubs had already begun to take shape. Some plants were in bud and gave no clue as to what their colours might be, and Joan always enjoyed leaving it to chance when this occurred, and it was sometimes chance that made for especial beauty.

Without the sun, it became startlingly cold, which Joan did not mind. She worked on. She did not even mind too much when a shower began. She stood in the small porch, flattening herself against the front door, holding a trowel, knowing the rain would blow over, and thinking that early May was really only late April. What she did mind was that she wanted a loo. She knew people in some of these houses, but not well enough to make that particular request. That request would have required a certain humour and perhaps sophistication that Joan did not have, even if everybody was not likely to be out at work. In the end, she was forced to walk back to her own house earlier than she had expected to. The job would now take a couple more mornings. Joan always cleared up after herself, which took time; and when she was finished, green sacks of garden rubbish would be lined up neatly in the front of the house.

When she arrived home, she hurried to the loo, then returned to the front hall to take off and hang her coat – not too wet. The rain had stopped already, and the sun was out again. She rubbed her short hair with a towel hanging for the purpose on the pegs. Perhaps it was because the towelling process kept her standing by the front door that she took particular note of her row of keys, keys of local houses to which she had ingress in her various capacities. One or two were long disused, and in one case the key's owner was dead. The key that took Joan's attention at this minute was one labelled 'Leopold.' That was a key she must belatedly return. She remembered the house it belonged to. A speculative expression, mixed with a touch of boldness, came into Joan's eyes.

The next day was another very ordinary day for Hazel. She went to work and came home, arriving at about six o'clock, with nothing special to do in the evening. She had some work to finish and some phone calls to make, but there was nothing to look forward to. She listened to her uninteresting messages, took her shoes off, and made herself a cup of tea. She drank it staring out of the kitchen window, experiencing the disappointment of her life. She had not wanted, nor expected, to be alone and childless at fifty. She had certainly not expected a colostomy.

Her small and pretty house, one of a row of Victorian cottages, had been a joy to her at one time. It was a good size and shape for one person, but it would also fit two. Most of the houses in her short street did fit two. But in hers there were not two. She stared out of the window at the Spring evening, full, for some, and certainly for the birds, of hope and promise. Perhaps she had better not get another cat, because of the birds. In the back of her mind she was wondering what to have for supper.

She finished her tea, sighed, and went for a pee. She did not pee. In the toilet bowl there was a turd.

Hazel had not seen a turd in a toilet bowl for two years. First she stared at it, then she turned back and put the light on, then she stepped forward and stared again. Staring did not make the turd go away. The fact that it could not be there did not make it not be there. It lay, partly submerged, absolutely still, utterly anonymous, as solid and undeniable as herself.

She was terrified, as if by a nightmare. Her mind ran in all directions, looking for an explanation. She collected herself as best she could, and sat on the edge of the bath to think. She was not alarmed at the thought that someone had entered her house in her absence. She desperately hoped that someone had. That would render the turd ordinary, innocent, a thing of the known world. She racked her brain for whose it could be. It was not the cleaner's day. However, her hands clammy and trembling, she telephoned the cleaner.

'Rhona,' she cried in a jolly voice, 'I'm sorry to trouble you, but I just wonder if you popped in today instead of Friday. Everything looks so nice and clean.' She forgot to announce herself, but Rhona knew who it was.

'Hazel? No, I did not come today. I will be coming on Friday as usual.' A baby could be heard in the background.

'I just wondered whether, for any reason...'

'No, I was far away all day in Hackney. It's my day for Hackney. Is anything wrong?'

'No, not at all. Thank you. Goodbye.'

Rhona turned to her husband. 'Funny woman,' she said. Her husband did not ask who or why, concentrating as he was on spooning food into a cheerful little face.

Hazel's next thought was the plumber, who was due to come in to do a few jobs, including, indeed, the cistern of the loo. She did not think she had ever given him a key. Yet she might have. Perhaps he popped in to look at the jobs and was taken short. She telephoned him. 'Just wonder if you popped in today to case the joint,' she said.

'Case the joint?'

Her attempt at humour had failed. She was white, and her hands were trembling. 'I just mean – well, you said you could manage to come soon, and I just wondered if you had come in today.'

'No. I haven't got a key. Remember, we said Monday, and that you'd be in.'

'Oh yes, I remember.' Now Hazel was afraid the plumber thought she suspected him of something untoward. 'Sorry, see you on Monday.'

Hazel continued to sit on the edge of the bath, now swaying backwards and forwards as she tried to devise an explanation. A terrifying fantasy was in her mind. She was afraid the turd was her own, that in some involuntary way, perhaps whilst peeing, she had delivered it. The old routes of her digestive system might stealthily have re-established themselves. What would that mean? Her understanding was that her rectum had been removed and the gut that led to it had been forced by surgery to emerge beside her navel. So there was no possibility that faeces could make their way down to her disused anus. But what if something had gone terribly wrong, and her body, homesick for its old ways, had insisted on re-establishing the known direction by a newly made path?

She stood, shaky and shuddering, and made her way to the computer. She brought up a map of the digestive tract, and studied it, her heart pounding, her mouth dry. She saw the colon, and assessed at what point in her case it ceased to exist, and, instead, broke surface on her abdomen. Without the gut, there was no way down. Therefore the turd could not be hers. But what if it was? She had not managed to establish another possibility. What if, like a cat knowing its way home, like snails performing feats to get back to the garden where they were born, her body had nostalgically rebuilt a thoroughfare? But surely, trying to calm herself, such a phenomenon would have showed up on her last scan. But her last scan was six months ago now.

Hazel was gripped by the horror of mystery. However, she flushed the toilet at last, and for a moment that was soothing. The destruction of the evidence made her able to feel that perhaps the turd had been a hallucination. She knew it had not. It was gone, but it had been there.

There was no supper and no sleep for Hazel, and she did not go to work in the morning. Instead, she managed to secure an emergency appointment with the GP.

It was a doctor she knew quite well. With cancer, you get to know all the doctors in the practice. Her lips twisting with fear as she spoke, she told him the story. 'Has another channel opened up, do you think, in my insides? And of course it won't work properly...Will I get peritonitis as faeces leaks out of cracks in its walls into my bloodstream?'

The doctor examined her. He was not persuaded by her fantasy, but hoped to reassure her. However, for her, the fact that he chose to do an examination lent her terrors added reality. 'I really don't think...' he said. She craved something more definite than that. She didn't like to hear him say, 'I'm just looking up when your next scan is due.' He was puzzled, as Hazel was, by the fact that the stool could not obviously be anyone else's, as far as was known. But his medical mind refused the inference that the stool could be hers. His private opinion was that she had entertained a guest she had forgotten, though it did seem rather odd. He wondered if she was a drinker.

Hazel went home, her nightmare contained but not comforted. It was lunch time. She should go in to work in the afternoon.

Joan returned to the garden that morning, but had more or less finished the day before. She only had to bag up, put the finishing touches, and stand back to admire. It was irresistibly lovely, and passers-by made it clear they thought so too. She made use again of her serendipitous key, in a house five doors up, and then returned to admire, twiddle and tweak. She watered. It was hard to tear herself away. But she put her gloves and garden implements in her nice sacking bag, and was ready to go.

Before she went, she must return the key to its owner. She wondered why Hazel had never called the key in. Most people did. Perhaps it was because Leopold's disappearance had been such a wrench, and Hazel could not bear to do anything that made it final. And then time had passed, and no doubt she had forgotten Joan that had a key, forgotten it as much as Joan herself had, though the key was hanging by the front pegs in Joan's house. Joan had heard about some kittens recently, and wondered whether to let Hazel know that they were on offer. Perhaps Hazel already had another cat, and a nearer neighbour was now the occasional minder.

Leaving that question, Joan dropped the key through the letterbox of Hazel's house, and heard the reassuring tick as it landed on the doormat. She did not leave a note for Hazel, although she felt she should, because of the obscure sense of guilt and shame about the use to which she had put the key. She let the key be anonymous, and set off home.

Hazel opened the door of her house. The post had come, and she had to shove a bit to get the door open. She automatically stooped to pick up the envelopes, although, in spite of the doctor, her mind was still working and her heart racing. Then, on top of the letters, she saw a key. She picked it up. Breathless with hope, she opened her purse to compare it with her own. She looked at the key, turning it this way and that. She tried it in the lock. She smiled, and there were tears in her eyes. She had no idea who the key came from, but she knew she was back in the ordinary world.

Teeth and Hair

Christine Poulson

NELL WOKE UP WITH a start. She could hear someone talking.

It was the first time she had been left in charge overnight. She and Polly were alone in the house. So what was Nell hearing? Polly didn't have a TV in her room and she wasn't allowed a mobile phone. She did have an iPad, but it stayed downstairs at night. Matthew, Polly's father, was adamant about that.

Nell sat up in bed and switched her bedside light on. She squinted at her phone. It was one in the morning. She got out of bed and went quietly onto the landing. A low murmur was coming from Polly's room. She trod softly, but one of the floorboards creaked. Instantly there was silence. She knocked on Polly's door, opened it without waiting for a reply, and switched on the light.

Polly sat up in bed, blinking. She had crinkly red hair, like a girl in a Pre-Raphaelite painting, and the pale skin and pale eyelashes that go with it. Grown-up and with the right make-up, she would look stunning, but at eleven, she looked washed out, like an over-exposed photograph.

'I thought I heard voices,' Nell said.

Polly hesitated and Nell thought she was going to deny it. But: 'I was talking to Daisy.' Daisy was Polly's favourite toy, a black and white stuffed dog.

Could that be true? Maybe. Polly still liked to be bolstered in bed by a company of teddy bears, pandas, and other animals.

'It's late,' Nell said. 'You ought to be asleep.'

She tucked Polly in and went back to her own room.

It was hot up here in the eaves of the cottage. She opened the window and leaned out. The soft night air caressed her face and the scent of cut grass rose up from the garden. Fields of ripe wheat stretched away, gleaming under a full yellow moon. The cottage was on the edge of a village in Cambridgeshire. Now and then she could hear the hum of the motorway half a mile away and see the flash of an occasional headlight.

It was the summer of her first year at university, studying English. Her mother worked at the same firm of City bankers as Matthew and that was how Nell had got the job. It was very well paid – she couldn't believe how much she was getting – but she had to live in. Matthew often worked late entertaining clients, and on those evenings he stayed at his London flat.

Still, how hard could it be? she'd asked herself. Polly wouldn't need *that* much looking after. But the job was more full-on than she expected, because during term-time Polly was at boarding school, so she didn't have any friends locally. And there was Polly herself. She was a nice enough kid, polite and amenable, fell in with everything that Nell suggested – they went shopping, painted their nails, did girlie things together – but she never expressed a preference. There was something withheld about her. She wasn't at all like Nell had been at her age, throwing herself headlong into everything, tearing around the playground, giggling with her friends.

Oh well, it was only for a month. Matthew had made other plans for the rest of the holidays. One week down, three more to go.

Nell got into bed. Wide awake now, she settled down to read *The Turn of the Screw*. It was one of the set books for next term.

'Oh – hell,' Nell said, just in time managing not to say 'fuck.' 'I've lost a button.'

And it was her favourite shirt too: well, blouse really, a vintage fifties number, red with white polka dots, a tie waist, and square mother-of-pearl buttons. It had been a charity shop find. That was where Nell got most of her clothes.

It was the following morning and they'd just got back from a trip to the swimming pool in Cambridge.

'They're such nice buttons, too,' Nell lamented.

'There might be one like it in Mummy's button box,' Polly said.

Nell knew that Polly's mother had died the previous year. An accident, Matthew had told her. She didn't know the details.

'Great,' Nell said. 'Shall we have a look?'

'I'll get the key,' Polly said with the first show of animation that Nell had seen.

The key?

Nell followed Polly out of the kitchen into the hall and to the door of Matthew's study. Polly went in and came back with a key in her hand. She wasn't meeting Nell's eye.

'Is this the key to the room that's kept locked?' Nell asked.

Matthew had explained that. 'My late wife's belongings – I haven't had time to sort through them. In the meantime, I don't want Polly going in there and rummaging around. Best if she doesn't think too much about her mother.'

'Just to get the button box,' Polly pleaded. 'I don't think Daddy would mind that.'

Nell wasn't so sure. But she did need a button for her blouse...

'All right then. Just for the button box.'

The room was in an extension that had been built onto one side of the cottage. The air was hot and stale as if no-one had been in there for a long time. Dust motes hung in the light that slanted in through the windows. There was a single bed, a sewing machine, and a dressmaker's dummy. A wardrobe stretched along one wall and shelves ran up to the ceiling.

'Mummy was ever so clever,' Polly said. 'She used to make her own clothes.'

She spotted the button box on one of the shelves.

It was just a plain cardboard box, but inside were riches indeed. Nell plunged her hand in and let the buttons stream like pebbles through her fingers. Mother-of-pearl and jet, diamante and glass, buttons covered in silk or linen, humble shirt buttons, tiny little black buttons – were they boot buttons? – and big bold statement buttons. All sorts of shapes – flat ones, globes, domes, squares, oblongs – and wonderful colours: coral, emerald, cerulean blue. It was so poignant, seeing them still here when the woman who had collected them had gone.

She looked up to see Polly gazing wistfully around. Nell couldn't let her explore further, though she was curious herself. She resolved to take the first opportunity to come back and have a proper look round.

'Come on,' she said. 'We'll take these to the kitchen.'

They tipped all the buttons onto the big scrubbed pine table, sifting through them until they found one to match the button Nell had lost.

'Can I keep the box in my room?' Polly asked.

But Nell thought they had better put it back.

When they'd done that, they locked the door behind them. Nell followed Polly into Matthew's study to see that she returned the key. And, also, so that she'd know where to find it again.

As Polly closed the desk drawer, she looked at Nell and a look of complicity flashed between them.

The following day Polly had a two-hour riding lesson, giving Nell some free time. Back at the cottage, she got the key and unlocked the sewing room.

As she stepped over the threshold, she felt a frisson. She was like one of those bold girls in fairy stories: Bluebeard's wife or Goldilocks. Or perhaps it was like *Jane Eyre*... Though Matthew was – sadly – no Mr Rochester. He was fifty-ish, overweight, and a smoker too. Nell disapproved, but at least he had the decency not to smoke around Polly.

There was a door on the other side of the room. A closet? She opened it and saw a small bathroom with a shower, basin and loo, and a cupboard. She opened it and gasped. A row of heads stared at her. They were wig stands, three of them – polystyrene heads with smooth expressionless faces and blind eyes. There were two wigs, one a feathery crop, the other shoulder-length, both a blonde so pale that it was almost silver. One stand was empty, just a shiny bald head. She picked up the nearest stand and took it to the window. The strands of hair weren't all the same colour, there were subtle shifts of tone and some glinted in the light. Surely that meant it was real hair? The thought made her uncomfortable. She put the wig away and went into the sewing room.

She gazed around. She didn't even know the name of the dead woman. She opened the wardrobe door. What a lot of clothes, and such lovely clothes too. She took a dress out of the wardrobe and looked at the label – Ghost – a chiffony, floaty affair. So sad... all those clothes left behind.

The alarm went off on Nell's phone. Time to go and collect Polly from the stables. She would come back and have a proper look another day.

They cooked spaghetti bolognese that night.

Nell wasn't expected to do any real cooking. Her job was just to look after Polly. The domestic routine ran like clockwork all on its own. Twice a week a woman came in to clean and take the washing away. A gardener came for an afternoon a week. There was a dishwasher and a freezer full of ready meals. But cooking would be a nice thing to do with Polly, better than spending all their time on Netflix or playing 8 Ball Pool on their iPads.

As they chopped onions and fried mince, Nell's thoughts kept drifting back to the wigs. She wondered if Polly's mother had been ill, had lost her hair through chemotherapy. Or perhaps she had one of those diseases where your hair falls out? A girl at Nell's school had actually pulled out her own hair, it was a stress-related thing.

When Matthew came home, they ate at the kitchen table. They'd almost finished when Matthew paused in mid-sentence. He ran his tongue round his lips and put his hand to his mouth. 'A hair.' Frowning, he struggled to grasp it. He pulled and it came and came and came like a stream of handkerchiefs from a conjurer's hat. He laid it on the side of his plate and looked at the two girls.

'Not mine,' Nell said. Her hair was just as long, but it was a rich dark brown.

Polly didn't speak, but it clearly wasn't hers. Her hair was a reddish gold and kinked. The hair on the plate was straight and so blonde that it was almost silver.

Where could it have come from? Could Nell have picked it up on her clothes when she had visited the forbidden room? Could it have come from one of the wigs? Matthew didn't say anything, but she thought he looked at her strangely.

The next time Polly went riding, Nell raced back to the cottage.

She let herself into the room, went straight to the bathroom, and opened the cupboard. The faces gazed impassively at her. The hair in Matthew's food couldn't have come from either of these wigs. Neither was long enough.

The sewing room itself was clean, apart from a little dust. She didn't think she had picked up the hair here. She decided to have another look at the clothes. There were one or two labels that she recognised, but most of them seemed to be handmade. At the back of the wardrobe there was something in a protective cover. Nell took it out and unzipped it and inside was a long dress in ivory silk. A wedding dress? She slipped it off its padded hanger and held it against her face. It was cool and slippery, and so heavy. Those little pearls on the bodice must have been sewn by hand. She remembered what Polly had said and wondered if Polly's mother had made this herself. There was something strange about the sleeves. They gaped open as if they'd been slit. She looked more closely and received a little shock. The tight-fitting sleeves should have been buttoned up to the elbow. The little loops were still there, but not the buttons. They had been cut off − carelessly, leaving jagged holes in the cloth. She turned the dress over. There should have been buttons down the back from the neckline to below the waist, but those too had been ripped away. One round pearl button remained, dangling from a thread. When she touched the little opalescent globe, it came away in her hand.

She slipped it into the pocket of her jeans, slid the dress back into its sheath and put it back in the wardrobe. She looked round to see that nothing was out of place. As she locked the door behind her, she noticed something that she hadn't seen before: a bolt high up on the outside of the door.

The vast Fenland fields and the huge empty skies stretched out on either side. Nell was a city girl, born and brought up in London. Driving back from the stables, she felt exposed and

15

vulnerable, like a beetle crawling across a table-cloth. It didn't help that her period was late and she felt bloated and sluggish. And the heat was building. She opened the car window, but even the breeze was hot. It hadn't rained for weeks and they were talking about a drought.

Nell couldn't stop thinking about the ruined dress. The violence was shocking, the desecration of something so beautiful – it could never be repaired – what would make a woman do this to her own wedding dress. But perhaps it hadn't been her? Perhaps it had been Matthew? No wonder he hadn't wanted Polly to see this. Nell wished that *she* hadn't seen it. And the bolt: she could understand there being one on the inside, but why was there one on the *outside*?

They got stuck behind a farm lorry. It lumbered along the road ahead of them, its load of bales a swaying tower. Specks and stalks of chaff eddied behind it like sparks in the draught of a bonfire. It turned off and a flock of pigeons swooped down to peck at the debris left behind. As Nell's car approached they scattered. But one, too laggardly, misjudged, hit the windscreen with a bang that made the glass vibrate, and was flung off to the side.

Polly cried out. Nell pulled over and she and Polly stared at each other, aghast. The bird must be dead, Nell thought, but she had to be sure. She got out and, followed by Polly, walked back to where it lay on the verge. She squatted down beside it. It looked uninjured – there was no blood – but the eyes were closed, the body limp. How beautiful it was when you saw it up close, the green iridescence on its neck, the elegant bands of slate grey on the paler grey of the wings and then the pathos of the little legs and claws curled under, useless now. The impact must have killed it instantly. A little life snuffed out in a moment.

Polly's eyes were full of tears and Nell felt like crying too. She put her arm round Polly. Polly leaned into her and put her hand into Nell's.

'Can we take it home and give it a funeral?' Polly asked.

Nell thought about that. Didn't they carry diseases? Fleas or something?

'I don't think we'd better,' she concluded.

They drove home in silence.

Matthew was home for supper and Nell made a risotto.

Matthew had taken only a few mouthfuls, when: 'What the –' He reached into his mouth and plucked out something between thumb and forefinger.

'I've cracked a tooth!' He held up a small, white object.

For a few moments Nell thought it was the actual tooth, but when he went over to the sink and rinsed it, she saw that it was a pearl button. He put it down on the edge of the sink.

'How did this get in the food?' he said.

He didn't raise his voice, but Nell could see that he was coldly furious.

'Polly?' he asked.

Polly shrank back, frightened and mute. She shook her head.

Out of the corner of her eye Nell caught sight of something. There was a slight slope to the edge of the sink and the pearl button was on the move.

Matthew saw it, too. He shot out a hand, but he was too late.

'Damn! It's gone down the plug-hole.' He spoke sharply. 'I'm asking you again, Nell: do you know how that object got in the food?'

She came to herself. 'What? No, I'm really sorry, no idea. I can't think how that could have happened.'

Matthew grabbed his plate and scrapped the rest of the risotto into the bin. Without a word, he left the kitchen, banging the door behind him. He went down the garden and stood by the pond. He got out a packet of cigarettes and lit up.

Nell and Polly finished their meal in silence. Polly went up to her room as soon as she had finished. Nell stacked the dishwasher and followed her up. As soon as she was alone in her room, she slipped her hand into the pocket of her jeans and felt about for the button. It was no longer there.

The next day Matthew left early before Polly and Nell got up. He rang later to say that he might be staying in London that night and that he had managed to get an emergency dentist's appointment.

It was still so hot and humid. Nell's period hadn't come and that seemed all of a piece with the thundery weather, the feeling of heaviness and something building up. If only it would rain...

Polly went to the swing and swung lazily backwards and forwards. Nell wandered off down the garden to where a weeping willow hung over the pond, its silvery fronds touching its surface. She sat below the tree and dangled her feet in the cool water. Here as elsewhere, no expense had been spared. The pond had been stocked with water lilies and other aquatic plants. Irregular slabs of stone were piled up at one end to make a shallow waterfall. The sound of trickling water lulled Nell and as she gazed into the depths of the pond, her eyes slipped out of focus... Her thoughts drifted... how strange... that plant, billowing out into the water, those thin silvery strands stroking her toes... it was like... yes, it was like hair... it *was* hair, long blonde hair! Nell jerked her feet away. She looked again. Of course it wasn't hair. It was just pale fronds of water weed waving in the ripples from the waterfall.

Just for a moment she'd thought... after all, there was an empty stand and a missing wig.

Where was that wig now, she wondered? A horrible thought occurred to her. Had Polly's mum been *buried* in it?

Shaken, Nell went indoors. Polly soon came in, too. They spent the rest of the day lolling around, watching TV with the curtains closed against the sun.

They had a pizza from the freezer for supper and at about nine Polly went up to get ready for bed.

Some time later a scream brought Nell up the stairs two at a time to find Polly cowering on her bed. The room was full of movement, a flapping, a blundering in the air. Something swooped towards Nell – a bat! It touched her and for a heart-stopping moment, she thought it was tangled in her hair – but then it was gone, back through the open window, out into the night, swallowed up as if it was a part of the darkness from which it had emerged.

Then Polly was in her arms, and she felt the thin body shuddering.

'Hey, hey, it was only a bat,' she said, trying to cover up her own shock. 'It was just as frightened as we were.'

She went over and closed the window, Polly still clinging to her. 'There, it can't get in again.'

'I'm frightened,' Polly said. 'Can I sleep in your room tonight?'

Nell hesitated. But after all, why not, there were twin beds in her room.

'Come on then.'

Polly picked up Daisy and her pillow. Something slipped out of the pillowcase and landed with a clunk on the floor. She snatched it up, but it was too late. Nell had seen what it was. A mobile phone!

'Give me that, please, Polly.'

Polly handed it over. Guilt was written all over her face.

'Where did this come from?' Nell asked.

Polly's eyes were filling with tears.

'My aunt Jessica gave it to me. So that we can talk to each other.'

'You're not supposed to have this, you know that. Was that who you were talking to the other night?'

'I hate Daddy,' Polly burst out. 'She wanted me to go and stay with her and Daddy wouldn't let me. She lives in California.'

'Is she your mum's sister?'

Polly nodded. 'Please don't take the phone away.'

It wasn't so long since Nell was Polly's age and it all came back in a rush: the awful powerlessness of being a child, the yearning for things that you weren't allowed to have, the knowledge that adults were in control and there was nothing, *nothing* you could do.

'Alright,' Nell said. 'But you mustn't let your father find out. I'd get into trouble, too.'

Polly's face lit up. 'Oh, I won't, I won't. I promise.'

Nell saw that a photo had been slipped inside the case. It showed a much younger Polly, five or six, standing between two women, clearly sisters.

'Is one of these your mum?'

Polly nodded. She reached out and put her finger on the photo. 'That's her. And that's Aunt Jess.'

'What's her name? Your mum's name, I mean.'

'Isabel.'

'She's pretty.'

Her hair was long and loose, the colour of the wigs. Her sister was blonde, too, but darker.

How poignant they were, old photos... It struck Nell for the first time that there were no photos of Isabel around the house. Wasn't that strange?

She gave the photo back to Polly.

'Come on. Let's get you settled.'

They went into Nell's room and Polly got into bed.

Soon Nell joined her, but try as she might, she couldn't get comfortable in her own bed. It wasn't just the heat. The mattress felt lumpy. She got out and threw back the sheet – it was too hot for a duvet. Nothing there, but she could feel that there was something beneath the undersheet, no, actually under the mattress cover. She stripped the bed.

A row of teeth ran like the nodules of a spine down the centre of the mattress.

She gasped and shut her eyes. When she opened them, of course they weren't teeth. They were pearls, pearl buttons, like the ones from the wedding dress.

But how on earth had they got there? The answer came to her in a flash. Polly! That explained everything. It was all down to Polly – the hair in the pasta, the tooth in the risotto, and now this.

Nell looked over at the other bed.

Polly was sitting up, staring, open-mouthed, wide-eyed. Then her gaze shifted to Nell and she read Nell's thoughts.

'It wasn't me! Really it wasn't!'

'I won't be cross.'

'I didn't! I didn't!' She started to sob.

'Hey.' Nell went and sat on Polly's bed and put her arm round her.

Polly went on insisting that she hadn't put the buttons in Nell's bed. When she had at last fallen asleep, Nell went quietly downstairs, taking the buttons with her. She got the key from Matthew's study and opened the door to the sewing room. There was a figure standing motionless in the moonlight. She gasped and her hand went to her chest. She fumbled for the light switch. It seemed an eternity before the light came on and revealed – the dressmaker's dummy. She let out her breath in a long sigh.

The button box was where they had left it. She put the buttons in it, went out, and locked the door behind her. She zipped the key into an internal pocket in her handbag, where Polly wouldn't find it. Then, feeling foolish, but unable to help herself, she went round the house and checked that she had locked all the doors and windows.

Sleep was a long time coming. There must be something wrong with Polly. Either she was lying or – even more worrying – she'd put the buttons in the bed, but she didn't know she'd done it. Nell wished she'd never taken the job. She decided to ring her mother the next day.

Nell did ring her mother, but somehow things seemed different by then and she accepted what her mum said, that it was just a silly joke. She didn't want to leave Polly. She thought of the small hand slipped into hers at the side of the road. Matthew was not an affectionate father. There were no hugs, no 'love you's and when Nell thought of her own ebullient father, she felt sorry for Polly. No wonder the poor kid was a bit disturbed.

By mid-afternoon, the cramping pains had begun and at the same time her mood lifted. She felt relaxed and sleepy. The weather was changing too. It was still stiflingly humid, but far away across the fens clouds were massing. Rain was on its way.

After supper Polly went up to her room. Nell stayed in the sitting room to finish *The Turn of the Screw*. She was woozy with painkillers and soon her eyelids began to droop. She fell asleep on the sofa.

She woke up, damp and sweaty with her hair plastered to her face and neck. She pushed it aside, but a hair remained stuck to her lips. She tried to get a grip on it, but it seemed to be actually in her mouth now and she gathered saliva to try to dislodge it. It didn't work. The sensation remained – and a musty taste. She went into the kitchen to try what a glass of water would do.

As she ran the tap, she heard something above the sound of the running water. It was something familiar, but she couldn't quite place it. She went into the hall and listened. Nothing. She was turning to go back to the kitchen, when her eye was caught by something. The bolt on the sewing room door had been shot. But who could have done that? Polly couldn't reach it. Then the sound came again and she knew what it was this time: the stop-go staccato of an electric sewing machine. It was coming from behind the door to the locked and bolted room. The hairs went up on the back of her neck.

And that was when she really woke up, still on the sofa, shuddering and gasping.

She lay there for a few minutes, letting her breath settle, until she heard a car pulling up outside. The beams of its headlights flickered across the room. Matthew must be home. She looked at her watch. Only half-past eight. She had better slip upstairs and check on Polly.

Polly was in bed and asleep. Nell went to her own room. She was still shaken by the dream and she didn't want to encounter Matthew just yet. Though in fact she hadn't heard him come in. He had probably gone straight into the garden to have a smoke. She looked out of the window. Yes, there was a pinpoint of light in the gloom and she could just make him out, standing by the pond.

Cool air flowed in through the open window. The storm was surely about to break. The sky was overcast and the sun had set, but a sullen light lingered in the garden, too dim to distinguish more than the shapes of things and making it hard to focus. The trees, the shrubs, seemed to advance and retreat. The figure by the pond seemed almost to flicker, to shift and jerk.

She saw a glowing arc as Matthew flipped the butt of his cigarette into the water. Later she found it hard to describe – even to herself – what happened next. She thought he was turning towards the house, but no, he swung back as if he had been caught by the shoulder. Nell strained to see. He seemed to writhe, as if something were shaking him to and fro – for an instant, the scene was illuminated by a flash of lightning – then, a cry and a splash.

The next half hour was a blur: the dash for a neighbour, the nightmare struggle to drag Matthew's water-logged body out of the pond, the neighbour pulling strands of water weed out of his mouth. All the time the rain fell in sheets. Attempts to revive Matthew were in vain. Amazingly, Polly slept through it all.

The post-mortem found that Matthew had not drowned. He had died of a heart attack that had caused him to pitch headlong into the pond.

Nell wondered if she should tell someone what she had seen. For a split second – stamped on her retina by the flash of lightning – she saw – or thought she saw – rising from the pond, a dark mass, all hair and teeth. But who would believe that? She hardly believed it herself.

A couple of months later, she got a text message from Polly with a photo attached. She was standing in the California sun, hand in hand with her smiling aunt. Polly was smiling too.

The Universal Stain Remover

Gaia Holmes

She's sitting cross-legged on a black bin liner in the middle of the lawn, eating a bowl of steaming spaghetti bolognese in the snow. Her pale cheeks are cross-hatched with the red sauce and there's a big blob of it on her chin and flecks of it on the white lawn.

The next-door neighbours go away every winter for a month to stay with his family in Sweden. Last year they got burgled, so this year they've got someone in to mind the house. That must be her, their house-sitter, the woman on the lawn eating spaghetti in the snow.

When I tell people what I do for a job, most of them assume I have it easy. They probably think I spend all day rooting through my clients' drawers and fridges or slobbing on the sofa in my pyjamas watching TV with their central heating turned up high but I don't do any of that. I take my job very seriously. No one's cat, goldfish or houseplant has ever died on me and, in five years, I have only once left any noticeable sign of my presence.

I've got five-star reviews from all my clients. Whilst they're away I clean those places that are neglected: under the fridge, the cooker. I dust down the backs of hung paintings. I scrub the grubby nooks beneath cup handles, polish whatever I can polish and leave their homes smelling of lemons and lavender wax and a bit more sparkly than they left them. When they return their air is purer and their homes seem a little bigger. It's just a little everyday magic that I do: stretching space. Making room for more good air.

I don't take much when I go to look after a house, just a small black suitcase and my toolbox. It's a red tin box with lots of compartments. It's meant for builders to keep their nails and screws and hammers in but I have filled it with bottles, cans, jars and dusters. I have a full set of Dr Beckmann's Stain Devils but, most precious to me is the half bottle of Universal Stain Remover. I use this with restraint and only as a last resort because I can't remember where I bought it from and despite extensive online searches, I can't find anyone who stocks it. I'm not sure it exists anymore. Sometimes I consider decanting it into a more worthy, fancier bottle – something made of green or blue glass with raised patterns because really it deserves better than the white plastic dispenser it lives in with its faded labels curling at the edges. Most of the text has been rubbed off. All that's left are the words UNIVERSAL STAIN.

I'm definitely not a slacker. Dust settles more quickly than you think. Tea can leave a tannin line inside a cup within half an hour. Dirty dishwater can coagulate and block a plug hole overnight. When I arrive at a new place I read the notes and instructions that the owner's left, familiarise myself with the recycling and refuse collection days, and then I get out my book, sketch a grid of the house and draw in the stains and, if I can, I classify the stain. If the shape of the stain resembles something else, I write that down as well. So, for example, here in the living room on the carpet by the back left leg of the coffee table there is a faint orange stain (possibly curry) the shape of a rabbit's head. On the surface of the table is half a cup ring like a horses hoof. It looks as if someone's tried to remove it but failed. In the big bedroom, there's a purple wax stain that looks like a wine gum beneath the window and, in the bathroom, above the sink, there is a small crack in the tile on the top row, second left. This inventory of scuffs, cracks, burns and smudges takes me almost a whole day to complete. I am very thorough.

In the early days, when I first started this job, there was an incident. I mistook one of their stains for mine, tried to remove it and, temporarily, made it worse. I worried the carpet with brushes and soap and baking soda and the small stain began to roar, darken and spread. I couldn't let it be and it wouldn't let me be. I obsessed over that stain. Every night when I'd gone to bed I lay there fretting that the stain was continuing to darken and spread, that it was creeping up the beige stair carpets and purpling the magnolia walls and I had to keep getting up to check. When I finally forced myself to leave it be and the carpet dried out, it seemed to disappear and I could finally relax and then I started worrying that perhaps, for some reason, they wanted to keep that stain. Some stains can be precious. If I got back to my flat to find someone had sanded and varnished my kitchen table, I would be furious and bereft. All those familiar cup rings, smudges, smears and friendly mistakes wiped away. Flensed. Without that timely patina of stains that table would not be my table. So, after spending three anxious days trying to remove a stain from their carpet, I put it back. That's why I started keeping The Book, so I wouldn't make the same mistake again and since then I haven't. I am always certain of my stains, where they've come from and who they belong to.

For years I have studied the science of stains. Name the stain and I'll give you a solution. I have tried almost every product on the market and created my own concoctions. I have successfully removed oil, sauce, ink, sweat and other bodily secretions. I have learned the timbre and nature of stains, how they spread and set and the direction they needle themselves into fabrics. I, myself, am made of stains. If you could take out my heart or my 'soul' or the bruisable, feeling part of me and open it like a bedsheet what you would see at first would be one big stain. Look closer and you would notice that that one big stain was an amalgamation of smaller stains with a few thin slivers of pure, clean bits in between. Most of my stains were his doing and they are heavy stains that curved my spine, pushed me down to the level of the low with the worms and the things that crawl on their belly. They are stains that flattened me, crushed me, turned me into a slanting italic version of myself. Stains of humiliation. Stains he made with words.

When someone keeps telling you you're mad, ugly and stupid you start to believe it. You fold in the edges of your life, try to take up less space. Each day a new stain blooms on the inside of your skin and your own colours are subsumed. After a few years you realise that you no longer have your own keys or your own friends and half your name is gone and he's taken control of your phone and your clothes and your post and your world but he's done it so surreptitiously you didn't notice it happening and when you do realise something's wrong you wonder if it's your own paranoia because, as he keeps telling you, you're not really normal, you're not quite like other people, you have lots of 'issues'. And when he shouts at you, it's your fault. When something breaks, it's your fault. When he sets the wok on fire or slips on the path, it's your fault. And the things that cause the stains are usually little things... *Don't be stupid... you silly thing... that dress/coat/haircut doesn't do you any favours... don't you know how to wash-up... can't you make an effort with your appearance for once... why can't you just be normal... why do you always have to be so bloody needy...* I regard myself as a good cook and in the past, people have complimented my cooking. In my student days, my housemates used to rave about my sausage casseroles but, for him, my cooking was never quite right. It was always too oily or too dry, over-cooked or too rare, too bland or too spicy, too sweet or too salty, and he'd shake so much salt on to my meals it was if he were trying to kill a plague of slugs. More little things. Subtle insults and putdowns.

He was one of those men that don't believe in menstrual cramps and PMT, one of those men who is utterly repulsed by the whole thing. One time when we fucked, the fucking brought it on. Afterwards, when he got out of bed to clean himself up and saw the mess on the sheets and his cock and his belly, he freaked out, thought the blood was his. I said it was mine, time of the month, apologised, told him it was normal, natural, but he looked at me as if I was a dog that had just pissed on his shoe and he went for a shower, spent ages in there scrubbing and scrubbing, came out pink, half-raw and slept on the sofa.

A few months later he shouted down to me from the bathroom. Said 'Could you come upstairs for a minute please?'

'What's that?!' He said pointing at several dried drops of my menstrual blood on the toilet seat. 'How can you expect me to use the toilet when you've left it in such a mess? It's quite disgusting really isn't it?'

'Sorry. I didn't realise. I'll wipe it off. Calm down. It's only blood.'

'I don't need to calm down because I'm not angry. I'm just disgusted. You're getting worse, aren't you? You can't even clean up after yourself. You can't even look after yourself. Your hair needs a wash and you stink. You smell like a fish market. You know, sometimes you really disgust me. You're lucky I'm so tolerant because no one else would put up with you… I'm going out now. I suggest whilst I'm out you have a bath… try to get rid of that awful smell. And tonight I'd like you to sleep on the sofa please. '

From then on he wouldn't sleep with me or eat anything I'd cooked when I was bleeding. I started trying to bleed as neatly, quietly and sweetly as I could.

If I start to bleed on the job, I take extra precautions. I will put a plastic sheet on the bed and wear double protection because when I bleed, I bleed heavily and my womb empties itself with gusto. I am not like one of those fantasy women in the Tampax adverts who just gets on with things as normal lugging heavy suitcases from country to country, skiing, swimming, abseiling and never leaking a bloody rose into the fibres of her tight white jeans. Since the onset of my menses at the age of thirteen, I have left many a bloodstain in my wake.

Once, after I'd left him, I stayed in bed for three days with a stack of novels and several packets of custard creams and I bled without restraint. I wanted to see how much of a gorgeous, spicy mess one womb-governed body could make. I wanted to turn the bed sheet into a Rorschach test, a map, a missive, a squeeze, a jubilant shout. I made scabs and poppies. I bred silky scarlet gloop and jammy crusts, liver spots, dropped plums. Then I let it dry and pinned it up on the wall. I spent a lot of time looking at it, deciphering the shapes. There were horses, waves, church spires, tulips, crocuses, lotus flowers, fiery dragoons. It was really quite beautiful and energising to see it hung like a painting, exuding the vague scents of malt, seaweed and yeast. It made me feel quite empowered. All that blood. All *my* thick, rich healthy blood. All those clever stains I'd created.

Along with cheese fondue and watching the late-night shopping channel, one of my guilty pleasures is to imagine people as particular kinds of stains. The surly teenager on weekend duty at the off licence is a brown sauce stain. The fat bus driver who drives the 325 is a yellowy chip fat stain. Jessica, my line manager from years ago, is mildew. My chain-smoking neighbour at Raglan Court is a black coffee stain. And him, he is a puce coloured stain consisting of oil and tannin and protein covering all of the five official categories of stains. If he dried and set on a tea towel you'd probably throw it away.

I love my job. I take it seriously and I'm good at it. When I'm looking after someone's house, I'm very conscientious. I understand the values of privacy and trust so I don't poke around. I don't open any drawers or cupboards I don't have to open. I try to eat clean foods, foods with a low stain risk, dry things; fish fingers, toast, things without oil or sauce. If I need to eat messy things, if I get cravings, which I sometimes do, I will eat them in the porch, and if there is no porch and the weather's OK, I will eat them in the garden. It may sound a little over the top but I can't risk causing a stain. Anyone that hires me has to be fairly well-off and from my own observations, I have come to the conclusion that the well-off tend to favour the paler, blander palettes, unassuming confectionary colours with names like vanilla, fudge and clotted cream. This place is all praline and plush cappuccino carpets. It has a pristine impractical kitchen with highly stainable marble worktops and faux sheepskin rugs. Yesterday, after staving off the craving for spaghetti bolognese for over a week, I succumbed. I prepared and cooked it very, very carefully and, because there's no porch here and I fancied dining out, I sat and ate it in the middle of the lawn in the snow washed down with a mini bottle of Bordeaux which I drank without a glass. It was lovely and it felt quite serendipitous to be sat there letting those cold flakes of winter season my meal as the stain of the cold darkened on my knuckles.

His reduction of me, his unravelling, his breaking down, his absolute staining of me was a slow timely process that happened over two or three years. As things in my life began to shrink: my social life, my desires, my confidence, my dependence on him grew. I stopped being able to tell the difference between love and need. They both had the same weight, the same tug, the same undefinable colour. I needed him. I needed his approval. I wanted him to praise me. I wanted to get things right but, more often than not, I didn't. When he lost his temper, he did it calmly, icily, eloquently, like the blade of an ornate Japanese knife. He never hit me. He never raised his voice. Never swore at me though he could make the word 'darling' sound like the most damning insult. I think sometimes I wished he would use his fists and raise his voice so that what he was doing was more obvious and, maybe then, someone might intervene and help me. Sometimes I wished there was some special kind of ultra-violet light that would make all the stains he'd left inside me show through my skin so that people could see them slowly moving around my body casting sinister shadows like sharks.

These days what he did to me is regarded as a criminal offence. You can get locked up for it. But back then it was regarded as too vague and abstract. There was no name for it and something without a name is hard to condemn. I did consider telling someone but shame buttoned my lips and anyway, what he was doing to me was so hard to explain without physical evidence. And what would I say: *I want to report my husband because sometimes he calls me stupid. Because he puts far too much salt on everything I cook. Because he keeps telling me to take my pills. Because he tells me I'm getting worse. Because he says he's only trying to protect me?*

Everything was my fault. The weather. The blocked pipes. When I confronted him about the dark pink satin knickers I'd found in the foot-well of his car, he told me I was delusional, imagining things, said I needed to go to the doctor and ask her to increase my medication. And then, six months later when I'd found the undeniable proof of his infidelity, he changed his tactic, said, yes, he was having an affair but it was my fault because I'd let myself go and he wasn't attracted to me anymore, but he still loved me and didn't want to lose me. After that, I tried to leave him but it was hard because he was good at making promises, saying he'd change. And he was good at crying when he needed to, when I had my coat and hat on and my suitcase in one hand, the front door handle in the other. His crying always melted the bits in me that were trying to harden but on my third attempt I succeeded and left him as cleanly as I could. I deleted him from my phone and changed my number, moved to a flat in another town and, after a few months I felt his stains inside me fading. I started standing straighter, thickening my voice, being more present, more certain, more solid and I signed up with the Guardian Angels House Sitting Agency.

My last day at a property is a very strenuous day. I have to make sure everything is 'just so'. I scrub, mop, vacuum, polish, beat the rugs and open all the windows to give the place a good airing. I don't listen to music very often, but on my last day, when I'm doing my final deep cleaning session, I always listen to Handel. Though Handel is good for little else, his music has got that formal pomp that's highly conducive to deep cleaning. I regard it as musical elbow grease.

Today there are no recycling boxes outside number 16 and I'm a little disappointed. Even though we hardly spoke, the sight of her beating the rugs on the lawn, the sound of her daily hoovering, the constant wafts of disinfectant and detergent, were reassuring. The other week I bumped into her at the end of their drive on recycling day. Her recycling boxes were a work of art. Every tetra pack pressed, every cardboard box flattened, every piece of paper neatly folded and arranged in order of size. They looked like they might have been ironed. All the jars, bottles and tins were rinsed out with their labels removed, not a scab of jam, a hint of glue or a smudge of milk. The rare January sun was bouncing off all the spotless glass creating a sort of halo which radiated from her rubbish so brightly that it hurt my eyes.

3 Raglan Court

I do love my job, those brief spells of luxury in houses with lawns and corner baths and central heating, but I always like coming back to my humble little flat with my books on the shelves and my pictures on the walls and the creaking floors and those familiar drafts. It's like climbing back into my own skin. Remembering myself. The 'working' me is quite different to the 'idle' me. The working me is always racing the dust, never allowing anything to develop a skin. The idle me may leave damp towels in molehills on the bathroom floor. She may let things clot and congeal and grow stale or sour. She may drink herself dizzy and sleep in her clothes. It's nice to be off-duty, a little more laid back. Usually on my first night home I celebrate by frying the more bloody of meats and drinking dark inky wine. I don't care if the fat sputters from the pan and freckles the floor and if I knock over my glass it is not a complete crisis. I leave my plates soaking in the sink overnight.

One of the many benefits of my job is that he can't track me down so the only thing that sours the reunion with my flat is the worry that he might turn up. Somehow, after a year without contact, he managed to get hold of my address. Obviously things weren't working out with him and the owner of the pink satin knickers. One night he turned up at my door and tried to beg me to let him stay for a few days because she'd chucked him out. I told him no. I told him if he turned up at my flat uninvited again I'd tell the police. The second time he turned up I thought I really needed to find out about taking an injunction out on him but I still haven't got round to it. When he came round the night after I'd got home I wasn't completely surprised. It was the same scenario as last time. Things aren't going well with him and whoever he's living with now and he's sleeping in the car again. He was in a terrible state, all crumpled and dishevelled smelling of sweat and takeaways. He looked pitiful and pathetic. I realised that, for once, I was in control. He needed me. And a tiny seed in my head, a fantasy I'd often had, started to grow. I told him that unfortunately I was busy that night, but if things hadn't changed by the weekend he could come round for a hot meal and a bath. That was on Monday and since then I have been very busy preparing things. Today is Saturday. Today is a day for Handel. And today my moon-cup floweth over! What a blessing! And in they go, the unused gloops and shreds and menstrual meats of me. Into the pan with the diced onions and the minced beef. It smells rich and gutsy but I won't be eating it myself. I've heard about women eating their own placentas. It's supposed to be a healthy thing to do. Apparently the placenta is packed full of vitamins and iron. I'm sure the old blood I'm seasoning the meal with will be too, but I'll leave it all to him because he used to love my chilli con carne. It was just about the only meal I made for him that he didn't criticise. I've got some of the beers he used to drink chilling in the fridge and I've put flowers on the table, lit some candles, turned the heating up.

When I lead him into the flat his unwashed stink makes me feel slightly nauseous. I tell him I've eaten already, sit him at the table, give him a plate of chilli and a bottle of beer and watch him eat. He thanks me and tells me it's so good of me to take him in, says the food is delicious and asks for more. I comply and whilst he's eating his second serving I go and run the bath for him and put the bottle of beer with the pill in it between the taps.

'It's ready now,' I shout to him.

When he passes me in the corridor he thanks me again and touches my hand.

Back in the kitchen, I scrub the hand he touched and get out my book. I draw a diagram of the flat and add a big stain to the square that represents the bathroom then put on the Handel CD, pour myself a large glass of red wine, sit at the table and wait. I play the CD twice, just to make sure, then I go to check on him.

He's out. Unconscious or sleeping deeply in the bath. I'm not quite sure exactly what the pills do but he's in the state I wanted him to be. The water's scummy and slightly grey. He must have been very dirty. I get the precious universal stain remover and pour the contents into the water above his chest. It floats there over his heart, slightly pearlescent, like petrol in a puddle. I consider giving him a good scrub with the hard brush I use to clean the doormats with but I don't really want to touch him so I decide I'll leave him soaking for a little longer until the hard skin on his heels is soft and pale as uncooked pastry and I'll drink another glass of wine whilst I consider my options. As I'm closing the door behind me I catch a glimpse of the bright, almost holy, blue of the Domestos bottle where it stands between the toilet and the sink.

( ) ((

Lara Williams

IT BEGAN WITH A collection of eyelashes, which was innocuous enough. It was a kind of tick she had developed to punctuate her evening skincare routine. First, she would double cleanse, sweep an oil dowsed cotton pad over her forehead and nose, then wash with a soy-based cleanser. She would press lactic and hyaluronic acid into the problem areas, then every second night she would apply a vitamin C treatment to spots showing signs of sun damage. She was trying to be low key. Finally, she would pinch her eyelashes between her forefinger and thumb and pull out any strays. She would study her fingertip: a tiny pillow, pink with coastline lacerations, topped with three or four half parentheses, ( ) ((

Her ex-boyfriend used to say her nightstand resembled some kind of old-time apothecary, covered, as it was, with powders and tinctures. Among the pipette droppers and tinted bottles sat a vintage pillbox which had once been her grandmothers'. She used the pillbox to store her tweezers, which she would reach for first thing in the morning, tidying up her eyebrows while she listened to the headlines on her phone. It felt good to pluck hair from her face while metabolising the news. It reminded her of the large hole her father had dug in the back garden, for no discernible reason, before his nervous breakdown. *Girls,* he would tell her and her sister, while they sat on the sofa watching daytime TV. *I'm going outside to work on my hole.*

It occurred to her the pillbox might be a good place to store her jettisoned eyelashes, once she had gotten to the point where she could no longer, in good conscience, send them fluttering to the floor. Who can tell the difference, she reasoned, between an eyelash and a single eyebrow hair? And would it not be reasonable for a few errant eyebrow hairs to be found alongside the implement used for their extraction? If someone were to open the pillbox, which no one ever would, and enquire about the mounting volume of eyelashes contained, she would simply explain it was the box in which she stored her tweezers, and that perhaps a few eyebrow hairs had found their way in. That really there was nothing to suggest what they were viewing was the beginnings of some sort of 'collection', though perhaps she would later casually concede, it was indeed a bit 'gross'.

She began collecting her eyelashes around the same time that she became interested in cacti. It was also around the same time she was diagnosed with rectovaginal endometriosis.

She became interested in cacti after visiting a newly opened lifestyle store in her neighbourhood, which specialised in plants. It was owned by a husband and wife who wore matching raw cotton pinafores and recycled clogs. It was damp and warm in the shop, and it smelled like a holiday. They kept the cacti in the back, away from the woven throws and expensive candles. She pressed her fingertips to their sharp spines; studied their phallic, otherworldly fronds. *They can live for up to 300 years,* the husband said, following her while eating a flapjack. *This one's a Bolivian Torch.* She bought it and took an Uber home; the cactus resting between her legs and periodically impaling her calves.

( ) ((

She was diagnosed with rectovaginal endometriosis via laparoscopic surgery a week earlier. Her ex-boyfriend had driven her to the hospital. En-route he had stopped at McDonald's after announcing they were still in time for breakfast. *But I can't eat anything,* she had said. He pointed at the twin McMuffins. *These are for me,* he replied. At the hospital she was dressed in a gown and slippers. An anaesthetist sat at the foot of the bed, tenderly explaining how she would be put to sleep. *You have to make sure I don't accidentally wake up,* she had said. *With a hole still in my belly.* He had smiled at her kindly, though tellingly made no promises either way.

For the surgery a thin camera attached to a long tube was inserted into her abdominal wall, basically to take a look around. She imagined the instrument an inquisitive and somewhat bureaucratic tapeworm, probing this way and that. She imagined her stomach a baked potato, pronged to let out the steam. On waking her a few hours later they told her what she suspected: that she had endometriosis, moderate to severe, and that while they had removed what they could, she would still likely experience a bit of a tummy ache every month with her period.

Back at home she was groggy, delicate on her feet. *I could eat one of those McMuffins,* she said, and her ex-boyfriend wordlessly reached for his jacket and left the flat, returning with English muffins, strong cheddar and burger mix. She watched him in the kitchen, wondering why people tended to swing pendulously in their treatment of her. She thought what she would like was someone right down the middle. No special favours. No fuck ups. Someone who was always more or less neutral in their interactions.

Her collection expanded when she noticed an unusually long hair sprouting from a mole on the underside of her forearm.

She pulled taut the skin to study it, Googled 'hair + mole = cancer?'. The results were inconclusive. She retrieved the tweezers from their pillbox and removed the hair: it was dark and curved, a bulb of sebum at the end. It left behind a pinprick-sized crater at the centre of the mole. She thought about her father, digging his hole. Coming back indoors sweat-stained. *Good work,* he would tell her. *Good work on the hole.* She placed the hair alongside the eyelashes, understanding that was where it belonged.

The first period following the laparoscopy began as usual: a gentle tug low in her abdomen, brown streaks in her knickers. Perhaps this will be as bad as it will get, she wondered, before waking up in the middle of the night with the familiar sensation of being repeatedly kicked in the stomach while something clawed at her uterus from inside. Pain shot up her legs and crashed into her pelvis; blackened clots on the sheets. But mainly pain, a lot of pain, enough pain to fill up a swimming pool, enough pain to fill up an aircraft hangar. She called in sick for work and drew the curtains. Her ex-boyfriend came to visit at lunch and turned on the TV. *Switch it off,* she begged. *It's like listening to a podcast during a plane crash.*

The Bolivian Torch provided some comfort from its place in the corner: bluish-green in hue and inching upwards in height. Penis Cactus it was sometimes called, or *frauenglück* in German, meaning 'woman's joy'. *Does it have to be kept in the bedroom?* her ex-boyfriend would enquire, occasionally throwing a towel over it when the pain was manageable enough for sex.

In the weeks that followed she started noticing a strange new symptom, studying her body after her monthly wax: an increase of in-growing hairs across her legs and bikini line. She wondered why bits of her body were always showing up where they were not supposed to: endometrial tissue outside her ovaries and inside her bowel, hairs which didn't know which way to grow. She used the tweezers to ease them out, and when that wouldn't work, she used a nail file and a needle: the nail file to flatten the skin and the needle to get beneath the hair. She began thinking of these exercises as 'procedures', later, 'operations'. She filed these hairs away with the others.

She went back to her GP, explaining she was still in extreme pain every month, it was like a white noise of agony. *What I am more concerned about,* the GP had told her, *are these marks on your arms.* She looked at her arms, speckled in red spots from the operations. The in-growing hairs were turning up everywhere now: on her arms and the tops of her shoulders, across her belly and breasts. Her evening skincare routine now involved a full body inspection, naked, in front of her mirror. *Could abnormal hair growth be a symptom?* she asked. *What other things can abnormally grow?* The GP printed something off from his computer, gave her the details of a support group in town.

The hair on her mole had returned, she was disheartened to find, sitting on the sofa one evening, slowly chewing toast. It was like a small eyelash, a dark crescent moon. She went for the tweezers before having another thought. Before her father had begun digging his hole, he pulled out all the plants and flowers from the garden, pulling them from the base of their stems, their dirt-covered roots. She needed to weed out the root of the thing if she was going to rid herself of it entirely. She searched her kitchen looking for a tool: this would be a slightly different operation. She wiped down her arm with vodka. A stainless steel fish filleting knife, a gift from her ex-boyfriend, bubbled in a pan of boiling water.

She made a space on her desk, an anglepoise lamp delivered a white circle of light. She waited for the fish slice to cool. The first cut was the worst but then things got a little easier. She needed to make several incisions all the way round, to get right under the mole if she was going to do this properly. Blood ran down her arm and dripped from her elbow. It was hard to see what was going on. Once confident she had cut deep enough into her skin, she used the slice as a kind of lever, pushing down to force out the mole. It came out in two parts, tearing down the middle. It left a red, wet hole. She placed it on a single square of toilet paper, before using the rest to wrap up her arm. Once dry, she put both parts in the pillbox, dusting her eyelashes and ingrown hairs with more dried blood.

Her ex-boyfriend had started asking questions about the scars, would force up her sleeves and demand to know what was going on. She still had the terrible pain every month, had to take taxis when she couldn't walk. Still excused herself to the bathroom, to lie down beneath the bowl and sob into her shirt. How could she explain that these excisions were the only thing that relaxed her? That standing in front of her mirror, digging sebum or whatever else from her nose, was when she felt most at ease in her skin, in the world?

The Bolivian Torch had grown a full foot in a month, it was turning out to be a very healthy boy. She would find herself absentmindedly running her fingers against its spines, sometimes humming beneath her breath: wordless lullabies for a baby.

Soon, she was performing one or two operations nightly, using the fish slice to dig out the in-growing hairs alongside other uncomely blemishes, any blackheads or spots. She kept them all in the pillbox, which had acquired a meat smell, a metallic smell: the smell of rot. She no longer kept the pillbox on her nightstand, instead slept with it beneath her pillow. Her ex-boyfriend was coming over much less, was always at band practice or working late, but still, she couldn't risk it. Plus, she liked falling asleep with it just beneath her ear.

At her monthly waxing appointment, her beautician refused to treat her. *I'm sorry,* she said, holding a jar of hot wax in one hand, wooden spatula in the other. *It's just not safe.* She considered this to be a disaster, the stuff of nightmares. At home she surveyed the damage: the hairs sprouting all over, the red lumps where they buried back into her skin. She administered a home wax, fixing honey-scented strips over her legs and bikini line, underneath her arms. It hurt to tear them off, they took scabs and dead skin with them, re-opened old wounds. She looked at the hair- and blood-coated strips, too big for the pillbox, instead placed them in a canvas bag and hung them from a hook on the back of the door.

On the train ride home from work she felt the beginnings of the pain, the certain contractions of her womb. She closed her eyes, got herself ready. The pain was seismic, knocked her out. She could feel her knickers filling with blood, clots sliding out of her, wet and still warm. She pictured the butchers' counter at the supermarket, the fresh kidneys and livers all lined up. When she reached her destination she did not look back at the spot she'd been sitting in to confirm the stain but she knew it was there. She made an appointment with the GP as soon as she got home.

Her ex-boyfriend came over, said he didn't like the sound of her voice. He brought a takeaway pizza but had already eaten two slices by the time he arrived. He sat at the foot of the bed while she lay shivering beneath the duvet, a pillow over her face. *What can I do?* he kept asking, more panicked than she was entirely comfortable with. *Just tell me what I can do.*

The Bolivian Torch was shedding its spines. They gathered like pine needles on top of the soil. The spines keep the cactus safe from animals, she thought, the spines help it absorb water. She tried forcing the spines back into the plant but it felt an unnecessary violence. Instead, she fixed them back to the plant with glue. She opened up her pillbox, scattered a few eyelashes and hairs onto the soil for good luck. She did her nightly operations next to the cactus, not wanting to leave it for even a second. Eventually, she slept, curled around its base like a cat.

She received a letter from her GP: she would not be receiving any further treatment. There was a long waiting list, a waiting list for the waiting list, and it seemed the medication she was on was working just fine. She clutched her hair in frustration, tore out a large clump. She looked around the room for somewhere to store it, eventually tucking it between the pages of a book.

Her ex-boyfriend still had a key to her flat, something she had forgotten about. He had let himself in to cook her dinner, something special to cheer her up. He rang her at work, asked her to come straight home. She walked into her apartment feeling nervous though she wasn't sure why. When she walked into the kitchen she saw what he had arranged on the table: her open pillbox plus other bodily effects. *Aren't you going to say anything?* he demanded, the sound of panic more prevalent than before. *I found a jar of fingernails! I found handbags filled with skin!* She sat down on the floor. She was exhausted. *You can keep them,* she said. *I'm not certain I need them anymore.*

Once he had done shouting, telling her she needed to get help, he left her alone. She gathered herself from the floor and went to sit by the Bolivian Torch. *Woman's joy,* she thought, admiring it. It was still shedding its spines. She plucked one from the soil and pressed its pointed tip to the pillow of her finger. She pressed until a pinprick of blood emerged, which she squeezed and eventually sucked dry. She took a few more and pressed them into various parts of her body. It hurt but then so did everything. When she was happy with her work she lay down beside it. She thought again about her father, digging his hole. She remembered calling to him, telling him dinner was on the table. How she had stood on the doorstep, shouting and shouting and watching him dig, but he couldn't hear her, didn't even know she was there.

The Reservoir

Meave Haughey

'I'VE SEEN THE PICTURES, you know. It spilled out and flooded the high street. Again, and again.' The woman jabs at the map on the supermarket wall, pointing to a spot near the foot of Meredith's road.

'It always floods round here. Have you seen the old photos? Them's rowing down the high street in one of 'em. When we was kids we was always messing about in the muck down there. The water's just under the ground here – always comes back, no matter what they done.' She turns and looks more closely at Meredith, who has one hand on her daughter in the shopping trolley and one on her belly. 'Another babbie on the way? You'll have your hands full won't you love? I remember them days.'

Once home, Meredith crawls, her face close to the worn floorboards, sniffing to find the source of the damp. Behind Matthew's desk with its orderly piles of paper untouched these last weeks, she finds three lost hair clips, a pencil, and a single domino, but the cloudy, musty smell vanishes the nearer she gets. She drags the remaining furniture away from the walls and, behind the couch in the bay window, she presses her fingers into a softening in the floorboards which she hasn't noticed before. The edges crumble like putty. She pokes her hand through – a blind visitor crossing into the unseen world of the subfloor and then withdrawing suddenly for fear of what might come. Her fingertips emerge smelling of sea, or the loam of a forest floor. Meredith walks more quickly than usual to the kitchen and fetches some wire wool from the cupboard under the sink to block up the hole. Boundaries after all, are boundaries.

That night, Meredith lies in bed and thinks about what Matthew told her about The Great Reservoir sitting at the bottom of the road. He's been working through the grid, mapping the historic character, and found it almost by chance. There were entirely imagined cities, he'd told her once, invented by cartographers to obscure what was really there. It reminded him, he said, of playing by the river as a child when the mist would come in, knee deep. Meredith pictures a milky layer of mist obscuring the ground. The idea unsettles her, makes her wonder which map she's been working from all these years. Down the hill, where she watches cars get stuck in winter, down there, she thinks, it was all water. Two hundred years ago, all those rows of terraces were not yet imagined. The Great Reservoir lay there, silent and still. Around it, the leasowes and fields which would become Watery Lane, Reservoir Close, Pool Meadow. The Great Reservoir drowning the barely workable land from which the poor tried to wring out a living, their cattle and sheep always ankle deep in mud. Its sodden ground marshalled to the now greater purpose of feeding the engineering vision of James Brindley and his six locks; the contained magic of water rising to a mile-long summit at Smethwick and then descending. From the front of her small Victorian terrace, she could have looked down the hill and watched the moon drop into its darkness. It is hard for her not to think of the reservoir and its cadaverous stillness and worry.

'Not to worry,' says Matthew, with a geographer's confidence, they are safe there on the hill. They'll never be flooded. 'One of the highest points in the Midlands,' he says. If they could see far enough, they'd see the Ural Mountains before there was anything higher, he says, and Meredith is amazed even if she isn't exactly sure where the Urals are.

On Bonfire Night, with Matthew and the baby able somehow to sleep through it all, Meredith closes the door, with its thick layers of paint, and leans her head back against it, looking into the dark for the Urals. She smells the burn of sulphur and coal from fireworks which throb above the trees in the park beyond the foot of the hill. A thick flow of people slides down the street, eddying round the cars which are cruising for parking spaces. The shuddering volleys of explosions with their echoing reports mix with the rush and the burning smells of fairground and bonfire and Meredith thinks of the reservoir they visited that summer in Wales with its chapel bells ringing underwater. She thinks of the protests and the bombs and what if she can't hold back the reservoir any longer.

A woman was killed at the bottom of the road last year. Just outside what was once the Post Office with its oddly prow-like shape. Meredith can imagine the men with their broad moustaches, and bowler hats, arms crossed silently across their waistcoats, standing in the doorway. As though they were captaining some invisible ship, watching her slip under. Doing nothing.

The cat wakes her, purring round her head. She pulls the phone under the duvet, cupping it in her hand to check the time without waking Matthew. He's been worse since the funeral, lying in for what seems like days at a time, the darkness flooding round him like a river in spate.

As she draws the sheet across his shoulders she sees his curled up body as though he were still the child he has told her about who spent long hours waiting. Most days, after school, he'd said, he would kneel on the same uncomfortable chairs, resting his forehead against the glass, looking down into the atrium of the library where his mum worked, watching her press date stamps neatly into boxes. Meredith feels rough green cloth under her knees, and she imagines her head against the glass, looking for her own mother, but her breath obscures the view.

It is just after 5am. Meredith tiptoes down to the kitchen on the edges of the stairs where they creak less and lights the gas under the kettle. Shivering in the blue light of the cooker, a thin blanket wrapped around her shoulders, she watches the neighbour's loose gutter clattering in the wind. It's raining again. On cue, the baby cries. Meredith's breasts ache deeply, her milk letting down in response as she climbs back up the stairs to reach her daughter. She sits in the rocking chair in the dark, the blanket wrapping round them both now, flowing into her child, the point of separation between them indistinguishable. How can she be pregnant again, so soon? Will she never be free of violent sickness and breasts that leak and drip? Meredith cradles one child and imagines the next crying at her knee as the tide of panic rises. She can't do this. She can't do this.

The local history library is small and badly lit, as yellow as a newspaper cutting. She's looked in before at the collection of balding men at low tables writing earnestly in notebooks in front of ancient microfiche readers or sliding their hands along the folds of enormous tablecloth maps. But today Meredith enters, struggling to push the buggy through the stiff double doors. The sign in the lobby was right. She finds a display of items which were once locally manufactured. Nails, mostly. Photographs of the foundries, factories, production lines. A small glass case on the filing cabinet containing original promotional boxes of nuts and bolts from the GKN factory. A postcard with that same image of the men standing outside the post office – arms crossed. Over-sleeves on their arms to keep themselves clean. A pile of free maps of the local area at different times. Meredith's hand is drawn to the one whose centre is marked *The Great Reservoir*.

'It's culverted now.' The librarian gestures towards the reservoir on the map and Meredith can see she wants to tell her more.

'Oh yeah, I know,' she mumbles. 'But thanks.' She's not in the mood to talk, folding the printout in half and backing through the doors with the buggy, heading for her car which is parked around the corner next to the old pub. She drives the short distance home and sits in the car across the road from her house. It appears faceless, its heavy nets, far too long, filling the bay window in great grey waves. Meredith has noticed mould creeping up them from the lower edges and wonders how to stop it.

That night, Meredith dreams of water again. This time, a lake, leaden and still. Before the pines, down the left side, the silhouettes of three or four log cabins, locked up for winter, follow its curve. Lawns, cropped short one last time at the end of the season, lead from abandoned porch swings and patios down to the open water. There is no sound.

There is an emptiness to the cold predawn light. Still dreaming, Meredith cannot resist inching her stiffened hand into the icy translucent water. Beneath the surface her hand appears white, luminous, hanging in the dark like a drowned moon.

All night, it seems, she has lain next to the lake and heard nothing, only once, an owl, but now from somewhere comes the doleful mute tone of bells. She wakes, realising there's something else. She reaches down and feels wet, the heat of panic instantly overtaking her – deafening her to all but the dark thud of her heart.

'It's a hind water tear,' the midwife says. She explains that a slow dribble of amniotic fluid can be caused by a small tear in the amniotic membrane. Meredith starts to cry. She is an inadequate vessel. Broken, like the forgotten reservoir seeping its dark secrets into the ground. They're holding it back for now, but what if the weather changes without warning?

Meredith goes to the place outside the shop where the woman's murdered body was left and stands there wondering what she expected. She's seen pictures on the internet of the exact spot the police had taped off for a few days. Now it's under a pile of bin bags. It is only when she looks closely that Meredith sees the brown stem of a flower, taped to the lamppost behind the buckets of cheap footballs in plastic nets, shiny pinwheels, inflatable hammers. A group of young men stand and sit around the door of the shop checking their phones and smoking. They don't look at Meredith with her thickening belly as she feigns interest in the bowls of vegetables and fruit.

Struggling to hold together a fragmenting space, she superimposes her memory of the map over the scene. It didn't last long, Matthew had said, they diverted the canal with a huge cutting, a deep slice right through the ridge, the contents of the reservoir running to waste. The outline of the Reservoir flows through the world in front of Meredith, swallowing up streets, the corner shop. As she'd walked down the street towards it, she'd seen the roof of the post office rising above the houses in front of her. She had felt the ground shifting.

She waits for the rich sweet morning: autumn air, slightly warm, even in the darkness; the sky just light enough to pick out the black lace of the trees. The world has a strange flatness, as though the trees are paper cut-outs in a magic lantern show. This, the only hour when it is quiet enough to really listen. There it is. The obsidian sheen of the water, dark as darkness. Her breathing is heavy now, the trickle of waters rushing out more steadily as she searches, confused. It's here, but then not – the Reservoir hidden again by halogen lights on the end of houses and the watching eyes of the CCTV. It is culverted, she says to herself, lowering herself to the pavement – pressing her head against the ground to listen – the tiny stones embedding themselves into her face.

The Leftovers

Margaret Drabble

YOU NEVER KNEW WHAT you would find when you first went in after one of Them had left. You found evidence of strange habits, strange predilections. One of Them left the freezer full of tubs of good quality and exotically flavoured ice cream, some unbroached, some with a few spoonsful missing. You found this odd, but in no way offensive. You finished some of it off yourself and threw the rest away. One of Them had broken the shower attachment but had gone to great lengths to fix it, leaving you a long letter describing his efforts, full of modest and justifiable self-praise. One of Them had broken a not very important glass jar full of cotton reels, and had replaced it with a much better jar. One of Them had nosed into a cupboard in a part of the house where he had no right to be. You would never have known about this had he not emailed you a not very good short story, unpublished and unpublishable, in which he made mock of the ancient contents of that cupboard – its tarnished remnants of family silver, its wellington boots, its heavy Olympia typewriter. You didn't think he came well out of that. The understanding was that They would look after the house and its contents and live more or less rent-free, in exchange for keeping an eye on things. They weren't expected to look in your cupboards.

One of Them had been heroic. He had had to weather the Beast from the East, in the terrible storms and snow of the winter of 2018. He had gone up into the attic to sweep out the snow, he had alerted the neighbours and found some builders, he had put buckets under the drips. He had had two dogs with him, this one, but there was never a trace of them when you went in after him. Not a hair, not a ghost of an odour, not a scratch or a mark to be seen. And fewer rabbits, for a while, in the gardens.

One of Them had embarrassed you slightly by asking where, in all the many bookcases throughout the house, she could find the poetry section. You had had to reply that there wasn't one, not really, or not as such. Books of poems were distributed randomly through the house, on shelves and on bedside tables and on desks. You were not, you had to admit, a very tidy or well-organised person. But you had trusted this one, and she had driven your car for a month or two without mishap. And you honoured her interest in poetry. So her request did her credit rather than otherwise. It was you that came out poorly from this exchange.

This time, you had to admit to yourself, you were apprehensive. You sensed there was trouble brewing on several fronts as well as the domestic. There was talk of a new plague, a new virus, which might change our ways of life. There might even be a possibility of travel restrictions at some point in the future – unlikely, but possible. So it was important to get there while you could, to make sure all was well, to wash the sheets and put out the recycling and empty the bag of the vacuum cleaner and clean the filter of the tumbler dryer.

You sense that she might not have washed the sheets or put out the recycling. Some of her recent emails had been disquieting. There had been a demand about a light bulb, which she seemed to expect you to be able to change from 250 miles away. You had responded a little tartly to this, saying it was either a screw or a bayonet, and there were spare bulbs in the cupboard. Then there had been a power cut and she hadn't understood about trip switches and fuse boxes and didn't know how to locate an electrician. And then there had been mentions of mice. A big old house in the country does tend towards mice, as everyone knows. You had warned her she would find herself in the middle of nowhere. It was not helpful to panic about mice, which might have got the upper hand because she wasn't very good with the recycling and the compost. The house had been free of mice for a couple of years.

So you had been apprehensive, as you parked in the drive. She'd been away for 24 hours, you hadn't wanted to overlap with her or to see her, you don't really like other people very much, and a person-free handover was fine by you, it suited you better than a smiling face-to-face. When you crossed the threshold, your first impression was that everything was in reasonable order. There was even a bunch of daffodils in a jug on the table, and a Thank You card, and a small gift-wrapped object. So far, so good. There was a note saying there were cheese, eggs and bread in the fridge, and you looked in the refrigerator, and there they were. At first sight, the contents of the fridge looked in good order, though you had been warned that one of the plastic shelves in the fridge door was broken and 'needed glueing.' That was a minor casualty, you thought, though you hadn't liked the word 'glue' in connection with a refrigerator. They made a toxic compound.

You adjusted, over the next week or two, but began to make more and more unsatisfactory discoveries round and about the house and to hear increasingly ominous reports from the outside world. Your radio told you that the virus outbreak was going from bad to worse, and you told yourself that it was a good thing you came here when you did, as life would be much more unpleasant in the busy densely populated northern city that was now your home. You were safe enough here, in this remote outpost.

You had plenty of provisions, for a long siege, and you had plenty of time now to go through the cupboards and wonder which of the past-their-use-by date tins and packages of rice and flour and pasta would be safe to use. A war baby, reared in adolescence on tales of Second World War hardships and the famines of Europe and the Soviet Union, you rather liked the idea of using up the backlog. You couldn't be sure where some of the stuff came from, stuff that dated back a long way. The oldest items you must have purchased yourself – the butter beans and tinned chestnuts and pearl barley from 2014 were yours, though the custard powder was probably your daughter-in-law's. Her children were partial to custard. It smelled remarkably fresh when you opened it. But you don't like, have never liked custard. You cooked some pearl barley and it tasted fine, but the reason why you hadn't cooked it before was, you realised, because you didn't like pearl barley very much either. But you ate it, just the same. This was an emergency, and in an emergency you couldn't always eat only what you liked.

As the days passed, you began to take more and more note of things that had gone a little wrong, things you wouldn't have noticed in busier times. You tended to blame them all on her, the last of Them, and to exonerate the ice-cream fancier and the poetry lover and the dog man. Those burn marks on the beautiful wood of the kitchen dresser were surely hers. She must have put the Le Creuset casserole dish straight from the hob onto the wood. Not once, but several times, in overlapping rings. Most of the clothes pegs were missing or broken. The tiles that had fallen from your bathroom wall could have fallen off of their own accord, but she shouldn't have been in your bathroom anyway. She had admitted to the broken shelf in the fridge and to a broken ovenproof dish and to some broken wine glasses (which, to be fair, she had replaced) and to the broken toilet seat, but she probably hadn't even noticed the large offensive dark patch on the pale blue fabric of the padded headboard in the room where she was supposed to have been sleeping. A large round head-shaped stain. She must have rested her head there, probably repeatedly, when her hair was wet or greasy or oily. It was unpleasant.

Inevitably, your irritation mounted, as you became more and more aware of what you saw as her shortcomings. Those plastic bottles of mayonnaise in the fridge, for example. They were of a supermarket brand unknown to you, and one of them was unopened, but there were also three that were opened and three quarters used. When she had got down to the point where you had to shake or squeeze or find a narrow spoon to extract the last quarter of the content, she had simply put the almost empty bottles back in the back of the fridge instead of washing them out and putting them in the recycling. And then she had bought another one. And why had she accumulated three half-empty bottles of soy sauce, two half-empty jars of horse radish sauce, two of malt vinegar, one of peri-peri and one of hoisin? Her condiment usage was excessive. She had clearly been in need of gross and violent stimulants. She had liked strong chutneys and poisonously bright yellow piccalilli. And she had used up all the Marmite and the stock cubes, of which you usually left a good supply.

It's not as though you were yourself a model of kitchen virtue. Far from it. In your fridge up north you often left a piece of cheese mouldering or deliquescing because you hadn't quite the heart to throw it out and didn't quite fancy eating it. The heels or tubs of cheese had turned into experiments, awaiting a scientific eureka moment. There were tins of fancy soup you had left on the shelf for years (you could do them now) and pasta that dated back a long, long way.

But that was different, you told yourself, it was your own rubbish going off in your own home, in an interesting manner. Your own rubbish is always pleasanter, more rational, than the waste products of others.

She was clearly not very well house trained, and hadn't thought to cover her tracks. You'd smelled a rat when she'd emailed about the recycling and asked where to put it as it was beginning to smell. As everyone knows, recycling doesn't smell. If it smells, it's not recycling. This was what you said to yourself, crossly, over the first fortnight: she just didn't know how to do the basics. But then, as the difficulties of shopping and getting anything delivered increased, you began to note contradictory and puzzling aspects of her behaviour, aspects that were now proving curiously useful to you. For instance, she had stocked up with several packets of muesli, most of them unopened. There were plenty of dishwasher tablets, possibly a year's supply, and some unopened bottles of washing up liquid. There were two boxes of toilet rolls. There was plenty of bleach and three varieties of detergent. There was even a big cardboard box of packets of coffee. For all of these you were grateful.

The mismatch of minor misdemeanour and forward-thinking was so pronounced that you began to wonder whether she had foreseen this crisis, this pandemic? Had she had access to secret warnings? Was she on a government hotline? Slob though she seems to have been, did she also have second sight? You didn't know much about her, really. You never knew much about Them. You didn't want to nose into Their affairs, or for Them to nose into yours. It was all a gentlewoman's agreement. It was a matter of trust.

You started to dwell more on the past, having little else to do, apart from cleaning windows and polishing furniture, activities that had not much attracted you over the years. You spent a lot of time tenderly rescuing woodlice, of which you were fond. You picked them up and dropped them out of the window, onto the outdoor window ledge, reasoning that they preferred to live outdoors, they wouldn't like being in a house, not even in a house as full of rotting wood as yours. They rolled themselves up into little primeval balls when you picked them up, and you watched anxiously as they fell onto the ledge. Sometimes they fell on their backs, and waved their many legs frantically for a while, but they always managed to right themselves. You had read somewhere that in the eighteenth century ground woodlice had been considered to have therapeutic qualities, but you hoped you wouldn't come to testing that supposition.

You began to cast your mind back to the holidays you had taken, as a child, in this large family house by the sea, with your aunt and your cousins. They had been happy times. Beachcombing, crabbing, gazing into rock pools, inspecting mussels and limpets and starfish, collecting pebbles, identifying butterflies. You see those butterflies now – the comma, the peacock, the orange tip. You have been out on the shore several times, gathering driftwood for the wood burner. Sometimes you see another person, at a great distance, with an armful of those light pale brittle sea-washed salt-imbued logs. You think of when you were children and picnicked on the beach. One year you all made a memorable fire, in a great hearth of stones, and you boiled a large pan of seaweed. The hot green vegetable odour returns in your memory. It hadn't tasted good, but the process had been thrilling. The seaweed smelled of ozone. You liked the word ozone.

Cousin Robin had been your particular friend. He was three months younger than you, and a clever lad. He had become an epidemiologist attached to a grand London hospital. He would have been enthralled by this epidemic, but he had died of bowel cancer a year ago, and thus had missed the drama of the century, the tragedy of the millennium. What emails you could have exchanged, had he still been alive. It was a pity he wasn't there to witness it, to interpret it for you.

You had played risky games, when you were alone together, and unobserved by your siblings. Tit and bum games, eminently suitable for pre-pubertal children. These were inventively secret games, slightly but not very shaming, and even more thrilling than driftwood fires and boiled seaweed. In adult life you had of course never mentioned them, but a kind of flicker of amusement lay behind your relationship, as you met at family or public events or exchanged news of books you were reading. It was he that had recommended to you a 1970s book about plagues and people, with its theories about epidemics in the Ancient World and the ambitions of the measles virus. And you had put him on to that gripping thesis about the origins of consciousness in the breakdown of the bicameral mind. You had both liked to wander on the wilder shores of speculation.

And here you were, on the wilder shores of Britain, at the very tip of your long rambling coastal garden, wearing rubber gloves as you harvested a crop of nettles for nettle soup. Going through your head were lines from Swinburne, from 'The Forsaken Garden', much of which you had known by heart as a romantic teenager:

> '*In a coign of the cliff between lowland and highland*
> *At the sea-down's edge between windward and lee*
> *Didummdiddy dumddiddy dumdiddy*
> *A ghost of a garden fronts the sea...*

How did it end?

> *Till the slow sea rise and the sheer cliff crumble*
> *Till terrace and meadow the deep gulfs drink...*
> *As a god self-slain on his own strange altar*
> *Death lies dead.*

Are those tears in your eyes? Surely not. It is the wind in your face, the salt wind only.

You were always susceptible to the potency of cheap poetry. *For the foam flowers endure where the rose blossoms wither...*

It is coming back to you now, that strange game, the strangest and most elaborate game Robin had ever devised. He had decided on an experiment. You would both cut your nails, and put the parings in a glass bottle with your own urine, and hide them here, at the garden's extremity, in a deep cranny in the dry stone wall at the roots of the hawthorn hedge behind the compost bins. Then, the next summer, you said you would come back and dig them up and see what had happened to them. Robin had provided most of the pee, for obvious reasons, but you had provided the bottle: a special bottle, an old glass bottle, which had been found buried in a flower bed closer to the house.

What had he expected? What strange alchemical metamorphosis? You don't know, because when you came back next year, you both forgot to look. That's how children are. An intensity of purpose followed by forgetfulness and indifference. You forgot all about the disgusting bottle. A year is a very long time when you are twelve.

Is it still there? You can't be bothered, you are too old and tired to rummage or dig for it. You stand, arrested by the past, in your pink rubber gloves, with a pail full of stinging nettles at your feet.

You are a bit phobic about gloves at the best of times, and this is the worst of times. You can tolerate greengrocer's mittens, but they aren't much good for receiving Amazon deliveries or picking stinging nettles.

Gardens are full of buried bottles. There is one of those bottles in the house now, standing in the ornamental Kettle's Yard display of pebbles on the marble-topped dining room sideboard. It is about six inches high, of thick clear sturdy glass, slightly tinted with green. It is a translucent sea green. It has high shoulders, and the raised letters on its front and sides spell out *WORLD FAMED BLOOD MIXTURE, CLARKE'S OF LINCOLN*. Its glass stopper is round and pitted but elegant. You've often wondered how it got there, how long it had been in the earth, what the Blood Mixture could have been. The fingernail-and-urine mixture had been more of a witch's brew than a restorative.

Shall you try to find the other bottle, in the stone wall at hedge bottom? No, you really can't be bothered.

If Robin had been still alive, you think you would have done. You could have emailed him about it, and you could have reminisced about how disgusting you had both been. But it's too late for that. It's too late for most things.

Perhaps you shouldn't have had such harsh feelings about the disgusting One, who had marked your wooden surfaces and your spare bed's upholstered headboard. We are all disgusting, it's just that we have different ways of expressing it, we have different levels and objects of disgust. And she had left you all that muesli, and all those cleaning agents. You ponder the paradox of a personality obsessed with acquiring cleaning agents but not very good at cleaning.

You set off slowly, back towards the house, with your tragic pail of nettles. At the back door into the house you pause. For there stands another bucket, a bright red one, which you hadn't noticed before. It is full of clothes pegs, none of them broken and some of them new. Had that been there when you went out? You don't think it had. Surely you would have noticed it?

You think of the story of the elves and the shoemaker, which as a child you had found mysteriously enchanting.

Had somebody brought them for you? Would there be other gifts indoors? Is this a good story, or a very very bad one? You haven't even unwrapped the little gift wrapped offering

She left. You don't want to know what it is.

Maybe you are losing your wits. It wouldn't be surprising if you were. Here, in this forsaken garden, at the end of the road. Alone, isolating, self isolating, with the masked Amazon delivery man your only friend. You have already had one or two hallucinations. You thought you saw a peacock in the hedge. You thought you saw a stag amidst the fireglow. You thought you saw an egret on the roof.

What will you find when you go indoors?

Maybe She is still in there. Maybe She never left.

You are afraid to go in to your own house.

You stand on the threshold. Maybe She is in there, maybe She has locked you out. Maybe she has locked you out of your own house.

You pick up the pail of problematic pegs.

You will go in, and you will make a start on the poetry shelf. From Auden and Browning to Wordsworth and Yeats. You will set your house in order. These fragments you have stored against your ruins.

An Enfleshment of Desire

Saleem Haddad

Two DISTINCT MEMORIES RESURFACE when I think of those ten days in October. The first involves a series of videos coming out of Iraq that I saw shared on Twitter, footage of tear gas canisters shot from close range by security forces embedded in the skulls of protesters. In one video, a canister lodges in the eye socket of a middle-aged, overweight man. He falls to his knees, his hands cover his eyes, a thick cloud of smoke blooms from between his fingers. In another, a man lies facedown in an expanding pool of blood as the back of his head smokes like campfire. The other memory comes from my first encounter with S., when he flipped me over in bed and grabbed my ass with both hands. He squeezed and slapped my cheeks painfully, assessing my body like it was a cut of meat at the butchers. My face, pressed against his mattress, could not see the look in his eyes. Was it one of admiration and desire? Or was he still undecided on whether my body was what he wanted, and needed to see how my flesh would respond to his beatings? I wondered this as I lie there, the sharp pain from his slaps shooting through my body, as his cock – pressing against the inside of my thigh, a foreshadowing of a future penetration – pulsed each time I cried out in pain.

This period began at the close of my three-week visit to my parents in Beirut. I had been living in New York City for eleven years, married to D. for nine of those. The last time I lived in Beirut was 2008, when I left shortly after the street battles that dominated the spring season that year. What drove me to leave Lebanon was a desire for something, opportunity perhaps, or at least a liberation from some ill-defined shackle I was too young and naive to fully grasp at the time. Arriving in New York at the age of twenty-four, I was still full of dreams, full of the kind of youthful idealism about the life I might be able to create for myself, the relationship I might find and the dreams to which I might aspire. When I met D., we lived happily together for many years in a thoughtfully furnished apartment in Brooklyn that we shared with an adopted beagle named Barbara. D. was kind and good-natured, a man of logic and reason, and we supported each other through our studies and the establishment of our careers. We enjoyed nights of domestic bliss, cooked together in our tiny kitchen, devised elaborate travel plans, derided the failures of capitalism, and binged reality television while snuggled against each other on an ancient leather couch that belonged to D.'s great-aunt. On occasion, a kind of tyrannical sadness would overcome me, a melancholic longing for a time and a life that never existed. But for the most part I was happy. D. had always been good to me, treating me with a respect and kindness that I secretly didn't believe I deserved.

The night the protests begin, I am having drinks in Mar Mikhail with F., an old friend I had known from my past life in Beirut, who has since moved to Vienna to pursue a career in psychotherapy. It is Wednesday evening and I am due to return to New York at the close of the weekend. My phone buzzes with a text from my father, telling me to return home immediately because something is happening downtown. F.

and I finish our drinks and make our way back, the streets suddenly possessed by an eerie emptiness.

At home, on the television, a presenter is interviewing people rioting in the street. The government of sectarian warlords turned business tycoons has just announced a new set of austerity measures. A proposed tax on WhatsApp calls, it turns out, is the final straw. A young man with a scarf draped over his face leaps into the frame and grabs the microphone. The reporter tells him to remove the scarf and asks where in Lebanon he is from.

– From Akkar.

– And who told you to come protest?

– No one told me anything. I came because taxes keep rising. First on cigarettes, now they are taxing WhatsApp. Soon they're going to stick a gauge in our ass and tax us on our shit too.

That night I follow the news from my phone. The bodyguard of a politician points his machine gun at an unarmed female demonstrator. She responds with a roundhouse kick to his balls. The bodyguard falls back, his gun points to the sky. The video spreads like a virus on the internet. Demonstrators break into a telecommunications company, shatter the front glass of banks – those that hold the country's debt, that facilitate the thievery of the politicians. Some demonstrators set a construction site on fire, and two Syrian refugees who had been sheltering in the site choke to death on the fumes.

The next day, I put on my running shoes and meet F. in front of the civil war museum. She is all smiles and excitement, a large camera dangles from her neck, and we walk to the protest together. Streams of people flood the roads. 'Everyone means everyone' is the chant that echoes down the streets and boulevards leading towards Martyrs' Square. This chant feels like a unifying rallying call, a rejection of the entire gamut of sectarian warlords that have sown mistrust and division while looting the country for decades. In the blink of an eye, we have implicated all our sectarian masters with no exceptions. They all must go.

Lebanese flags are everywhere, draped over backs, flapping in the air or painted on sweaty faces and grime-stained walls. Smoke from burning tires and piles of trash rise up in the humid air, the putrid smell collects on our skin and clothes.

Many people are carrying signs. Young people mostly, but also old, and from all over the city: anarchist buzzcuts mingle with tightly-draped headscarves, toned and naked torsos sculpted by manual labour press against the garish plastic surgery of the upper classes. There are families too, rich and poor, carrying their children on their shoulders or pushing strollers through the quieter parts of the square. F. and I make our way to the dense centre. On the frontlines, women hold hands to protect the men from the security forces guarding the road leading to parliament. Here the air is a thick broth boiling with righteous indignation, but it feels easier to breathe somehow, easier than it has felt in a long time in Beirut.

F. takes photographs of the demonstrators while I stand beside her, my heart beating to the chants. My T-shirt is rapidly soaked with the sweat of others and myself, and the smell of this sweat hangs with the cigarette smoke in the air, the smell of bodies and burning. All at once, a powerful desire grips my body, a desire to dissolve inside the absence of fear, inside the collective public defiance, the call for unity and freedom that has erupted on the streets.

Surrendering to the sway and pulse of the crowd, I find myself wishing for violence, a climax to our transgression. When the violence finally comes that night – as security forces attack the crowds, lobbing tear gas canisters across the dark streets – the numbers only grow. The message is clear:

the more you attack us, the stronger we become.

In a phone call with D. that evening, I try to explain what has happened, but it is like trying to describe a vivid dream. My words are unable to recreate the power of the moment, they tumble from me hollow and vague. You're so fortunate to be there, D. tells me, before informing me that he cooked the most delicious shallot pasta dish from a recipe in the *New York Times*. His description of the caramelisation of the shallots feels more powerful than anything I have tried to describe, and I find an excuse to get off the phone before the despair overwhelms me.

The next day the crowds multiply, the numbers surging into the millions, people flock to the streets in every town and village across the country. The mood is one of excitement, passion, confusion and despair. The message is consistent. Everyone means everyone. The warlord politicians, and the sectarian system that upholds them, that privileges the wealthy and powerful, that exploits cynical privatisation schemes and networks of patronage and nepotism, that increases the poverty and indignation of the underclass, all must go.

F. and I walk through the crowds in a euphoric daze. People are pressing and moving through one another, chanting and singing and clapping hands. In the thickest sections, people collapse, from the heat, from the vibe emanating from the bodies. Ambulances drive through crowds to pick up the fallen, and crowds disperse like parting waves to let them through. When minor skirmishes flare up, they are quickly extinguished by the crowds.

A giant clenched fist is erected in the centre of the square, a symbol of the thawra, the revolution. Malaise – the moral ill-being that had engulfed us in a fog – is now replaced with desire. And this desire – no one tells you how horny a revolution makes you. The subversion of tyranny, the orgy of bodies pushing up against one another in joy and defiance, the voices rising in unison and collective understanding, is an immensely vibratory experience. We are all fucking or else dying to fuck and yes we want all of the impunity and corruption and fear to go away but we also want to fuck too, gloriously, to lick and suck and press our sweaty bodies against one another, to connect in all the ways possible.

Were it not for this revolutionary desire, I would never have met S. Like everyone else I was yearning for something, an intimate hunger both political and erotic. On Friday afternoon, I take a break from the crowds and find a quiet corner behind the square, where I download a hookup app. Later that evening, F. and I follow the crowds spilling out of the square and into the bars and restaurants along Gemmayze. We order drinks and stand in the street smoking cigarettes and talking.

We enter into a heated discussion with a group about which of the two evils is more powerful: sect or class. We discuss what would happen if someone were to raise a Palestinian flag alongside the millions of Lebanese ones. After all, aren't the Palestinians who have lived their entire lives in Lebanon also suffering from the same problems, stuck in a never-ending limbo with their cause held as a noose around their neck, the young punished for the mistakes of their forefathers? Too early, F. says. Let the Lebanese solve their own problems first. But isn't that what is always said? Let us get our rights first and yours will follow. In the Palestinian camps, someone mentions, an eerie calm has prevailed. Even the drug dealers and armed factions are lying low, waiting.

My phone buzzes in my pocket. It is a message from the app, a message from S.

– Hey.

His profile contains a single photograph, a sweaty post-workout selfie in the bathroom mirror of a locker room. He is wearing blue shorts, a pair of Bluetooth earphones hang around his neck. His eyes partially hidden behind locks of brown hair, his nose long and straight, his mouth pursed in concentration. His chest is large and muscular, peppered with hair that trails down his abdomen. A constellation of rebellious freckles scatter across the left-side of his stomach.

I respond.

– Hey. What are you looking for?

– Sex.

– What are you into?

– I am top.

His omission of the article 'a' bestows a sense of non-negotiability to his sexual position, rendering it a totalitarian state.

– Okay.

– Meet now?

The app informs that he is thirty-five years old and 672 metres away. I imagine a circle – with me at its centre – extending 672 metres across the city in all directions, encompassing the crowds and chants and fires, with S. somewhere on the circumference.

– Not now. Maybe tomorrow.

Tomorrow is more of the same. Young men on motorcycles speed through the streets, snaking through the crowds, sucking on cigarettes through the small holes of their masks. More tires are burned to block the main roads. Demonstrators take over abandoned and derelict buildings downtown. Previously closed off to the public, these buildings become lecture halls in the muggy afternoons and techno raves in the evenings. Inside the buildings, the chants dissipate into a quiet murmur of childlike curiosity, as revolutionaries explore the insides of the crumbling structures that have been boarded up for so long. Beirut's downtown – reconstructed in the aftermath of the civil war as an exclusive and impenetrable ghost town of high-end stores, banks, and businesses – is taken over and transformed. Previously empty streets fill up with pedestrians, food stalls, impromptu hair salons and shisha stations. The process is not one of colonisation but reclamation, the people and the streets are two lost lovers rediscovering each other's bodies.

On Saturday, I message D. and tell him I am considering delaying my flight back. It's a once-in-a-lifetime opportunity, I explain, and I am ready to fight him about this, but he only tells me that I don't need to explain myself, that he understands. But does he truly grasp what is happening, and do I even want him to? It would be like a needle meeting a balloon. I do not want him to grasp what is happening inside of me, I realise with surprising bitterness, as the schisms between me and the comfort of my New York life begin to reveal themselves.

That night, the protest transforms into a massive rave. Revolutionaries dance in the dark streets, drunk on unity and power. Working-class young men, lean and shirtless and wearing Guy Fawkes masks, grind against each other, posing for the cameras of foreigners and the upper classes. F. and I hold hands among the crowds, our bodies swaying, buzzing, as bodies brush up against our own. Above us, clouds of smoke float up into the night sky. Music and chants blast through speakers. F. grabs my head with both hands and shouts into my ear to be heard above the noise.

– I've spent my whole life trying to leave this country. Now I wish to return.

At this moment, I make the decision to delay my return. I grab my phone from my pocket and message S.

– I need to fuck.

– Come over.

I walk F. home, we stroll past the row of police wearing helmets and carrying plastic shields. Further along the road, cars and motorcycles shoot by waving flags and honking. I follow S.'s directions, crossing Bechara El Khoury and taking a turn into a dark street behind Sodeco that smells of rotting garbage. At his building, I ring the apartment number and the door clicks open with an electrifying buzz.

His smile is the first thing that greets me when I disembark the elevator. It is a thick and warm smile that leaves me entirely disarmed. Inside the dark apartment we stand facing one another, our bodies navigating around each other like two cautious predators meeting in the wild. He is tall, an imposing presence, but his eyes are large and like warm honey. His dark brown hair flops playfully around the edges of his face, and is longer than in the picture on his profile. He is also heavier than in the picture, and this suits him. His apartment is spacious and opulent. He is a rich man, I begin to understand, and he carries himself in a way that suggests he has been rich all his life.

We sit down on his leather sofa at a respectable distance from one another. The awkwardness feels electric and dangerous. Finally, his words penetrate the silence.

– Shall we move to the bedroom?

The bedroom is dark and it is difficult to see. His large hand grabs the hair on the back of my head and pulls my head back and up, exposing my lips. He leans forward and touches them with his fingers. My hunger for him is an overpowering stench and I can smell the same from him. After some moments I pull myself from his grip.

– Maybe I should shower. I've been on the streets all day.

– No. I want you this way. As you are.

He pushes me onto the bed, turns me over, claws at my skin, gnawing on the flesh of my back, my sides, my flank. The next morning, while getting dressed in my bedroom, the sight of the bruises revolutionises me. Looking at my bruised body in the mirror, I think of Beirut, a city beaten-up and scarred, of its bullet-ridden buildings and the tires burning on its streets. My body feels like a site of experimental transformation, a dangerous struggle for power. The bruises feel like an enfleshment of my desires, all of them.

But that night in his room I only feel my soul leaving my body and floating up to the ceiling, and beyond that to the sky along with the tear gas and smoke bombs that are set off that night. We repeat five words to each other, over and over, as we fuck.

– I want you so bad.

In his shower I wash him, wash the day's revolution, off my skin. When I emerge in a towel he is already dressed. He stands in the living room, a black cat curled around his bare feet. I notice the nail of his little toe has blackened and is about to fall, and I wonder how it must have happened. But the lights in the apartment have brightened, a shift in tone that makes the question feel too intimate. Outside, there are sirens. Inside, his voice is tender, his mannerisms reluctant.

– How long will you stay?

– I am supposed to fly back to New York on Monday but I will delay my return.

– You have someone in New York?

– A husband, yes. I need to get back to him.

– Mmhm.

– But I want to stay.

– Riddle.

The next day the protests feel more serious and confident. The hundreds of thousands of defiant revolutionaries press against one another, stimulating the body, enfleshing the politics. The chants cut through the thick air like a blade through flesh. Anger is brewing, I can feel it pulsing through my veins as I chant. Mao Tse Tsung once said that a revolution is not a dinner party; it cannot be refined, leisurely or gentle. Rather, a revolution is an act of violence.

A revolution is not a one night stand, either. S. messages in the afternoon.

– Hey sexy.

We meet in the early evening. He is naked when he opens the door, all the blinds in the living room are down, and he descends on me like a beating, tearing off my clothes, scratching my skin. He licks my nipples and I moan. Then he bites down harder. I squirm out from under him, it is the first real pain he has caused me, but he holds me in place and looks me in the eyes, paralysing me.

– I wish I could be with you every night.

In response, I slap him gently on the face. It is more of a tap, a guidance. He looks at me and I do it again, and he understands and strikes me back, first gently and then harder, until my skin burns and the inside of my cheek scrapes against the edge of my teeth and I can taste blood. The pain runs down my spine, electrifying. He kisses me and smiles.

– I wish you were mine.

– I'm yours right now.

– Yes. But I wish you were mine all the time.

He utters these words and I am caught in his trap, radicalised by this desire. I want nothing more than to say the same to him, that I wish I was his all the time, but D.'s face appears in my mind. I can picture his round bookish glasses, his unassuming smile, and then his face disappears as the sound of banging pots and pans echoes outside, a denouncement of the government from those unable to head out to the streets. I am caught in the revolution's trap too, I know, cannot tear myself from the city. I wish it were mine, wish the revolution were mine forever. It is a hopeless desire, I know, and one that is not without consequence.

Later, when towelling myself in S.'s bedroom, I notice a painting on his bedroom wall that resembles two half-rotting skeletons embracing one another. When I emerge into the living room, S. is standing in the centre, his long hair is wet, the blinds are up and we are revealed to the city. This exposure introduces a formality that feels like a betrayal.

– The painting in your bedroom. Did you paint it yourself?

– No. I commissioned it.

It is then that I notice the walls of his living room are covered in large paintings in differing styles. Dark and textured, bordering on the abstract.

– And these?

– I commissioned most of them, yes. All Arab artists – mostly Syrian and Iraqi. I ask them to paint pain and desire.

– Pain and desire?

– Arab artists only paint pain and war. I want them to paint this pain, but in the context of desire. I have asked them, show me this pain, but with a desire.

He moves towards a large square painting above the leather sofa.

– What do you see?

I consider the painting. I can see the shape of a man, a head and a body, and just above the man is a shadow of another face, smaller, looking towards the sky, the mouth open in a grimace or a howl, somewhere between ecstasy and terror. The painting brings to my mind Jung's concept of the shadow.

– Is it a man and his shadow?

– Everyone sees this one differently. The artist based this painting on a photograph taken in the aftermath of a bombing in Syria. A photograph of a man running from the site of his destroyed house, carrying his son on his back. But I like your interpretation also.

He moves towards the painting by the front door. The largest of all the paintings, this one takes up an entire wall that runs the length of the dining room table. The painting is of soldiers attacking a group of women, tearing off clothes, thrusting themselves upon their bodies.

– This was done by a Kurdish artist. A scene of the rape and pillaging of a village during war. See this woman who is being raped. What is the look on her face? The artist told me her face is in pain. Do you see pain in her face?

I look at the woman's face, her mouth is twisted like a rotting apple on the pale hue of her skin. Before I can speak, S. answers his own question.

– I can see only desire.

Returning home that night, my mother turns from the scenes of violence on television and studies my face.

– You have a redness on your cheek.

– Do I?

– From the protests?

– Perhaps.

Every day that week F. and I meet at the entrance of the civil war museum near Sodeco square and head down to the thawra together. There is so much to see, so much to do. Demonstrations, roadblocks, meetings, symposiums, film screenings. Every day of the thawra, every moment of it, is composed of a different vibe. I surrender to the mood of the day, to whatever emotions the street decides, to the hundreds of thousands of emanating bodies. Emotions come suddenly and without warning. I tremble with fear, howl with joy and weep tears of rage. My body does not belong to me. The main chant, 'Hail-a hail-a hail-a hail-a ho, *Gebran Bassil kes emmo*',[1] possesses a meditative quality, the 'O' sound resembling a Buddhist chant. For the next several days, my lips find themselves around the 'O' at unexpected times, while making a cup of coffee, while brushing my teeth, while trying to fall asleep at night, while debating whether I should ever return to New York.

Some chants are popular, others less well-received, hinting at fissures.

– Politicians out out! Refugees in in!

A few murmurs of dissent from the crowd.

When the chants turn to Iraq and Sudan, someone behind me grumbles.

– Let's focus on our country first, please.

The fissures grow. Unblock the roads, people need to get to work. No one should go to work until the system falls. Everyone means everyone, all sectarian parties need to go, and Hezbollah is one of them. Hezbollah is a red line, do not be swayed by foreign strategies to weaken the resistance. Feminists chant about bringing down the patriarchy, homophobia, sectarianism, to counter the patriarchal and homophobic chants of some of the revolutionaries. Together on the streets we are discovering that betrayals and injustices cut a million different ways like reflections from a broken mirror. And we are also discovering, though we are not ready to admit this, that unity is but a desire, and that a desire must by its very nature remain elusive.

It is hard to think, impossible to plan. I understand that outside of all this I have a husband and a job and obligations, duties of a past life. But all this solidness melts away with disorienting ease. Emails and messages accumulate with requests for meetings and I don't even know what will happen in five minutes let alone in a few weeks. Every moment new things are happening, people are mobilising, everything is changing. My entire present and future is at the mercy of the street, at the mercy of the emotions of fear, hope, anger and love that passes from one body to another.

And at night, I am at the mercy of my carnal desires. I make my way buzzing to S.'s apartment in Achrafieh. He greets me at the door, his tall, large body in the shadows, and he pulls me inside. He takes off my clothes, wet with the day's grime and sweat, and leads me to the dark bedroom, where we excavate from one another the day's vibe, the intensity of our desire bestowing a clumsiness to our behaviour, full of stops and starts. Afterwards I shower, wash him off me and emerge cleansed, my skin red and pulsing from the hot water, to see the blinds in the living room are up, allowing an easy view into the apartment, signalling an end to our time together. We do not discuss the thawra, what it means, where we stand on it. Does S. attend the protests? I have no idea, and a part of me does not want to know. He possesses an ambivalence that indicates he might react to the protests in the same way he reacted to seeing a photograph of D. and I together: revealing an ironic smile that could be read a million different ways as he simply said 'cute couple'. I don't want to know where he stands, I realise. My desire to remain ignorant of his politics is a deliberate blinkering, a redaction. When I leave his apartment he offers only a hug, and I make my way home through the silent streets.

One morning the army is mobilised to clear the roads, beating civilians who try to stop them. Messages sent through WhatsApp ask people to go to the areas the army is targeting, and soon the numbers are large enough that the army can do nothing. Some of the men in uniform have tears in their eyes, they hug civilians. Many say the army is composed of people just like us, that they are for the protection of the people and a friend to the thawra. Others remind that the army is a brutal structure, part of the system of oppressive power that must be neutralised, that cannot be trusted.

That afternoon in the squares, a teenager distributes condoms with a sign that says: Free condoms so you can fuck the politicians.

F. walks up to him.

– Fucking is a beautiful act. Why must we use it as a threat of violence?

The teenager stops to think, then he looks F. in the eye and points to his own chest.

– I'm the one that will be doing the fucking.

Later that evening, F. and I walk to Hamra. In front of the central bank, a group of activists sit in a circle in the middle of the street, discussing ideas for a new Lebanon and strategies to get there. Before speaking, each person introduces themselves and says where they are from. Beside me, a man with long dreadlocks sketches each of the speakers in his tiny notebook, alongside speech bubbles that highlight key words that come from their mouths. Someone hands out water and cookies.

More and more people speak, the voices accumulate on top of one another like the Babel Tower, and the weight of the week's events descends on me. This is huge. It's huge and the road is long and uncertain. We are a nation that has collectively decided to embrace this uncertainty, to head into the unknown. One man with glasses speaks about mortgage rates and central bank corruption, and to my left a young man heckles that this advice is only useful to the middle-classes.

– I don't even have a bank account, man.

A woman begins to speak, and the heckler interrupts her.

– We told everyone to come. Be prepared. Around one thousand people are heading this way now. From the square.

Thirty seconds later men on motorcycles begin to arrive. We can hear chanting as silhouetted figures appear on the horizon, heading our way. Thawra, thawra, thawra. The group of activists stands up and dissolves into the incoming crowd.

I hail a taxi to take me to S.'s apartment. Upon entering the car, the driver, young and angry, turns to me and says I must pay in dollars.

– And the petrol prices. Do you think this is worth it? To drive you across town at these prices?

He grips the steering wheel tightly, takes a sharp turn and heads east.

– We are all hungry. We are all suffering. I agree with the protests, but this will bring more suffering.

And then.

– They are all thieves, conspirators destroying the country.

– And you? You are coming for a visit? From where? Is this the time to visit? What is there to see in this shithole?

We speed down the empty highway towards Ring Bridge. The road is blocked. The driver is furious.

– There is nothing for you here. Go back and forget about this hopeless place.

He turns and speeds under a bridge.

– This is as far as I can go. You have to get off here.

I get out of the car, which disappears down the empty highway. I cross the road and walk the fifteen minutes to S.'s apartment. He opens the door for me and quickly pulls me inside. I need you so much tonight, he whispers. He is panting, weakened by desire. I try to smell the revolution on him, the smell of the streets, but I am intoxicated by my hunger for him. When he is inside of me, he holds my face in his hands and looks me in the eye.

– I want to come inside of you.

– That's not part of the rules. You know that.

His hands slide down to my throat.

– I am so jealous of him. Your husband.

– Don't.

– I don't even know him but I want to destroy him.

He is pushing the boundaries now, I know, of my relationship, my rules, my body. He is testing the red lines, bringing to mind the chants of the anti-revolutionaries: The resistance is a red line. Berri[2] is a red line.

– Stop talking about my husband.

– I can't help it. I'm jealous. I want you all for myself. I want to come inside of you.

It rains on me as I walk home that night. I lie in bed and think of what it would feel like to have his seed inside me, the transgressive significance of the gesture. Had I not been married, and married to a foreigner, would S. have wanted so badly to stake his claim to me, to make my body the site of his own revolution? When I fall asleep I dream of S., of holding him in my arms. But every time I reach for him his face transforms to someone else, an ex-colleague, a famous actor, an old high school tormentor.

The next morning, as the government continues to call on the people to unblock the roads, it rains so hard the streets are flooded and no one can move, the bitter irony of a government trumped by its own infrastructural neglect.

Lying in bed, my body throbs with desire. This desire – for S., for the revolution – feels not like an estrangement but a return from an estrangement. Gripped in this fever I feel that I have found something again, something that makes me who I once was but also never was, a fantasy of myself to which I have been longing to return. I listen to the monstrous thundering of rain and fantasise about riding on the back of a scooter with S., racing down the old beach road from Batroun to Beirut. The coastline is unpolluted, free of garbage and debris, the air in our faces fresh and clean. I fantasise that I am with him in a bar in Beirut, our bodies intimately close to one another as I push the hair from his face so I can whisper in his ear. I fantasise that we are both in his living room, making plans for a Friday night. S. is in a towel looking at his phone, I am sitting on his brown leather sofa, the black cat on my lap.

All of these fantasies involve an anticipation, the destination never fully fleshed out. The focus is on the journey: the drive down the unpolluted coast, a whisper in a crowded bar, the intimate planning in the living room. I try to conjure up the destination: the plans being made, the arrival at our location, the words being whispered. But the destination of these fantasies is just out of reach. And that's the thing with desire, I am learning, once the destination is reached, desire ceases to exist.

That afternoon, for the first time in seven revolting days and nights, the president finally appears on television. It is a 'live' broadcast that is obviously pre-recorded: the camera cuts in odd ways, a stack of books behind his senile body keeps re-arranging itself. I agree with you about the evils of the sectarian system, he says, but it is too difficult and complicated to change. Corruption has eaten us to the bone, he says, but what you are calling for is impossible, a fantasy.

When he is finished speaking, D. messages from New York.

– Can we chat?

– I need to go protest.

– Just for a few minutes.

Even through the computer screen it is clear that the uncertainty has infected D. in New York. He tells me about the routines of his day, the meals he has cooked, the films he has seen. As he tells me about Barbara's latest misbehaviours, I think of our life together – the cuddles on the couch, the home-cooked dinners, the long walks in the park – and the feeling of returning to my comfortable exile is akin to a bucket of water dousing a fire inside me.

– When do you think you will be back?

– I don't know.

– But your flight back is tomorrow?

– Yes.

– But you won't be on the flight.

– I don't think so.

– Barbara misses you.

– Barbara is a dog.

– I miss you. Why are you delaying your return?

– I don't know.

The patchy internet freezes my body into a permanent shrug. I observe my image on the screen, frozen in a moment of uncertainty. I don't know how much of my desire to stay is driven by S. and how much is driven by the thawra. D. has always been good to me, loyal and caring. He is handsome, intelligent, funny, and well-loved by my friends. He has taken care of me and understands many parts of me, enough for us to progress happily in our lives. And the parts that he does not understand, I realise, are taking shape now, on the streets and in S.'s apartment. I am discovering parts of myself that I have shut away in a closed room for a long time in New York, frightening parts, parts that are not understood by D., parts that perhaps I do not fully understand myself, but which are now being taken out and unfolded in front of my eyes.

And in my frozen eyes on the screen, I see a resentment simmering underneath my veil of ambivalence. I've come to blame D. for my estrangement, for being exiled from myself. And although D. is pleading with me to let him in on the parts of myself I have kept from him, I fear that he will believe this estrangement to be his own fault somehow, and look for ways to correct it therapeutically or medicinally, to diagnose and fix the problem like it were an upset stomach. Or perhaps the reason I have kept these parts from him is because I have become too comfortable in my own estrangement, and fearful of what I may lose by reconciling all these different parts of myself.

When the image unfreezes, I tell D., You are the most important thing in my life.

Not anymore, he replies. He smiles when he says this, and the internet glitches again, freezing his face, giving me time to explore all the sadness and shame and doubt lingering behind his eyes.

Just then the electricity cuts off in the apartment. D.'s frozen face disappears. My news feed comes to an abrupt halt.

Everywhere is silent as the appliances die. There is nothing but the sound of traffic and the distant roar of the crowds in the streets, nearly indistinguishable from the sound of the thunder in the sky. I don't know what the world will look like when the electricity comes back on and suddenly I am petrified.

When I see S. that evening, my body is stiff and useless in his arms.

– You are nervous.

– Saying that only makes it worse.

– You are holding back from me.

I shake my head weakly but he is right. I am holding back the full force of my desire. The greater the desire, the greater the danger, and I am fearful that if not repressed my desire will swallow the both of us whole, will uproot the entire order of society as we know it. Does this desire for S. extend beyond his body, beyond his bedroom, encompassing the crowds, the rat-infested streets and the tear gas and chants and polluted seawater and privatised beachfronts? It is hard to put my finger on this desire, to civilise it with language, to limit its tremendous power, animalistic and primal. Is it love, a powerful love, or is it a force that is out to destroy me?

S. rolls on his back, pulling me on top of him, his muscles flex as he holds me close to his chest and smiles into my nose.

– Let me love you a little.

He kisses me gently on the lips, the cheeks, the nose. The roughness with which he had reached for me during our previous encounters melts, his touch is softer and more tender now. And for now this is what I desire, to be loved and to feel helpless. There is a power in this, to brandish my helplessness like a weapon. A chosen powerlessness.

S. whispers in my ear.

– Just let go. Surrender to me.

To let go? To surrender? To surrender to the erotic desire, like giving in to the movement of the crowds, to the idealism of the revolutionary chants? If I could only surrender freely to desire, knowing that what I desire is within my grasp, not just a dream or a fantasy. In a relationship one projects their desires onto another and edits out the rest. The process is akin to a mutilation. All revolutions fail, do they not? And those that succeed only sow different seeds of rot. And our revolution, our relationship, would be no different. A person can project anything they desire on a leaderless insurrection, and that too is akin to a mutilation.

And the next day I watch from home with my heart in my throat as Hezbollah's leader comes on television while his supporters beat protestors and tear down the makeshift stalls of the small businesses and initiatives that have been set up in the squares. And in a soft and gentle voice, he implores the protestors to be honest and admit the dark and shadowy foreign agendas funding the revolution. And a menacing smile is drawn on his face as he admonishes the use of 'bad words', warns of the dangers of chaos and political vacuum, reminding that everyone in the country has weapons and everyone in the country has emotions, and these emotions can be easily triggered by bad words. And as his supporters tear down the revolutionary tents they chant: the resistance and its weapons are a red line. And when he is done speaking he tells his supporters to leave the squares, and like a tide retreating to the ocean they disperse and disappear, leaving the revolutionaries to clear up the wreckage. And as soon as his face vanishes from the screens the streets fill up with people coming out in defiance. And F. and I descend to the squares, and it is this defiance in the face of fear and accusations of treachery that hold us together, I believe, because the source of the fissures lies in fear and treachery, and it is only in our steadfast denial of these tactics that we have any hope of staying together. And that evening, next to the statue of Samir Kassir, a young woman grabs a loudspeaker and begins to shout.

– Celebrating in the streets is not enough! We need to go to those politicians' houses and step on their necks.

And I grab my phone from my bag and send S. a message.

– I need you to annihilate me tonight.

And he replies ten minutes later.

– My pleasure.

I arrive later than usual that night. He opens the door for me, behind him on the leather sofa I see a blanket and a glass of water. On the television, an episode of Law & Order: Special Victims Unit is paused on the screen. What kind of person watches Law & Order in the midst of a revolution, I wonder, and this drives me to finally ask him the question.

– What do you think of the protests?

– Why are you still wearing clothes?

He watches me undress. When I am naked I kneel down before him, pick up his foot, and put my lips on the blackened toenail. I can feel it loosen further in my mouth, and then he picks me up. My legs wrap around his waist, and he carries me to the bedroom. He lays me on the bed and turns me over on my stomach. I can feel him insert a finger inside me, then another, then another. I squirm from the pain, but he pushes my head down into the pillow with one hand as he explores me with the other. I recall then the gas canisters lodged in the heads of the protesters in Iraq, the videos I had seen on Twitter over the last week. When all five fingers are inside me he manoeuvres them around in exploration, and I cry out in fullness. I think of the clenched fist erected in the centre of the square, the symbol of the revolution. I'm not sure how much time passes, but I feel a sudden withdrawal, an emptiness.

– There is blood.

I lift my head from the pillow and turn to him. He is staring at his hand.

– Wash yourself.

I stand up and do as he says. He washes his own hand in the sink, ribbons of pink water swirl in the white porcelain before disappearing down the drain. Cleaned, he leads me back into the bedroom, pushes me on the bed and falls onto me, inserting himself inside of me with a heartless thrust, his wet hand over my mouth, his skin smells of soap and blood. He stares at me but his eyes are opaque, like black water. And then he moans and I feel his release, a foreign body, a canister, travelling inside me, emitting its poison, brutalising my insides.

In the shower, I make the decision to leave Beirut. I feel not sadness or joy but a disappointed sort of hunger. In the living room I tell S. about my decision.

– Okay.

– You're not upset?

– You will for sure come back.

I cannot grasp his tone. Is it one of reassurance, order, or smug confidence? It seems that whatever understanding we had of each other is now gone.

As a goodbye he high-fives me. His gaze is icy, there is a break of the spell. He is so terribly handsome, like a Disney prince. But who is the real S., I wonder, the man in the bedroom or the cold ghost in the living room?

Leaving his house, I walk down the dark wet streets, past a group of men lingering on the sidewalk, my flesh holding many secrets, in the creases of my skin and the holes of my body. At home, the decision having been made, I swallow any lingering unease and quickly fall asleep, after two weeks of barely sleeping.

At some point in those final two days I again have the dream where I am riding on the back of S.'s motorcycle along that unpolluted coastline from Batroun to Beirut. A warmth travels through my body like a sunburn until I remember that if a Lebanon like that exists then the S. I am dreaming about would not, he would be different somehow, in even the slightest ways, but enough to alter my desire for him profoundly. It is an impossible thing to hold both of these fantasies in one's hands, in one's mind, in one's heart.

At the airport, the calm resignation I have felt in the last two days evaporates. If I were younger, perhaps this is the moment I would turn back and take a taxi back to my parents' house in Beirut. But I am older, and idealism is something I can discard like an old piece of clothing. And I am safer because of this, although poorer too.

There's nothing to do now but to learn to live with all of these feelings, it occurs to me, as I pass through immigration at the airport. I buy a bottle of water for three times the amount it normally costs. I want to yell at the clerk but know he has no say in the matter. Then, when the officer checks my passport before boarding the plane, I have a sudden desire to be pulled aside, prevented from leaving, sent back to the revolution. But the officer waves me through, and that too is a feeling I need to learn to live with.

I return to my old life. D. does not ask any questions, but a chasm has opened between us and we are not as close as before. A natural gulf perhaps, one created slowly over years of commitment, the gulf between two individuals making decisions to stay with one another even as life moves on, changing them in the process. He does not ask many questions about my time in Beirut. I resent and am thankful for this. One time over dinner, some weeks after my return, he asks.

– So how was it?

And I shrug. He asks this the night that anti-revolutionaries set fire to the giant fist erected in the centre of Martyr's Square. When we return from dinner, I watch on social media, from thousands of miles away, as the fist burns in the night, and I recall S.'s own fist inside of me. And for the first time I mourn our failure, to move beyond the language of desire, to translate the passion into something else – love, the creation of a new world – if such a thing even exists.

Notes

1. 'Gebran Bassil, his mother's vagina!'
2. Nabih Berri, Lebanese politician, Speaker of the Parliament of Lebanon since 1992. He heads the Amal Movement, associated with Lebanon's Shia community.

Bind

Matthew Holness

*'A visual feast of spring colour, today! Small miracles of
floral fantasy. See the recurring marvel of the loveliness of
spring flowers. Refined, unexpected plantings.'*

IT SEEMED AS THOUGH I'd always had the invitation in my
possession. The attractive elegance of the card's design,
however, belied the location of the exhibition itself, which
began in a sparsely-furnished room resembling the reception
area of a school I'd known well.

The bare walls surrounding me were painted a pale blue,
brightened by sunlight which shone through tall, rectangular
windows spaced high above. Through these neglected panes of
glass, I could see only the vast, cloudless sky beyond. Positioned
in front of them, upon an adjacent ledge and disrupting the
perfect symmetry of the intersecting frames, I glimpsed a lone
daffodil, stem balanced against the slim neck of a glass bottle,
straining its flowered head toward the light.

Set against one wall of the room was a desk, upon which
a tray had been placed, containing a single, ordinary drinking
glass. There was no chair behind, and I felt my sense of
excitement fade as I realised there was no-one present to
confirm my invitation and welcome me in.

I wondered whether he himself might make an appearance, having arranged this entertainment especially for me. Then I recalled that I hadn't seen him in a long time, and had great difficulty, even, in visualising his face and features.

I picked the glass up from the tray, noting how the liquid within was unusually still, even when held in my hand. I raised the drink tentatively to my lips, caught a trace of something sharp in its scent and immediately placed it down again, transferring my attention instead to what lay beside it. This was a sheet of blue paper, evidently a brochure for the exhibition itself. I examined it closely, realising with mild disappointment that it was a cheap photocopy; far less enticing than the finely-wrought invitation.

The words upon it had originally been typed and were hard to discern, worn letterheads having failed to impress themselves sufficiently against the faded ink ribbon. There was also a diagonal crease across the middle, where the page had been previously folded, and the top half of the exposed side had faded with sunlight to a pale grey. I turned it over to read the descriptions spaced unevenly along one side.

The name of each display was embedded within the description that followed. Together, these formed brief, cryptic passages, awkwardly phrased and oblique in meaning, yet the combined effect was to convey a sense of anticipation in my mind.

As I made my way toward the closed door at the far end of the room, where I presumed the exhibition must begin, I sensed the ghost of a familiar glow somewhere within. A vague impression of lost familiarity. Childhood, perhaps, or an emotion I associated with it. Either my own, or that rekindled with Natalie during her fairground years. With a sting of unexpected sadness, that my daughter was not here with me to enjoy the entertainment, I grasped the door's handle in my hand and pushed it open, moving through in search of the first exhibit.

*

'A scent of gentle but ephemeral perfumes.'

The corridor I entered was long; empty but for another row of tall windows halfway down. These, like those in the reception area, were situated high up, close to the ceiling, and projected rays of sunlight down into the passageway ahead.

As I passed beneath these particular windows I looked up and again saw nothing beyond them but a deep, cloudless spread of azure sky. When I turned my head back to the corridor before me, my sight had become temporarily dazzled from the arcing light. The pale blue of the adjacent walls now appeared greener than before, matching my dim memories of the hospital and surgery corridors I'd been carried through as an infant. As if in sympathy with my thoughts, the walls now appeared to glide past me as I moved, as if I were suspended still in the arms of a nurse, or my mother, soon to be weighed in a silver tray, my alarm and confusion soothed with sugar against the needle's piercing jab. I wondered what traces, if any, remained in the worn veins and tissues of those struggling arms, then thought immediately of Natalie's unexpected, spontaneous laugh upon receiving her own, and the smiling sunflower pin they'd rewarded her with.

I glanced down to rest my eyes and saw that the worn carpet tiles beneath my feet were stained by a spillage of some sort which still emitted, I thought, a faintly chemical scent as I passed over them. It may have been that I was experiencing a sensory hallucination akin to my experience with the glass, a symptom of the lingering dysmosia I'd developed following an infection of impetigo caused by Natalie crawling over rented floors. But the smell appeared to fade again as I looked up and concentrated my mind on the path in front.

I could see now that the corridor opened up into another running lengthways in both directions. As I arrived at the junction, expecting to see paintings of pastoral scenes spaced evenly along each wall, I found that these were now merely rectangular patches of faded, flaking paint, where the frames and nails had been removed. The corridor itself was of equal length to the one I'd left, and ended in either direction at a closed door.

It was then that I first became aware of the sound. It seemed to come from a great distance away, although its true nature and proximity were smothered by the formless network of intervening rooms and walls. Whether the source of it lay beyond, or was instead contained within the confined space of one of the exhibition rooms, was impossible to establish. I thought, however, that it was a human voice, and sensed, upon listening to it carefully for a minute or two, that whoever it belonged to was in the habit of repeating a specific phrase, over and over.

The cry, for that is what it had now become, seemed to reverberate more from the left-hand corridor. It sounded increasingly like somebody weeping, the longer I concentrated my thoughts upon it. Unnerved by its unusual timbre, which itself had begun to transform in peculiar ways, I opted instead for the opposite path. Swiftly, I moved along it, away from the sound, concerned that there had as yet been no indication, no sign in place to point me in the direction of the first exhibit. Then at last I reached the door ahead of me, and immediately recognised the child's hand-writing upon its front.

★

'Unforgettable florescent carpets and the
magnificence and splendour of floats.'

The sheet of paper sellotaped to the glass pane, obscuring my view of the room's interior, was also decorated with a child's drawing of a house. The words themselves had clearly been copied directly from the typed brochure at some stage, and the manner with which the letters dipped frequently below the ruled lines, mixing with other faintly erased markings, reminded me of educational scientific animations, depicting cross-section diagrams of plant roots under soil. It made me think again of Natalie, struggling to keep her own letters above the line, and myself, too, reprimanded once by a teacher for piercing my arm with a sharpened pencil.

Easing the door gently open, I discovered long shreds of torn paper hanging from the immediate wall. As the door swung further inward, it revealed a large, untidy heap of coloured sheets, strewn across the floor within. Some of these had evidently been torn and flung, others screwed and crumpled forcefully into various piles.

As far as I could tell, the ruined sheets formed individual illustrations. Yet upon kneeling down to inspect them more closely, I saw that the various flowers they depicted were largely incomplete, forming instead part of a much larger, cohesive decoration, that had presumably been arranged in full against the wall.

I suspected from its description in the brochure, however, that the exhibit had not been vandalised, but in fact constituted the final composition of the work itself – a torn classroom display. Upon realising this, my immediate thought was that I had inadvertently spoiled the piece myself by touching it. But there being no way through the room without walking directly over the heaped piles, I reasoned that this must therefore form an essential part of the experience.

I stepped onto them and immediately felt something break beneath my feet. I reached down and drew out several fragments of a child's decorative model, concealed beneath the fallen paper. The crushed egg cartons and crumpled felt-tipped cardboard looked immediately familiar, and I recognised it as a present I'd made for my mother on my first day at infants' school. The gift had been a crude potted sunflower, its paper petals daubed with uneven splashes of yellow paint, with my mother's name copied so carefully from the teacher's guiding hand that she'd displayed it with unabashed pride on her bedroom dresser for years, alongside the photograph of me standing proudly next to the real thing we'd managed to grow, at long last, the following summer.

I dropped the ruined pieces to the floor, indifferent to the loss, which I suppose had already been suffered, having torn the thing up in front of her during a bad argument in my teens. It meant nothing to me, now. Only what any flower consisted of in real terms. A combination of form, colour and scent designed with a single aim; the biological purpose of attraction.

I felt other items breaking beneath my feet as I walked through the room toward the opposite door. I briefly examined one or two that I also recognised, and had kept safe for many years in a box by my own bedside. Yet these, like all the rest, were mere components of assembled material, once more fragmented. I crossed the room quickly and shut the door behind me.

*

'A unique planting of subtle splendour, richly adorned.'

I entered a dim room, illuminated only by a suggestion of windows somewhere above. Immediately before me was a wide staircase. The steps were wooden, with horizontal gaps spaced evenly between. As I ascended, I glanced through them and thought I saw a figure lying in the corner of the room below, its back facing toward me. Its form felt oddly familiar, and when I reached the pinned notice at the top of the stairs I realised I'd walked straight past the brochure's next exhibit. Recalling at last what it had resembled, I leant my head back over the adjacent balcony rail beyond the stair's reach, to see whether I could make out more of the display without having to get any closer.

The figure was moving – a shuddering motion, as though it were wracked with some stifled sobbing fit. The overtly dramatic nature of the movement felt unconvincing, however, like a deliberate gesture bordering on the histrionic. I watched it for a minute or so, curious to know whether it would turn its head to face me. This, after all, was what it had wanted. A voice to answer it in the darkness.

I scrutinised the floor close by it, almost entirely masked in shadow, and saw immediately what I knew was there. A bouquet of yellow roses for my wife, choked with twine and withering visibly inside their plastic wrapping. At the sight of them, I let out a sharp, involuntary breath.

For a brief moment the tremors ceased, the figure's head inclining slightly to one side, as if acknowledging my presence. Then it immediately resumed its former movement, rocking its body back and forth repeatedly against the wall. Suspecting it would never move anywhere beyond that place beneath the stairs, I turned and pushed open a set of heavy double doors, which led through into another empty corridor.

Ahead, opposing rows of elevated slatted windows lit the upper region of the passageway, revealing a suggestion of multiple doors spaced evenly along each side of the aisle. I wondered which of these rooms, if any, might contain the next exhibit. However, as I made my way along the corridor,

I saw that none of the doors were real, and were in fact merely paintings. Each was illustrated in exquisite detail, employing a repeated visual motif of spring flowers. The specific artistic styling of the designs resembled fairy-tale illustrations from a child's storybook.

Centred around each painted handle was a proliferation of familiar white flower-heads. My mother had called them morning glory and I recalled how I used to pop their heads off with my fingers until the entire lane behind us was strewn with white. Which hadn't mattered, she'd assured me, as they weren't flowers at all, but weeds. Their true nature, she'd said, was to strangle and destroy the real thing. The only thing you could do with them was to poison their roots, and kill them dead.

I looked down into the gloomy space below the painted handle of one door and saw, almost struggling to be noticed amid the suffocating shadow, the remnant of a single sunflower, starved of light, its bowed stem choked with green, twisted weed.

Instinctively, I reached out to remove the binding from its neck, quite forgetting that it was only a painting, and felt my nails scratch uselessly against hard plaster.

Then I heard the sound again. It was nearer now, though still some distance off, I thought. I wondered how long I had been hearing the cry in my subconscious without realising. Again, I listened closely, trying to determine precisely which words it continued to repeat. Yet this particular aspect of the cry was different now. In fact, it no longer sounded like a cry at all. The human quality had changed considerably, resembling more the agonised wail of some wounded animal; one whose throat appeared to be struggling against a physical obstruction of some kind.

I spent a great deal of time in the corridor, listening to it. The noise began to trouble me greatly, and I was reluctant to walk further, concerned that I was moving, inadvertently, toward its source. I grew angry with the creator of the exhibition, whose card had promised so much. Whose presence, it seemed, was entirely absent. I waited there a long time.

Until, unexpectedly, the painted door in front of me opened.

★

'The exuberance and delicacy of spring flowers.'

Its movement felt timid, faltering slightly, as if someone small were encountering difficulty opening it from the other side. I stood up from my position on the floor, watching the emerging light slowly fill the darkened corridor. I waited for my eyes to adjust, then reached forward and pushed the door fully open. It swung back with ease, revealing a shred of paper on the floor below it, announcing the next exhibit. As I looked up from the ground, my eyes were blinded again by the sun's rays shining down through the tall windows high above. I shielded my eyes with my hand and stepped through into a small room.

The walls were pale green and a faded paper frieze ran the circumference of the interior, depicting yet more painted flowers. These were mainly bluebells and yellow buttercups, again illustrated in the style of a child's story book. The floor, meanwhile, was strewn with a number of small tufts of dead, yellow grass.

Upon closer examination, I discovered that these were formed from the remains of tiny, wilted flowers. Some had been tied together in small, intricate sheaves, others connected delicately at the stem. I knelt down to retrieve a withered daisy that drew my eye, straw-coloured and shrivelled like a lifeless insect. As I lifted it gently from the floor, another rose with it, then another, before the fragile chain crumbled in my grasp, and fell apart onto the ground.

I sifted further through the clumps of dead grass, tenderly separating the aged leaves, knowing instinctively that what filled this sad space was every flower, leaf and small blade of grass that Natalie had gifted me during her childhood walks. I lifted up another daisy chain, scattering it accidentally into pieces, then another, which also fell apart in my grasp and collapsed into fragments.

I stood up, appalled at my clumsiness. A deep pain, long suppressed, emerged like a dark wave inside me. I stumbled across the room toward a black door in the far wall, horribly aware that each movement I made was destroying forever all that had once been precious to me. But this door was not real, either; merely an empty space, and I fell, like a stumbling child, into its darkness.

*

'The weeping April rain, or autumn in spring.'

I crept about blindly, searching in vain for any trace of light, then turned back round. The room of Natalie's flowers now resembled a book illustration, its pale green walls and frieze completely lifeless. I reached my hand out toward it, wanting to go back there, to retrieve just one small handful of my daughter's flowers to keep in my pocket, but the room back there was now a picture only; a static scene daubed upon the enclosing wall.

Then all was dark, and I cried out for her, calling her name over and over, trying to recall when I had last seen her. In horror, I realised I couldn't remember the moment, and wondered frantically whether they'd shown her photographs of me, or encouraged her to forget. I cried aloud because I no longer knew where she was; whether she was dead or lost, or had ever remembered anything about me.

As I wept I thought of her mother, too, and the poverty and loss I had inflicted upon them. I recognised at last their poor fragility; my own reckless cruelty. Then I thought of petals falling from a purple hyacinth, and rocked myself back and forth in the darkness, crying out for them, and for my own mother, and forgiveness of my sin.

As I cried those bitter, self-pitying tears, I grew conscious of my own physical movements. The pathetic motion of my body's convulsions as it thrashed itself around like a helpless child. I stifled my tears and ceased my involuntary gasping, which only reminded me of Natalie's helpless infant sobs; those heart-breaking sighs I'd failed to soothe while trying to whisper her softly toward sleep. I wiped the tears roughly from my cheeks, rose from my position on the floor and straightened myself.

Then heard the sound again.

It was close now, only a short distance ahead. Like my own cries, it was repeating her name, over and over. But there was no longer anything remotely human about the noise.

Sensing a change in the light ahead. I stared anxiously into the darkness and at last discerned a small, rectangular shape of pale grey. As I groped forward in the dark, feeling my way like a blind man, the shape grew slowly larger, and I realised at last that it was another door.

I knew then that there was no escape from what lay ahead. My anticipation, my hesitancy, were merely part of the overall design; the desired effect before this final display.

For his entertainment.

I approached the door, recalling at long last the terrible sound I could never escape, hearing it grow louder with each step I took. I walked forward to meet it, no longer slowing my pace in apprehension of what lay ahead, remembering the moment clearly at last; what had caused my cries to distort so unnaturally. I recognised fully the unbearable rasp of my vocal cords dissolving, their fragile tissue liquefying as I fought to scream against the bottle of pesticide I had drunk down.

★

*'For full absorption, apply in spring and
autumn when weeds grow more strongly.'*

I pressed my hand against the grey paper sheet announcing the final display and stepped forward into the last room I had known.

The smell hit first; a sharp, unpleasant chemical odour mixed with the stench of something more nauseating.

Then I saw it.

I was on all fours beneath the window, arched over what I'd already spilled of myself onto the classroom tiles. Much more was spread unevenly across the wider floor, where my convulsions had thrown me.

It was still some way from the end.

The thing I had been raised itself upwards onto its knees, as if sensing my presence, then arced its head toward the adjacent window, searching again for where it thought the sun had been; trying to feel a trace of warmth upon its disintegrating body. Though its face no longer possessed the ability to express, it was horrified still, I knew, by the sporadic visions of mental clarity.

The convulsions resumed then, hurling its body hard against the wall, the head cracking the stained and spattered pane of sunlit glass. As its body fell backwards, collapsing to the ground, the legs kicked out so hard they sent the bottle I'd used halfway across the floor toward me, the small skeletal image on its label, which I had focused so intently upon, barely visible through the mess now coating it.

Then I heard a light crackling, like popping candy, and watched the body rise from the floor to resume its sitting position, causing more of itself to flow out through the rents in its throat. The face mouthed her name still, over and over, but there was no longer a trace of my voice in it. Only the harsh sputter of flesh and tissue, a tortured rasping for her presence, and I knew I must get out of this room before it sensed me.

But as I moved quietly past, the head turned suddenly in my direction, both eyes staring manically toward me, wide open, yet seeing nothing. It held out both arms, clutching at the space between us, sensing something in its vicinity.

I froze, revolted by the sight of its ruined husk, appalled at the grotesque, distorted, fingers, clasping vainly for the touch of my own. The stench of its poisoned organs thickened as it drew close. I stepped back instinctively, shamefully aware that it wished only for comfort. To feel the touch of another as it endured its final, lonely journey.

But I reeled from it, rejecting its advance. I watched the lips mouth her name again, its agony masked by the horror of its dissolving features. Then I retreated further, terrified it could sense me still, and would attempt once more to claw its way toward me.

But instead it collapsed, strength suddenly exhausted, sensing, perhaps, that it had lost me for ever. It slumped backward onto its knees, dejected, feeling around the bloody floor with quivering hands. I watched its fingers grasp at the sodden carpet tiles of this place it had known well, searching and sifting through the terrible remnants of itself.

At length, it turned its head turned back slowly to face the window, where the sun continued to shine down from the blue sky above. It crawled forward toward the light, sensing what it needed must be there, and arced its neck upward with the last of its dying strength, straining like a flower toward the sun.

I left it there.

★

'Come again. Bring a friend.'

The door led back into the reception room. The bare walls surrounding me were painted a pale blue, brightened by sunlight which shone through tall, rectangular windows spaced high above. Through these neglected panes of glass, I could see only the vast, cloudless sky beyond. Positioned in front of them, upon an adjacent ledge, I glimpsed a lone daffodil, long dead, stem bent against the slim neck of the glass bottle it had died inside.

The desk ahead of me still held the same silver tray, with its lone glass refreshment, but I saw now that there was another person in the room with me. I stared at the familiar figure, aware, instinctively, that he could not see me, and watched as he picked the glass up, smelt it, then placed it back down upon the desk. He picked up the blue brochure beside it and scrutinised the faded sheet, then moved away from the desk towards the door opposite.

I was about to call out to him, to warn him that the displays were poor and not worth his time. That his feelings were best left numbed. That it would only serve his tormentor to play the game again, when I saw a second, smaller figure at his side.

He held her small hand securely in his, and though her back was faced toward me, I would recognise those movements anywhere in time. She looked up at him excitedly as he

102

pushed open the door toward the first exhibit, and before I could realise that my pitiful screams were soundless here, that nothing I could do would stop them going inside together, my beloved Natalie had vanished with her father, into the consuming darkness.

Mindless, I ran forward to the desk, grabbed the glass of liquid in both hands and drank it down.

Rejoice

Sarah Schofield

IT IS ALMOST DARK when I get to Dad's. Through the window I see him and April sitting round the table in the lounge. They are colouring in. She laughs, showing off the gap in her teeth. Her square black handbag sits on the windowsill.

I let myself in. 'Sorry I'm late.'

'Cuppa?'

I nod.

'How was work?'

'Busy.'

'Our NHS heroes.' He rests his head against mine. I know he is thinking about Dan and doesn't know what else to say. He goes into the kitchen, tossing his paper to me on the way past. 'Another chunk sold off. Like I said...'

There are VHS cassettes scattered across the carpet by the TV and another cardboard box stacked with curling newspaper cuttings and magazines. Margaret Thatcher looks up at me from the cover of one. I step over it to stand beside April and drop a kiss onto her forehead. She ducks and picks up a video cassette.

'Dad. I've told you...' I call through into the kitchen. The ringing in my ears begins to spike again. Always there now.

'Ah.' He looks in for a moment before returning to the

kitchen. 'She's just curious about the VHS machine. I've been meaning to put them onto DVD.'

'No one watches DVDs anymore.'

'Well, you know...'

'And why would you want to?' I take the video out of April's hand and drop it back into the storage box.

He comes back through and hands me a cup of tea. 'Lest we forget...'

April comes over and lifts the cassette back out of the box. She takes it to the dusty video player, slides it in and presses play. The Commons. Thatcher is fielding questions and the braying from behind her grows with every haughty rise and fall of her voice. She wears an emerald green suit; a silk bow at her throat. April returns to her colouring at the table, glancing at the screen from time to time. As she colours, I detect her twitching interest. She has mastery of it now; just a momentary pause, a prick of her ears, gives her away. A creeping dread starts across my shoulders and cascades to my stomach. I watch the pen squeak mechanically back and forth across the scrap of card in the little girl's fingers.

'You know, this is all on the internet now, Dad. You don't have to keep this in your house.' April flinches as I turn the TV off.

He shrugs. 'This whole business. It's made me...'

'Nostalgic?' I raise my eyebrows.

'No!' He looks hurt. 'No.' The phone rings and he takes it into the other room to answer. I sit down at the table with April.

'How was school?'

'Okay.' She puts her pen down and selects another.

I strain to hear what my father is saying on the phone. I go to the kitchen. He stands tall, hand in one pocket, looking out of the back window. He is nodding. 'Mm hm. Yes,' he says. 'When is that? Yes – of course.'

From the front room, I hear the clunk of the video player and the whir of a cassette rewinding; an instantly familiar sound. I stand unseen in the doorway. April has abandoned her colouring – carefully cut pieces of Rice Krispie box are scattered across the table. She stands in front of the TV with the remote in her hand, her handbag clamped into the crook of her arm. She bends forward to press play. The TV is set on mute. A Challenger tank bounces across scrubland. A figure in white stands erect out of the hatch, a Union Jack fluttering wildly beside them. The camera cuts to a close up. Thatcher, goggles strapped over a white headscarf, holds onto the hatch with one gauntleted hand. She looks from side to side as the tank rolls along. Her chiffon scarf billows. The footage ends and April stoops to press rewind.

'We're going, sweetheart,' I say.

She jumps away from the TV.

'Go and find your shoes.'

My father comes back into the room. 'You're off?'

'Don't be taking too much on,' I say. 'And please don't let her watch this stuff.'

On the drive home, April sits quietly in the back holding the bag on her knees.

'Are you hungry?' I say. 'Did you have fun at Granddad's?'

She nods and looks out of the window.

I wonder, not for the first time, whether I am right to simply ignore it and, like nose picking or shouting, it will just stop. Since she first watched Dad's recordings a few weeks ago it seems to have become an obsession. I have seen the search history on my phone's YouTube app. I should block it. Or stop her using my phone. I definitely should do that.

Dan would've thought this is funny. I should think it's funny.

We pull into our drive and I turn off the engine.

The house is cold. I gather the post on the doormat and set April up watching cartoons. While I heat up a tin of beans in a pan I flick through the post and open a letter. *We are writing to you because we believe you are eligible for Coronavirus Life Assurance scheme 2020 but you have not yet claimed. Since we last contacted you –*

'Do I look like her, mummy?' My daughter stands in the doorway, holding the bag in the crook of her arm. She presses her hands together under her chin.

I stare back down at the letter.

'Mummy, I said –'

I crumple it into my pocket and stir the beans. 'Go and wash your hands,' I say. The molten sauce thickens and the beans roll in the pan. I carry two plates into the lounge. April sits upright on the sofa with my phone. I watch her scrolling, pausing, smiling. She mouths something.

'What's that, baby?' I go over to her. The heat rises in my cheeks. The familiar prickle behind my eyes.

'Nothing,' she says.

I snatch the phone out of her hand. On the home screen, there is a new picture behind the app tiles of her and me drinking milkshakes. I hand her a plate.

I sit and scoop a forkful of beans into my mouth. The sauce blisters my tongue. I swallow. 'Eat up before it goes cold,' I say.

She stares at her plate.

'Come on, my lovely.'

'Bathtime,' I say.

She goes upstairs. I follow her and turn on the taps. While she gets undressed, I go downstairs and take my phone from the sofa and tuck it high on the bookcase. I go to the sink and wash my hands, lathering the foam between my chapped fingers. The antibacterial soap stings in the cracks in my skin.

In the bath she lines up a flotilla of plastic boats. She sits, the water lapping around her tummy, crashing her arms down on the bobbing toys. 'You're this boat, mummy.' She hands me one. 'I'll be this one. Ready?'

I reach for the shower gel. 'Let's blow bubbles.'

Later, when I carry her to bed, she grips the hair at the back of my neck and I hold her close. She tells me to sing to her. I stroke her cheek like I did when she was tiny and I look at her face. I see Dan, but I also see myself there, around her eyes and in the corner of her mouth. It is elusive – and when I look too hard it evades me.

'Mummy.' She strokes my cheek and yawns.

It's my weekend day off and I ask April what she would like to do.

'Charity shop treasure hunt,' she says.

We are in the Barnardo's shop. I pull a mask from my pocket while April stands beside me, holding her handbag. The woman at the counter smiles through her face shield. 'I like your bag. Just like mummy, hey?'

The skin across my face tightens but I force a smile into my eyes. Sweat is gathering on my top lip under my mask. But when I glance down at April, she looks as mortified as I feel. And it's as close to joyful I've been in months.

I send April to the toy section while I look at the books. 'We need new puzzles,' I call to her.

I pull out a gardening book and flick through it. 'What do you think, for Granddad?' I turn towards the toys, holding out the book. But she isn't there. I scan round the small shop.

I can't see her.

She isn't here. I step around the clothes rails. 'April?' Sweat prickles under my arms. 'April?'

I turn to the shop door. It is propped open.

I run out onto the street and look up and down. 'April?' I

shout. Which way? Would she head towards the library? Surely she wouldn't just go on her own. Someone must have grabbed her. The weird looking guy by the –

Someone touches my sleeve. 'Love?' The shop assistant points back into the store. Halfway down the left side aisle. April. She looks like she is genuflecting. She has something held in her hands and gazes up at me. I must have walked straight past her.

The terror rolls back. I take a deep breath. I stride over and take her by the arm. 'Why didn't you answer me? I was calling for you.'

She tries to peel my fingers away but I hold firm.

'Come on, we're going.'

Her eyes are wide.

'Come on,' I say again. I loosen my grip on her arm and she wriggles free.

She turns away from me and strokes the thing she is holding.

'What is that?'

'Nothing.'

It is something white. Synthetic fabric. A handkerchief? My own hands, empty, are shaking. I press them into my pockets. On her arm, a red oval grows where I'd held her.

I soften my voice. 'Is that the treasure today?'

She caresses the material.

'Would you like it?'

She nods.

'And then a snack-stop?' I say quietly. She looks up and I tilt my head towards the café across the road. 'Chocolate milkshakes?'

She stands, carries the material to the counter and lays it down. It is bigger than I'd realised. Not a handkerchief.

'Thanks,' I say to the shop assistant, as I pay. 'Thanks for before...'

April picks up the fabric and moves away. A moment later, I turn to where she is standing. She has found a mirror. She is balancing on tiptoes and putting the scarf over her head. She is tying it in a bow under her chin.

People stare at us as we walk across the road to the café. I tweak my mask up higher and swear silently behind it. Once inside, we go to our table. I slide the scarf off her head and tousle her fringe. She frowns and rubs the red patch at the top of her arm.

'Can I play my game?'

I pass her my phone. I watch her as I wait at the counter behind the taped distancing markers. I know she isn't playing a game because her thumbs aren't moving. Her eyes flicker my way and she slides down in the chair.

'Usual?' says the woman behind the counter.

'Yeah. Thank you,' I get out my card while she makes our drinks. I don't take my eyes off April.

'She's getting so grown up, isn't she?' The woman puts the drinks on the counter.

'Six going on sixteen,' I say.

'Hm.' She smiles and points at the card reader. 'When you're ready.'

I hold my card against the machine. It takes a moment to register. When I glance back up at April, she has pulled the scarf back up onto her head.

'Got to be careful though, eh? There's all kinds of weirdos online, aren't there?'

Heat rises up my neck. My breath is hot and sour inside my mask.

As I approach our table, I am sure I hear a strident orotund voice coming from the phone but when I peer over her shoulder she is watching Peppa Pig.

'Bedtime,' I say. April kneels on a chair at the dining table surrounded by cut out, coloured rectangles. They are stacked on a Snakes and Ladders board we found in a charity shop some weeks ago.

'Mummy, don't touch anything,' she says. 'I can't tidy it up yet.'

'Perhaps we can have a quick game,' I say.

'This is the money. And these are the coupons.' She pushes some cardboard squares towards me. 'It's the one with the most at the end that wins.' She looks up. 'Most money, not coupons.'

'I see.'

'It's really better with more than two players,' she says.

'Well,' I fold my hands. 'I'm sure we can –'

'More than two is what it's meant to be.' As she explains the rules to me there is something odd yet familiar about the way she is speaking. A slow, sonorous emphasis to the oration. And then I hear something else. I close my eyes and strain my ears to confirm I am right; a rhotacism. As if her 'r' is a tiny dignified challenge. Like she is stoically trying to conceal her endeavours. My heart beats in my throat. I look up from the board, really look at her – her mouth moving – and I remember her newly missing tooth. I breathe deeply.

'Things tend to take longer than you expect.'

Something still niggles. But it feels too big to look at right now. 'Perhaps you can explain as we play?' I say.

She unclasps her handbag and takes out a dice. She doles out the money, slipping extra onto her pile.

'Hey, that's cheating!' I say.

April's eyes flush with tears. 'Let's not play anymore,' she says. 'I don't want to.'

'I'm sorry.' I reach for her hand. 'Come on. Who goes first?'

'No. Let's put it away.'

'If you show me, we can play with Granddad tomorrow?'

April hands me a counter. She rolls the dice three times, finally rolling a six. 'A six!' She counts along the board. Then she rolls again.

'Isn't it my turn?' I rub at a headache nudging at my brow.

'If you roll a six you go again.' April shakes the dice vigorously between cupped palms. It is an action so reminiscent of Dan that I nearly tell her. She rolls another six and plays again. Then a four, jumping the squares with her counter. I stare bleakly at mine still waiting at the first square. I think about tomorrow's consultations I need to prepare for once April has gone to bed. The post-Covid backlog.

'You turn, if you want to.'

My head snaps up.

'What did you say?'

April is holding out the dice.

'What did you say?' I reach out and squeeze her fingers in mine.

'Your turn.' Her eyes are wide. I look down. My knuckles are pale; her little fingers crushed together inside my fist. An ugly knot that is both myself and something other, something unknown. A lithopedion.

'Mummy.' She pulls against me. I let go and April jerks back into her chair.

We meet eye to eye.

'Teeth,' I say. 'I'll be up in a minute.'

I bleach the surfaces in the kitchen. My hands sting as I wring the cloth out in the sink.

Later, when she is asleep, I press April's hand against my lips. I stroke the outline of my sleeping child. I feel the hard edges of her handbag tucked under the duvet.

It is late. I sit at the kitchen table with my laptop, reading over patients' case notes. April's board game lies beside my laptop where I'd promised to leave it set up.

I touch the stack of money.

I stand and stretch and I go to the bin across the room and pop the lid. I sit at the table and take a bank note, screw it into a tiny ball and flick it towards the bin. I do this over and over, until they are all gone.

Later, I pick through the rubbish. I sit and uncrumple the bank notes. I set up the ironing board and press each one until my fingertips are cross-hatched with iron brands.

★

After work the next day, I let myself into Dad's house and listen at the door. They're in the lounge.

'Not again!' Dad says and laughs.

I go through. They look up from April's board game.

'It's brutal, this...' he smiles at April. 'But quite wonderful! How was your shift?'

'Busy,' I say. I lean against the doorframe.

He pulls out the chair beside him. 'We need another player. Cuppa?'

'Thanks, Dad.' I squeeze his hand.

'You're exhausted.'

'I'm okay.'

He lays his hand on my shoulder and then goes to the kitchen.

I sit down beside April. We both stare at the board game and then I wrap my arm around her.

'How was school?'

'Good.'

I lean in to her. I look closer. Her lips are coral red. Slightly shimmery. Badly drawn. 'What's that?'

She raises a hand part way to her face. 'It's yours.'

'Come here.' I pull her towards me and scrub at her mouth with my fingers. She tries to pull away.

Dad comes back into the room. 'Steady, love.' He stands beside April. 'We didn't think you'd mind...'

I stare at the stain on my fingers.

'Just an old lipstick of yours. April found it in your room.'

April fiddles with the stack of bank notes. She looks at me.

'Come on, let's get going,' I say.

'Stay for supper,' Dad says. He turns to April with exaggerated delight. 'I'm doing courgette surprise.'

I think about the empty fridge at home. I haven't had time to shop.

In the kitchen, Dad sets the garlic sizzling in a slick of butter. He slices yellow courgettes and tosses them in. He is nimble, but I see his wrist strain under the weight of the pan.

'Can I help?'

'Relax,' he says and points to the breakfast bar. I perch on a stool and move a box of printed leaflets to make space to rest my elbows. I pick one out and read it.

'This is a bit old school.' I lay it back into the box.

He smiles and dices a block of feta. He pulls basil leaves off the plant on his windowsill.

Dad serves up and we eat.

April stabs a courgette slice. 'I don't like it.'

'Just try it...' I say. 'I'm sorry, Dad.'

'No. It's okay!' He gets up and pulls open the freezer. 'I've got fish fingers somewhere.'

After supper I offer to do the washing up. I drop the plates into the sink and run the hot tap. I watch the grease pooling on the surface.

'What's up, love?'

'Nothing.'

He looks at me. I pull the crumpled letter out of my cardigan pocket. I pass it to Dad and he puts on his glasses.

'It's for Dan.'

I turn back to the sink and scrub at the frying pan. After a couple of minutes he takes his glasses off again.

'I don't want their money,' I say.

'It's not their money.'

I dry my hands and stack up the plates from the draining board. April is standing in the doorway.

'Give it to charity, then,' he says.

My hands tremble as I open cupboard doors. 'They did this. If they had provided him with any sort of adequate PPE –'

Dad takes the plates off me. 'April, go and play in the lounge, sweetheart.'

'I'm waiting for you to play my game,' she says.

'We'll be through soon.'

April rolls her eyes and goes through into the lounge. I hear the clunk and whir of a VHS cassette sliding into the machine.

'It's just an insult, Dad. Don't get me started.'

'I know love. I know.'

'After all that fucking clapping.' I stare out of the window. 'And now they're just selling it off bit by bit.'

'That's why I'm, you know...' he points to the stack of leaflets. 'Come on the march with me. It's just local. But it's something.'

Just before we leave, I go upstairs and stand in my old bedroom. April's room now, for when I'm on nights. My old denim curtains still hang at the window but the sill is busy with new cartoon figurines. The overpriced kind they sell in the supermarket toy aisle.

My dolls house stands on the chest of drawers. I touch the door's brass knocker. It is double fronted, papered to look like wooden slats and sandstone. It has cream shutters at each window and an attached garage with a flip-up door. Someone has painted ivy up the front. I swing the front open. I know these spaces intimately. Fancy wrapping paper ironed flat and pasted into each room, wood panelling around the dining room fashioned from cuprinol-dipped lolly sticks, the baby grand; a birthday gift from a great auntie, and tiny beaded chandeliers hanging from the ceilings. I reach in and draw the Liberty fabric curtains across the window. I remember when I'd found that fabric in a jumble sale box of off-cuts – immediately I had wanted it for my dolls house. I had imagined how it would look in the windows, from the inside, if one were to look out. And I realise that that was always the way I'd seen it. To be inside. To sit at that piano, to lie in that four poster, to waltz down those stairs with their tiny brass stair rods and to gaze up and admire those chandeliers. To decide what to buy next. To look round at all you had built up and feel enclosed and pleased with yourself. A house where there wasn't food parcel deliveries and angry banners painted at kitchen tables.

A sudden recollection makes me recoil. Dan and I looking for our first home together. Weeks, it seemed, lying together in this bedroom scouring listings. I had dismissed each one. There was always a plausible reason – too far from the hospital, too noisy for night shifts – Dan getting more and more frustrated with me until, eventually, he slipped out of the house one evening convinced it was he, not the houses, that was the problem. I swing the front door back and forth on its tiny brass hinge. My throat feels suddenly dry and tight. How did I talk him round? We'd found somewhere soon after, I'm sure.

A noise at the door makes me turn.

'April's getting her stuff together.'

'Where did this come from?'

'Ah... Remember Derek, at the Branch? Derek's girl was a few years older than you.'

I nod.

He puts his glasses on and peers inside. 'You can take it home if you like. April spends hours up here playing with it.'

'We don't have room,' I snap shut the front of the house. 'She'll grow out of it. Pass it to someone else.' I point towards the windowsill. 'And stop buying her all this plastic rubbish. She's got enough.'

Back home, I let her stay up late. We watch cartoons together and I make her hot chocolate with marshmallows. We read stories in her bed and she rests her head against me.

She comes into my room in the night. I look at the clock but it flashes zero.

'Mummy,' she says.

I turn to her in the half-light and reel back. She is withered and sunken. Maggots crawl from her hairline. She has Dan's desperate breathless eyes.

'Mummy.'

I open my eyes. April is standing beside my bed. She is wide eyed. I pull back the duvet and scoop her next to me.

I lie in the dark until I feel her relax into sleep then I get up and go to sit at the top of the dark stairs, with my hands pressed against my ears. It's almost enough to hold the screaming sound inside.

I go into April's room and slide the handbag from under her duvet. Unclasping it, I breathe in. Desiccated lavender and liquorice imps. Within are two video cassettes. Her board game is also in there, the counters slide around the polyester lining at the bottom.

I unlock the front door and slip out into the street. I lift the lid of the grey bin and force the bag inside, rupturing bin bags and spilling their contents. I quietly lower the lid.

I stand at the front door and let the cool into the house. I look at my watch. 3.16 am. This is the time of night that Dan and I sometimes spoke about. Usually with a glass of wine in hand. This odd time when on a night shift, patients often seemed to slip into an in between place of holding on and letting go. Bodily and cerebrally – you could pause here and look back at yourself. Like catching your own reflection from the side. I go to the kitchen and pour myself a glass of wine. I sit on the doorstep and let the tears run down my face.

It is 4am. I am wiping congealed baked beans and the contents of the vacuum cleaner off April's handbag. I work Mr Sheen into all the stitched edges and over the curve of the strap.

Dad picks us up in the morning. I've packed a rucksack with a thermos and sandwiches. From over her bowl of cornflakes, April has been eyeing her handbag on the kitchen table.

'Go on,' I say and she reaches for it. She checks inside it before arming it and running to Dad's car.

The day is bright and crisp and there is something optimistic in the gathering of people; a crowd carefully observing social distancing. Someone hands me a mask with the NHS logo on it. While Dad gets banners from the boot, I watch April trying to fix her headscarf in the car mirror. After a few moments, I go over and adjust it, tying it securely under her chin. She watches me closely.

We hold hands as we move into the procession. Some people look at her and smile but no one says anything about her scarf and we travel with the flow.

Dad darts ahead, greeting people and tapping elbows. He looks vital and well. The sun is warm on my face. The traffic has stopped for us and I notice the quiet. I like how April's hand feels inside mine.

On the way home, Dad puts the radio on and hums along. I scroll my newsfeed.

'It's trending.'

'Oh yes?'

I read on. 'There's some photos. Local councillors were there apparently. Did you see them?'

'That's great, that's something.' Dad's eyes are shining.

'Nothing concrete, but...'

'Just rejoice at that news,' says a small voice in the back of the car. 'Just rejoice.'

My father turns to me. His face is momentarily unreadable. And then he hollers; his deep, hooting laughter that I haven't heard since before Dan died. He wipes his face and grins over his shoulder at April.

I smile. I force out a corner of laughter. But inside, I coil tightly back in. The screaming starts again, highly pitched in my eardrums. I clutch the phone in my hand and watch the world hurtle past as the breath is squeezed from me.

It's a Dinosauromorph, Dumdum

Adam Marek

JINGMAI HAD MESSAGED ME and said can you come over? Bernie misses you. So now we were driving to Folkestone. It was the first opportunity we'd had to make a long journey in the new car, but Serena had insisted that she wanted to sit in the driver's seat. Even though no actual driving was involved, I felt envious. The small responsibility of paying occasional attention to the dash display gave an illusion of control.

'Why did she message *you*?' Serena said. It was the first thing she'd said in an hour. Had it been on her mind the whole time?

'Well because she was worried about him. She didn't say this specifically, but I get the impression he's sort of retreating into himself.'

'So what does that matter? Some people prefer their own company.'

'Bernie can be outgoing. At college he was even more outgoing than me in fact.'

'I don't want to know about how you were back then,' Serena said.

'I'm just saying it's not like Bernie to spend 18 months in a new town and not make any effort to connect with anyone.'

'Well I always thought of him as an introvert,' Serena said, and then, 'Shut up a minute,' as the car's autopilot chimed and spoke: *You don't have enough energy for the journey home. There's a charging station five minutes' detour from here. Do you want me to go there now?*

'No,' she said.

'Chewie no,' I said.

'I asked you to change that.'

'But I…'

'Anyway,' she continued, 'I don't know why Jingmai messaged *you*, is what I'm saying. She's known us both for exactly the same length of time. In terms of friendship we're equidistant. Equilateral. Whatever the equivalent for friendship is.'

'I don't think there is a word for that.'

The car indicated that it was turning off the M20 and began to slow. The steering wheel swung anticlockwise and Serena watched it intently.

'See how much smoother it is than the old one?' I said.

'Obsequious is what I'd call it,' she said. 'The old one felt more impulsive.'

'And is that what you want in a car?'

'It was more exciting to drive.'

At the roundabout onto the flyover that led into Folkestone was a billboard on which a looped animation of a herring gull was playing. The gull began in the distance, as a silhouette in a blue sky, then came in to land, so that its head filled the enormous screen. It turned its bill left, then right, showing both sides of the red dot on the underside, and then the clip began again.

'Now I feel like I'm at the seaside,' I said.

Serena said, 'The codeword for if I decide I don't want to stay overnight is *equidistant*.'

'How are you going to weave that seamlessly into the conversation?'

Serena leaned towards the windscreen to check the road-sign as the car turned off. 'You leave that to me.'

The truth is, Jingmai had only meant for *me* to come and see Bernie. But I'd assumed it was a dinner invitation, as that had been our only method of connecting for years now, and mentioned it to Serena before Jing's later message revealed that that hadn't been her intention. And now it was too late and a dinner was happening anyway. Even though Jingmai didn't really want Serena to come, and Serena didn't really want to go either.

The car asked whether we wanted to park on the road or in Jing and Bernie's driveway.

'Chewie driveway,' Serena said, but then, noticing the driveway was heaped with inches of dead leaves, said, 'Chewie cancel. Park on the road.'

'Bloody hell,' I said, looking up at their place: an enormous Victorian end-of-terrace. Looming over it was a lime tree – the source of the copious leaf litter.

'How did Bernie and Jing afford this?' Serena said.

'Enormous debt, I assume.'

I started to unpack our overnight case from the boot. 'Leave it there,' Serena said.

From the doorstep we could hear chaos. Crashing and shouting. I paused a moment and waited. And then, when I heard laughter, I pressed the doorbell. Jingmai answered.

'You made it!' she shrieked, and hugged us both. And then, over my shoulder, she said, 'Oh my, is that a new car?'

'Work helped pay for it,' I lied.

'It's so shiny.'

'Is everything okay?' Serena asked, peering around Jing. 'I heard a crash.'

'Oh yes,' Jing said. 'It's just Wilson's new pet. It was his birthday yesterday.'

'His birthday?' Serena said. She shot me a look of alarm. 'We didn't know. This isn't a…?'

'No, no, it's not a party. And don't worry!' She threw her arms wide emphatically. Had she been drinking already? 'Well come in,' she said, but then she stopped at the threshold, took out her phone, and said, 'Oh, but you two aren't wearing your glasses.'

'We're trying to limit our time on them to just work,' Serena said.

'Well how virtuous!' Jing said. 'But I have to insist. It's just half the house is MR. There,' she said, swiping her phone's screen, 'Just say yes to all.'

I put my glasses on and tapped my screen to accept Jing's invitation, then swiped down the long list of Magic Reality categories, of which only a few were greyed out as private. When I tapped 'Confirm' the knocker on the front door morphed from a rusted hoop to a gleaming bronze phoenix.

Jing stood on the doorstep waiting for Serena to put on her glasses and accept the permissions, and then her smile returned and she stepped aside to wave us in.

'A new pet, did you say?' I asked.

'He's a bit rambunctious.'

'Real or MR?'

'MR of course,' Jing said. 'He's a lot of fun. He's had us all in stitches.'

'This place is huge!' Serena said, standing in the hallway with her hands on her hips looking up the centre of the staircase, which went up and up.

'You have three floors?' I said.

'And a basement,' Bernie said, coming into the hallway and drying his hands on the apron he was wearing.

'Crikey you've lost weight,' I told him as I hugged him. 'I can feel your shoulder blades for goodness' sake.'

'Do you think? I've not been trying to.'

'You should look at their new car,' Jing said.

'Ooh,' Bernie said. 'What did you get?'

'It's an Avatar 3,' I said, my face reddening.

'Nice.'

'Serena thinks it's obsequious.'

'But this place,' Serena said.

'If you sold your penthouse,' Jing said, 'You could buy up half of Folkestone.'

An animal, dog-sized, bolted from one door, across the hallway, and into another. It was closely followed by Wilson – their clumsy 8-year-old boy, and then Andi, their 6-year-old daughter, trailing behind making a sweet clip-clop sound.

'A whippet?' I asked. And then the creature bolted back in the other direction, followed by its giggling entourage. It stopped still at the end of the hallway and stared at us with its flame orange eyes. A reptile. Lean, with longer back legs and a whip of tail held aloft. Dainty fangs protruded from the slit of its mouth. It dipped its tail and rose up onto its hind legs, curling its shorter forearms in front of its chest, and sniffed the air.

'Wilson has a *dinosaur*?' Serena said.

The children caught up with the beast. Wilson raised his eyebrows precociously. 'It's a *dinosauromorph*, dumdum,' he said.

Serena looked to Jing, waiting for Wilson's rudeness to be scolded, but it wasn't.

'Has Wilson got braces?' I asked.

Jing gave me a confused and worried look.

'Just his voice...,' I said.

'No,' she said, flatly.

'Dinosauromorphs came before the dinosaurs, didn't they Willie?' Bernie said to Wilson, and then to me, 'We're learning a lot about dinosauromorphs.'

The dinosauromorph leaped off again on all fours, with a cheetah-like lope, into the adjoining room.

'Not the kitchen!' Jing yelled after them.

Bernie followed, calling back over his shoulder, 'I'll get them.'

'You two go through to the living room,' Jing said. 'I'll get us some drinks.'

We sat on the sofa and Serena told me not to drink too much, 'In case you need to drive later,' she said, and then, smirking, 'What did you think of Bernie's hair?'

'I didn't notice,' I lied.

'I bet that was Jing's idea. Maybe I'll buy you some MR locks for your birthday.' She ran her fingers through my hair and laughed.

I called out into the wider house, 'This room is incredible!'

Serena shuddered at my bellowing, and then in a conspiratorial whisper said, 'If you're an eighteenth-century aristocrat.' She slipped her glasses down her nose and peered over the top of them. 'Ha!' she smirked and shook her head.

'Be nice,' I said, and pushed her glasses back into place, as I heard someone coming down the hallway.

It was Wilson beckoning to his creature in a sing-song voice, 'Come on Gaston, come on'. And then he came into the living room, followed by the creature. Gaston moved with controlled caution, while flicking his head this way and that, sniffing all the while.

'Must be confusing for him,' I said, 'being zapped millions of years forward in time to a Georgian living room. What kind of *dinosauromorph* is he?'

Wilson ignored me, until Serena said, 'Wilson don't be rude. Tell Ben what kind of creature it is.'

'Prorotodactylus,' Wilson said, struggling with the word a little.

'Ah,' I said. 'He's very convincing.'

And then as if to assert how real he was, the prorotodactylus suddenly leaped up onto the sideboard and skidded along its mahogany top, scattering candlesticks and, devastatingly, an ornate vase made of dozens of yellow glass tentacles.

I instinctively darted forward and grabbed for it, but the vase passed right through my hands. It crashed to the floor and exploded into a thousand pieces, tentacle fragments tinkling as they scattered everywhere.

'Jesus Christ,' Serena said.

I started to explain what had happened as Jing, alerted by the crash, came back into the room, expecting her to be furious. But she calmly swiped her phone, and the pieces of the shattered vase flickered for a moment. The shards became animate, reversing their trajectories, and returning to full integrity on the sideboard with a theatrical whoosh and pop.

'Can't you just set the dinosaur so it can't interact with other MR stuff in the room?' Serena asked.

'It adds to Gaston's believability,' Jing said. Besides, it's fun watching broken things reassembling. My favourite thing about the Chihuli vase is watching it repair itself.'

'Something smells delicious,' I said.

'Freshly caught this morning,' Bernie said, entering the room with a tray of pink gin and tonics.

'By you?' I laughed.

'No no. If you get down to the harbour by 7am, the fishermen are there and you get fish that's fresh out of the sea and cheap as chips. But Jingmai did some foraging, didn't you darling? There's a sea buckthorn bush in the coastal park and no one else seems to know you can eat the berries.'

'Sounds idyllic,' I said. 'So you're happy you moved?'

'I've not regretted leaving London for one second,' Bernie said. 'The pace of life is slower, the living is cheaper, and there's a terrific creative community here, just so many artists.'

'You've met some interesting folks?'

'Jingmai's made some great connections. There's a sound artist called Luka Babić who's got a new piece on the Harbour Arm. We could go and see it tomorrow. Or listen, rather. He's made some kind of underwater enclosure filled with food, to attract spider crabs. All their bubbling and hissing is filtered through a music-generating AI and piped over a PA system. It's like... crustacean trip-hop. Pretty extraordinary.'

'And how about you?' I asked. 'Are you working on anything?'

'In a small way,' Bernie said.

'I'd love to see.'

'Ah, it's nothing really. I've been taking my sketchbook down to the beach and drawing seaweed, mainly. Something interesting is working its way through slowly.'

'You did that twice,' Jing said. 'That's not often enough to say you're doing it.'

'How often do I have to do something before I can say that I'm doing it?' Bernie asked.

'More than that.' And then to Serena, 'Hey, I love your necklace. Are those seedpods?'

'It was a gift. From a community we're working with in Sumatra.'

'Ooh, Sumatra,' Jing said, with an obvious streak of sarcasm.

Gaston bounded up onto the coffee table and lay down on his side with our glasses poking through his leathery body.

'Oh Gaston!' Bernie said, 'You lazy beast.'

Jing swiped her phone screen and the prorotodactylus winked out of existence before popping back into reality sat on the floor. He paused a moment as if reorientating himself, and then he was off again out of the room in one muscular leap.

'Ta da!' Jing grinned.

'Neat trick,' Serena said.

'So, Serena,' Bernie said. 'Sumatra?'

'It's quite an amazing project,' Serena said. 'The community were slashing down the rainforest to plant palm oil trees, but instead we've got them cultivating a rare fungus that only grows there. It's used in a cancer treatment. The forest is preserved and they're making triple the income.'

'And are they happy with their new life?' Jing asked.

'We built them a school and a medical centre, and put solar energy in for them.'

'I've always been a bit sceptical about how we swoop in and bring poor communities up to date,' Jing said. 'Is that what they really want, you know?'

'Well, for the women who used to have to give birth in a little shack lit by nothing but candles, the electric lighting and the medicine fridge are a big plus. They're less likely to die now.'

'Then thank goodness you came along,' Jing said.

'And how about you, Jing,' I said, 'how are you enjoying Folkestone?'

She paused and thought for a moment. 'There's a real sense of honesty here,' she said.

'How do you mean?'

'Authenticity I mean.'

'How does that authenticity manifest itself?' Serena asked.

I put my hand lightly on her arm, but she moved it away.

'Well,' she said, and paused again to think.

'We don't have a Starbucks,' Bernie said, and we all laughed. 'In the morning we'll walk into town to get brunch. You'll see there's hardly a chain store anywhere. It's all small businesses.'

'So you've found the perfect town?' I said.

'Except for the seagulls. They're forever raiding the bins and vomiting fish-heads on our doorstep.'

'Oh Bernie, you do exaggerate,' Jing said.

'I saw a billboard on the way in advertising seagulls. It's no surprise they feel welcome here,' I laughed.

'That's art,' Bernie said.

'I got that,' I said.

'We've got more outdoor artworks than anywhere in the UK. Sometimes you walk past a piece a dozen times before you realise it's art.'

'Aaagh!' Serena suddenly barked.

'What!' We all jumped.

'A mouse! There was a mouse!'

We all looked for a second, and then the mouse ran across the floor, and I could see that it was not a mouse at all. More like a gerbil.

'Is that an escaped pet?' I asked. And then, as if he could hear us, Gaston came bounding into the room, his feet thumping magically on the floorboards.

He leapt into the air, head drawn back, and pounced onto the gerbil, then closed his jaws on the poor thing.

'It's MR,' Jing said. 'Some kind of prehistoric rodent. It's what he eats.'

The prorotodactylus squatted, long tail curled around himself, with the hind quarters and tail of the gerbil protruding, splayed, from the clamp of his jaws. The prorotodactylus stared at us with puppy-like sincerity, as if waiting for our permission to finish the little beast.

Then Wilson came in and congratulated his pet. 'Well done Gaston! Good boy!'

'Wilson, don't give him too many of those things,' Jing said.

'Can MR pets get fat?' I joked.

'There's just one more he hasn't found yet,' Wilson said.

'Oh great,' Serena said and in protest took off her glasses.

Bernie's eyes widened in alarm.

'Please!' Jing said, her arm flying out towards Serena

instinctively. But Serena was already putting her glasses back on. She lowered her head and looked uncharacteristically devastated.

A buzzer went off in the kitchen.

'I'll er…' Bernie said, and got up.

The atmosphere in the room had suddenly congealed. I felt simultaneously embarrassed by Serena and guilty for putting her through this moment.

'Why don't you give him a hand?' Jing said to me, her voice taut.

Bernie retrieved a tray of aluminium foil parcels from the oven.

'What can I do to help?' I asked.

'You can unwrap these.'

'What's inside?'

'Hake.'

'Is everything okay?' I put my hand on his shoulder.

He nodded, not looking at me. His lips were pinched tight together.

'I'm fine,' he said.

I watched him for a moment, giving him room to say something else, but he just pointed to where the serving platters were kept.

Sweet lemony steam burst out of the first hot parcel as I picked it apart. Bernie took a bowl of tabbouleh and a tomato salad from the fridge, then set-to with a curved herb-chopping blade on a heap of coriander and dill.

'You've levelled-up somewhat,' I said.

'How do you mean?'

'You used to be more of a pasta-and-jar-of-sauce man.'

'Hah, yes.'

'Do you remember when you were with Helen, and Serena and I came round for dinner, you made that bean chilli, but you'd forgotten to soak the beans?'

'I do.' He sighed, and some of the tension in his voice evaporated.

'Do you ever speak to her?'

'God no. That was so long ago. She's living in the States now, doing some high-flying lawyering gig. Last I heard anyway.'

'So are you *really* happy here?' I asked.

'Of course.'

'It's just… Jing said… I think she's worried about you.'

'She did?'

'And I remember when you went through that phase at the end of college. I wanted to make sure you weren't going through something like that again. Because if you are, you know I'm always here for you.'

'Ah, we've had a tough time recently. Andi's having these awful nightmares. And Wilson wasn't getting on at the local school, so we've ended up… well *I've* ended up home-schooling them both.'

'You're kidding?'

'And I know it looks like half the house is decorated in MR, but we've actually done a huge amount of work here. It's all been expensive, and I've not had that many commissions lately.'

'You're worrying about money? Because you know a lot of my clients are going back to real paintings in their homes. Before you were doing client work… do you remember those amazing mushroom paintings?'

'Yeah, well I don't think the world is holding its breath for mushroom paintings.'

'Well maybe not the whole world. But you only need a couple of rich clients. I can recommend you to some.'

'Ah, I'm so rusty. I think my creative organ has shrivelled up.'

'Nonsense. You know you were always…'

Something about that caused Bernie's eyes to redden.

I went to give him a hug, but then Jing's footsteps came booming along the hallway and Bernie stepped back from me.

'What do you two look so guilty about?' Jing said.

'Bernie was just telling me how hard you've been working on the house,' I said.

'Well,' she said, 'just make sure he doesn't overcook the hake again.'

Bernie mumbled something under his breath.

'The hake looks exemplary,' I said, holding out the tray for Jing to see. 'Look, he's got brown shrimp and capers in there and all sorts.'

'Good,' she said, and then left.

'Well,' I said, 'Who'd have thought you'd grow up to be the kind of man who'd overcook the hake enough times for it to be remarked upon.'

He rubbed one eye with his knuckle and gave a sad sort of smile.

'This looks strangely familiar,' I said, of the dining room, which was decorated like a Tudor country kitchen.

'It's the dining room from the Burrow,' Bernie said, 'Where the Weasley's live.'

'Ah, Harry Potter,' I said.

'Our one concession to the kids.'

'I think you're spoiling them rotten,' I laughed. 'With all this, and the dinosaur thing – that must have cost a fortune.'

'It's very effective,' Serena said, looking around. Her tone was contrite. Had Jing bollocked her while I was out of the room for taking off her glasses?

The oak beams, worn tartan furnishings, Welsh dressers heaped with china, and tarnished mechanical gizmos on the walls were completely incongruous with the design of the rest of the house, but it was cosy.

'Are the kids not eating with us?' I asked, noticing only four places were set.

'They ate already,' Bernie said.

We all filled our plates without another word and began to eat. The tension in the room was so profound I didn't even feel I could make a compliment about the delicious fish.

'So,' Serena said, eventually. 'Have you guys explored the area much? When I was putting your address into the car I saw there are lots of seaside towns within 10 miles of Folkestone.'

'We've explored a little,' Bernie said. 'Margate and Sandwich. And Jing's been spending quite a bit of time in Whitstable.'

'Margate,' I said. I've always meant to make a trip to the Turner there.'

'So, are all the towns *equidistant*?' Serena said, and raised her eyebrows at me.

'I haven't been to the Turner yet myself,' Bernie said.

'Ah, then we should make a date of it.'

'So, why have you been spending so much time in Whitstable?' Serena asked Jing, her voice unusually gentle.

'My boss is opening another shop there,' she said. 'I've basically been setting it up solo. Ordering in all the stock and getting the displays built.'

'When it's open,' Bernie said, 'Jing might be left to run the Folkestone shop.'

'That's exciting,' Serena said.

Jing studied her for a moment as if hearing insincerity where there was none.

'I've done so much of the set-up, I think I could open up my own shop.'

'That sounds wonderful,' Serena said. She wasn't being herself, and I put my hand on her leg under the table and gave her a questioning look. She shook her head at me, minutely. The tendons in her neck were tensed.

What was going on?

'Would you like to have your own shop?' I asked Jing.

'I'd like to have a place that didn't just rely on weddings and funerals,' Jing said.

'I guess those are the times most people buy flowers,' I said. 'How would you make them more popular at other times?'

'I've been reading a lot about *hyggebana* – have you heard of it?'

'I haven't,' I said.

'It's like feng shui for flowers. It's a whole system for bringing peace and energy into your home through the flowers you choose and the way you arrange them.'

I looked around the room to see whether there were any unusual flower arrangements here that I hadn't noticed before. But there were no flowers.

A message popped up in the corner of my glasses, from Serena, typing discreetly under the table: *We need to go.*

'Has MR impacted your business at all?' I asked, ignoring Serena.

Jing seemed flummoxed for a moment.

'I only ask,' I continued, 'because interior design has taken a huge hit. No need for people like me when you can get a world-famous designer's creation set up in your home in an instant.'

'Not everyone can afford interior design,' Jing said.

'Oh god,' I said, 'I didn't mean that to sound judgemental. Gah! I've dug myself into a rotten hole here!'

Serena sipped her wine.

'What do you think of it?' Jing asked Serena, nodding at her glass.

'It's delicious,' Serena said, tilting her glass sideways as if now suspicious of it.

'It's from a local vineyard,' Jing said.

'Oh.'

'French producers have been buying up land all across this part of Kent.'

'Is that so?'

'I think what you've done with this place is great,' I said. 'And you know, with a house this size, MR is the only way to go.'

Jing got up.

'Where are you off too my love?' Bernie said.

'To get another bottle from the basement. Is that alright?'

Bernie sighed into his glass and took a gulp.

Another message from Serena popped up. *Please.*

And then, from upstairs, Andi yelped. Bernie sprang from his seat and ran from the room in such a panic that I felt compelled to follow behind.

Another message popped up in my vision: *Take off glasses. Wilson.*

From the top floor I heard Bernie shout, 'Shoo!' and then clap his hands.

'Everything okay?' I called out, following the sound to what I presumed to be Wilson's bedroom, and knocked lightly on the open door.

'Just a damn gull,' Bernie said.

Andi was sat on the floor with her nightdress pulled up over her whole face. Wilson was on the bed, his prorotodactylus sat, dog-like, beside him, practically purring as the child ran his hand down the creature's serpentine neck. Bernie was at the window.

'Shoo!' he said again, and banged a knuckle on the glass.

Outside, there was a huge, mean-looking herring gull perched on the windowsill, staring in sideways. There were flecks and streaks of seagull spittle on the glass.

'Shoo!' Bernie said.

And in response the seagull flicked its head sideways, slapping the glass with the tip of its beak and making an alarming *clack* sound.

'Cheeky bugger,' I said, and then to Wilson, 'You should set your dinosaur on him.' But of course the seagull wouldn't be able to see the virtual pet.

Wilson ignored me.

'They're tenacious little fuckers,' Bernie said.

Bernie almost never swore, so it was odd to hear him cuss in front of the kids.

'Wilson,' I said, 'did you know that birds are the direct descendants of dinosaurs? They're the only creatures that survived when the asteroid hit the Earth 70 million years ago...'

I discretely wrinkled my nose to push my glasses down a little, then peered over the top.

'It was 66 million years ago,' Wilson said.

'Of course,' I tried to say, but the words stuck in my throat. My face flared red and hot.

'Bugger off!' Bernie said, and rapped the glass again.

At this point Jing came in, flustered. 'What happened?' she said, and then, making a quick assessment of the room, rolled her eyes, strode to the window and pushed Bernie aside with her shoulder. She looked hard at the gull as she undid the latch and flung open the window, scattering the bird into the cold night with her hands and a hiss.

I pushed my glasses back firmly into place, thoroughly ashamed.

'There,' she said, and then to the kids, 'You should be in bed my lovelies.'

'But I'm scared,' Andi said.

'I'm not tired,' Wilson said.

'Come on,' Jing said to Andi. She hoisted the girl up onto her hip and stroked her head.

'Well I'm tired,' I said, faking a big yawn. I was shaking.

'Come and brush your teeth,' Serena said to Wilson, and wiggled her fingers for him to come. Wilson got up, and the dinosauromorph followed at his heels. Jing put her arm around Wilson protectively and gave me a suspicious look. I made a meek smile. The effort required was extraordinary.

Bernie cleared his throat and looked out of the window, standing guard for a moment to make sure the seagull wasn't going to return.

'They are a nuisance,' he said.

I put my hand gently on his shoulder. 'Bernie,' I said. 'Jesus Christ. What happened to Wilson?'

The atmosphere could not be repaired, and in the circumstances, our leaving early was accepted without complaint. We hugged Bernie and Serena, and apologised. We were sweating, and just needed to be out, making an awful mess of trying to be polite and nonchalant and understanding, but so obviously and embarrassingly discombobulated.

'Should we have stayed?' I said, in the safety of the car.

'What's wrong with them?' Serena said, shaking her head. 'I just can't believe…'

She started up the car and said, 'Take us home.'

'Chewie take us home,' I said, when the car didn't start itself.

The car piped up: *Alcohol is detected. Please breathe into the mouthpiece.*

'Oh for fuck's sake,' Serena said, and undid her buckle. 'Swap seats with me.'

We both got out of the car and changed places. The sounds of our doors opening caused the curtains of the front door to twitch, and a face appeared in them, but it was too dark to see who.

I smiled and waved at the face that everything was okay.

I sat in the driver's seat, and again asked Chewie to take us home, and this time, thankfully, the car started.

You don't have enough energy for the journey home, the car said. *There is one charging station within range. Shall I add it to your journey?*

'Goddammit,' Serena said, 'this place is cursed.'

'Chewie yes,' I said.

The car moved off, and when the house was out of sight we both breathed a huge sigh of relief.

'Did he tell you what happened?' Serena said.

'A dog,' I said, still incredulous. 'He said it was when they were camping in the Pyrenees, last summer.'

'And there's nothing that a plastic surgeon could do?'

'He's had seven surgeries already, apparently. And his hand... they're on the waiting list for some kind of amazing new prosthetic. Bernie tried to sound upbeat, but...'

'Jesus Christ. I can't believe they didn't tell us. What's wrong with them?'

'I can't bear to think they didn't trust us enough to say something,' I said. 'Did Jing say anything to you?'

'Not a thing. I don't think she even realised I saw.' Serena looked distraught.

'I just wish I'd been given the chance to... but the shock of it... I couldn't help but show it. I feel so ashamed.'

'What were they thinking?' Serena said.

'I guess they thought... with the glasses...'

Serena massaged her forehead with her fingertips and shook her head in disbelief.

'What if that's the end of it?' I said. 'They probably won't ever want to see us again now.'

'Well would *we* want to?' Serena said.

'They're hurting. They're grieving for... No one in this day and age should have to deal with trauma like that. I mean, what's poor Wilson going to do when he grows up? Wherever he goes. I feel so bad for them all.'

'I just want to get home,' Serena said.

I wondered whether Jing or Bernie would have told me in advance about Wilson if it had just been me going there. And if so, then this whole outcome was my fault, for misunderstanding Jing's invitation.

At the flyover, we passed the billboard again. I hadn't taken my glasses off when I left the house, and now, through them, the gull appeared as an enormous hologram. It swooped in to land on the roundabout, glaring left and right as if surveying its territory. I took my glasses off.

'Serena,' I said, 'Do you think they all wear their…'

'Can we just not talk about it any more?' Serena said, and that was the end of it.

The lights of the charging station appeared ahead. The car indicated that it was turning off and began to slow down. Serena had nailed it when she said the car's handling was obsequious, but, in my rattled state, I was so grateful for the gentle courtesy of its movement.

It was late and there were no other cars in the station, or on the road. In the bright payment kiosk, an older man in a blue sleeveless shirt was reading a magazine, his glasses perched at the tip of his nose. The ordinariness of this scene was an extraordinary comfort.

misisedwuds

Karen Featherstone

EVE PRACTISED SAYING THE baby's name several times a day
while it was pre-verbal. At a time when, she thought, it would
have no need of it. She was preparing herself. Little and often.
Building a homoeopathic tolerance to it.

In her words to the baby, seconds ahead, Eve felt the name
coming. She shouldn't swerve it, or halt. If she went over it fast,
she need barely notice it, but she did notice. Her husband's
name was not right either. And Fergal's laugh sounded off. It
was good that her husband laughed often – not all husbands do
– she reminded herself, but it was a short, brittle laugh with no
depth. So his name was not quite right and he had this laugh
and when he talked, it was too much about him. Eve couldn't
prove this had started with his name, but she imagined their
baby growing up socially clumsy too, perhaps disliked.

She should have stood up to his family. The baby's name
was that of Fergal's great-grandmother, a matriarch who'd sold
land when the airport was built at Heathrow. No one in Eve's
family had done anything so impressive. So the names on his
family's side took precedence and she hadn't wanted to look
like she didn't understand things.

The baby was growing. It crawled and Eve still wasn't ready.
The baby would become her name, that's what Fergal said. It

was just a word, Eve told herself, and if this word assigned to the baby, which meant the baby to others, was so *not-her*, what did it matter, as long as she was healthy. As long as she, Eve, wasn't throwing the baby into life with a disastrous name, like launching a ship one degree off course and having to watch it dash on rocks.

The child walked, bringing items to Eve to play with: a shoe, a spoon. Eve didn't know what she was expected to do with them. She took steps to avert catastrophe. On the internet, Eve repeated a familiar search for ideal baby names. It kept her awake, this responsibility to land on the perfect one, yet every day and night it escaped her.

She answered a pop-up ad for bespoke, neon name signs from a company called *Osmosis Interiors*. The sign, said the company, would make *a striking focal point of a cherished, loved one's name, transforming the feel of your home*. With great deliberation, she ordered one to hang on the bare brickwork in their sitting room. She hoped that the name, made prominent and celebrated, would be a hearth at which she and Fergal would warm themselves.

After placing the order, scrolling on her tablet, Eve's eyes were distracted by a further ad: *Caught you looking! Osmosis Interiors: Feel Good Inside*. She thought she'd ticked the box for no more advertising but, resenting its pull, clicked on it anyway. The site featured furniture with bright, confident colours in bold forms. *Osmosis Interiors* promised to be *a unique resource, using the learned tastes and behaviours of its users to produce composite design outcomes*. She supposed the company wanted to suggest a load of homewares to flog. It was tempting, but Eve didn't want to be hand-held in her work.

Strictly speaking, neither Eve nor her husband had to earn an income, but they'd established that Fergal's work was to be an architect and Eve's was to manage interior stuff. Their new, shipping container-inspired, three-storey home had been designed by Fergal and its secondary purpose was to be a showcase of his talents to prospective clients, so it needed careful dressing.

She was used to Fergal's mother dropping into conversations the names of decorating firms holding Royal Warrant, brands which Eve had never heard of. Eve felt she had to pass this test. She had drawers of plush fabric swatches, look-books of opulent wallpapers, some made of silk, and strips of leather from the last manual tannery in England, a few of which she'd had flown to Marrakesh for hand scudding.

She closed the ad and continued mulling over her spending options. Fergal was discerning. When discussing books, films, art, and on the topics of buildings and interiors especially, she lacked the confidence or education to counter his views. That would come. Fergal was quite a bit older. Forty-four to her twenty-three. She knew how it looked. There was that pop up again.

Eve browsed auction sites. Nothing on them was right. Fergal was drawn to mid-twentieth century pieces, but he'd claimed lately to be tired of them. They should forge their own style, he'd said. Fergal had even suggested she go on a course and make furniture. It was easier and more satisfying to buy things, but she let Fergal imagine her joining the maker movement and finding reward in the sorts of labour which for generations her family had sought to break free of, and which his family had consistently outsourced.

When the sign arrived, Fergal gave a neutral response. He told Eve it reminded him of Tracey Emin's work in the 90s and Eve nodded, not understanding whether this was a good thing or not. They mounted the sign on the wall, switched it on and stood back to assess it.

HARRIET

In red neon, the name was an assault. Eve looked away from it, then back, opening her heart to let the word rush in and find its rightful place there, but this failed. She confided to Fergal that she was finding her work hard. He answered that interiors were her thing and he didn't want to clip her wings.

Forgotten something? Eve cleared Cookies, but the ad persisted.

The site now offered a discount if she signed up that day, after which she could cancel at any time.

She needn't tell Fergal. Knowing that blocking the ad in any case was futile, (*Osmosis Interiors* was lodged in her brain now, and she would likely resort to Googling it at some point) she signed up. There was a form asking for room dimensions. With it, Eve was asked to send photos so that the site could synthesise her first outcome. It took no time for the result to fill her screen, along with a message *Are we getting this right?*

The image delighted her. There was the sitting room with their Charles Eames replica sofa from Heals, shown as a modular block of scarlet, rather than in the indigo of its real-life colour. (In the shop she had wanted the red version, but Fergal had wanted blue.) An image of a generic man, seen from behind, was at one end of the sofa. He had his arms around a dog.

The man had a Play People block of brown hair, the colour of Fergal's, and there was the beginning of a bald patch in the centre of the scalp. He had flesh-coloured cubes for hands. His body looked crudely assembled as if by a bot with rushed instructions for making humans.

Eve looked closer. The man's jumper was exactly the russet of a merino one she'd bought Fergal for Christmas. She'd hardly seen him wear it, so she was glad to see it in the outcome.

Had she unknowingly sent a photo that included Fergal? She recalled sending only unpeopled scenes. The site must have pulled their family photos from the Cloud or somewhere to lend realism.

She requested successive outcomes, and they appeared at once, only with slight changes. In one the dog and the man had swapped places, in another the wall colours had altered, or a pot plant was added or removed.

The single unchanging feature of all the outcomes was the room's ugly carpet. It was an odd choice. Its brown and cream swirls reminded Eve of the landlords' carpets of her childhood summers when, bored and shut in, she would lie on her stomach and trace the progress of silverfish; mercury commas, writhing deeper into the bare threads of the weaves. The memory hadn't bothered her in years. Tired of playing with the settings, Eve rejected all the outcomes.

It was Fergal who suggested to Eve that she needed help with Harriet. Eve was run off her feet, he said. It must be difficult to concentrate on her work. He'd tried to pitch in, but with Harriet demanding to play all the time, and with neither of them in a position to prioritise her, things were becoming impossible. Fergal put it to her gently. Perhaps Eve could contact an agency.

Eve refused. But perhaps Fergal had a point. Things were becoming difficult. Eve promised to spend more time playing with Harriet. Or maybe, Eve suggested, they could get a dog. What child wouldn't love a dog as a playmate? She remembered the dog in the outcome and marvelled at how the site must have picked up on her desire for one. Had she really been considering a dog at that time?

Fergal came home one day with a large, elegant Irish wolfhound pup. It looked great draped over their new Dwell ottoman. Eve Googled, learning that Irish wolfhounds, as well as being esteemed for their looks, can be energetic, with a high prey drive and (she read with satisfaction) with the right owner, they have a good propensity for play.

Unfortunately, the dog largely ignored Harriet and Eve, and from the start it chose Fergal as its favoured master. As it grew, it became paranoid and easily triggered to defend itself or Fergal from imaginary attack. When given exercise, it strained on its lead, half-throttled. It barked until hoarse at its reflection in the sides of bus stops, until Fergal dragged it home after another stressful walk.

Harriet was terrified of the dog. It was bigger than her. Once, Eve looked up from her device to see Harriet, bored of playing on her own, toddle over to the dog. As Harriet neared it, Eve stood, ready to act. The dog fixed Harriet with a persecuted stare. It was enough to make Harriet retreat, inconsolably rejected. Harriet approached her mother, but Eve had sat back down to Google *introducing dog to toddler*. Harriet sucked on the curtains, self-soothing, her eyes not leaving the dog.

When Mrs Edwards arrived at their home, it was a bit embarrassing because Eve had no idea she was coming. Mrs Edwards apologised for the shock, but thought Fergal would have told Eve that his old nanny was arriving to lend a hand. Eve's brain fought to make sense of the woman's turning up. It hurt her to think Fergal had contacted Mrs Edwards without Eve's knowledge. She grudgingly made Mrs Edwards a cup of tea, resolving to confront Fergal about it.

As Eve and Mrs Edwards sat discussing Harriet, thick purple veins showed between the hems of Mrs Edwards' short trousers and her loafers. It was like the plumbing had come out of her legs; something that should have stayed inside, had crossed to the outside.

Eve was back at her caesarean. In the rush, they had erected a surgical tent over Eve's lower half. She felt the surgeon's hands in her womb. The rummage and tug. The shocking strain of his exertions and the flash of oxygenated blood mirrored in a chrome ceiling fixture. The tent was knocked aside. She hadn't been supposed to glimpse the terrible, bright secret of the pulsing gash. *High-velocity arterial flow* someone said. The mechanisms of her imminent death were given commentary. As they moved her, to weigh the sheets, to calculate the volume of blood loss, Eve stayed pressed against the thin membrane between death and life. She hadn't known it would be so porous.

That was an example, thought Eve, of something she was supposed to have got a partial view of, but she had failed at this. She kept failing at this, habitually seeing, not a part but, against her will, the whole.

She was tired. It would seem rude in front of Mrs Edwards, but Eve closed her eyes. Fergal had been right to summon help.

While Eve rested, Mrs Edwards went on about the importance of *child-centred play*, about Harriet's *vital personhood*. She expanded on her recent enthusiasm for teaching phonics. Mrs Edwards demonstrated this, pointing to a button on Harriet's cardigan. *Buh buh buh button,* she said to Harriet.

Buh buh buh buh, replied Harriet.

Listen to them! Eve thought Mrs Edwards was trying too hard.

Yet Mrs Edwards was soft and cooing and Harriet took to her, curling her oddly muscular fingers around strands of Mrs Edwards' wiry, grey hair. It crossed Eve's mind that Mrs Edwards could bundle up Harriet and take the girl to live with her and Eve felt only flatness at the thought.

By the time the introductory meeting was over, Mrs Edwards had got Harriet to draw a yellow horse. It was a revelation. Eve stared at its wobbly, good-natured stride on its wrong number of legs, its imprecise, coloured-outside-the-lines joy. Yellow was Harriet's favourite colour, Mrs Edwards noted. This was news to Eve.

When Mrs Edwards left, Eve kneeled next to her daughter and asked Harriet to draw a horse for her. Harriet wanted to play hide and seek. *No*, said Eve. *It's drawing time.* On Harriet's face, Eve detected a new scrutiny.

Harriet had always been a watchful child. Eve had caught her eyeing them all in the evenings; thumb in mouth, watching the dog, watching Fergal, watching Eve. What happened in those long seconds? What did Harriet see in her?

Eve avoided confrontation with Fergal over Mrs Edwards' recruitment. He was becoming volatile. Despite hustling, he could not get commissioned as an architect. He phoned old school friends in the city and offered to dig out their basements for mates' rates. Some of them went so far as to pay for plans to be drawn up, but none went ahead with a build. His bitterness grew as the realisation dawned on him that he would not be given the work of an architect just because he badly wanted to be one. His mood swung from petulant to stoic, then back again. He sourced gadgets off the internet, including a complicated fitness tracker which didn't work to his liking. Small, consumer niggles which Eve thought a man with his disposable income should have thought little of, absorbed him. He would tap the blue digits on the tracker's screen, complaining that he'd been kept up half the night by a car alarm, yet this piece of junk claimed he'd had an excellent night.

Another thing, Fergal began to show more affection towards the dog. When Harriet sat up straight at the noise of a wrapper, or rested her head placidly on Fergal's lap, only to have him move it, Eve understood what Harriet was doing.

Eve worried, knowing how parents can get away with things. When parents didn't get away with things, it was often the mother who bore the brunt, but this was only right. It wasn't fair that a mother should be let off the hook. If something happened to the child, out of a sense of her importance in its life, which was a love of sorts, Eve wanted to be responsible.

Several mornings per week, self-exiled to a back bathroom so that she could watch them through the window, Eve observed Harriet and Mrs Edwards making daisy chain necklaces in the garden. Mrs Edwards would put one around Harriet's neck and say something. Was she teaching phonics again? No, it looked like:

I love you.

Or was she saying something else?

Day after day, Eve endured them garlanding each other with daisy chains. One brave morning Eve joined them on the patch of grass. Her presence changed the dynamic; she had subdued them. She smiled at Harriet.

Can I have a necklace, Harriet?

Harriet rubbed her eyes, ready for a nap.

One rainy morning, with the back garden out of bounds, Eve eyed them through a gap between Harriet's room door and the frame. She couldn't hear what words Mrs Edwards said to her daughter, just picked up on the anaesthetic purr of her voice.

On and on they went, in their exclusive, fucking world. On the wall behind Mrs Edwards, rows of multi-coloured, crayoned horses reared and galloped wonkily in exuberant cavalcades.

Feeling the usual churn at their closeness, Eve turned away, but something in Mrs Edward's voice made her pause. Through the gap, Eve saw the woman utter something. It was clear Mrs Edwards was calling to Harriet. But her lips did not form Harriet's name. She was calling her something else.

Eve shoved open the door. It banged against the wall.

What name did you just call her?

Mrs Edwards gathered Harriet to her, but said nothing. Eve tripped across the landing and down the stairs.

She found Fergal teaching the dog to beg. It was slow progress. When Fergal held up a treat, the dog would simply rise up on its hind legs and eat it.

Mrs Edwards has to go.

Why's that?

I'm firing her. She's gone too far. She's changed Harriet's name! Fergal.

But Fergal was too interested in the dog's actions to answer. He instructed the dog to sit and, even though the dog remained standing, Fergal fed it an amaretto biscuit.

Fergal?

His eyes didn't leave the dog. Eve had to somehow disrupt Fergal's absorption in the dog.

Can I have a biscuit, Fergal?

There aren't any left.

Fergal dipped into his pocket. He took out another amaretto. He tossed it towards the dog, which was already drooling. It leapt into the air with awesome power and snapped its jaws around it, just missing Fergal's fingers.

Mrs Edwards was vocal in claiming the right to a notice period and Eve wondered tetchily if she was practised at being fired.

Eve was prepared. When Mrs Edwards turned up the following morning, Eve announced she'd arranged for the family to go on a trip. A travelling funfair had come to the neighbourhood and they planned to set off mid-morning to beat the crowds.

But Mrs Edwards wouldn't leave. Sensitive to Mrs Edwards' upset, Harriet's face puckered. She and Mrs Edwards nestled together, so completely heedless of Eve that Eve wondered if they knew she was there.

Eve didn't know where the desire to give Mrs Edwards a sharp slap came from. A spasm of fury coursed through her arm. The gesture was over before Eve had thought to consciously do it. Harriet gave a scream of betrayal.

Eve let Fergal deal with the aftermath. She didn't trust herself around any of them. She locked herself in an upstairs wet-room, lying with her forehead against the cool, Carrera marble floor, waiting for the fracas to die down. She heard Fergal offering Mrs Edwards money not to tell his mother.

With Mrs Edwards gone, Eve asked Fergal to change Harriet's clothes and strap her into her buggy. Fergal didn't believe going out was a good idea, in the circumstances, but Eve insisted. This was a day they would weather.

Eve made an effort. She took from her walk-in wardrobe a pair of tights in a shade called warm mink. Bizarrely, Harriet never reacted well to her mother wearing tights. Harriet would pinch and pull at them. When Eve dressed this way, it usually meant she and Fergal were going out, enjoying time without her. Eve blotted her lipstick on a tissue and added a feline flick to her eyeliner. Well, Harriet would have to learn that her needs couldn't always come first. Eve picked out a tiny, impractical Louis Vuitton clutch.

She looked at herself in the mirror. It seemed to her that she spent most of her life wrestling with the gap between how things seemed and how things were, trying to get the two sides to meet. This was the stuff of adult life, being a coherent person.

Ignoring Harriet's calls and Fergal's tired, entreating voice, Eve went online to check the fair times and the ticket prices.

Missing us? Eve hadn't thought of *Osmosis Interiors* in weeks. Unless it had come up with something a little more exciting than her last outcomes, she wasn't interested. But Fergal was calling for Eve to help with Harriet, who would not put on her socks, and Eve was still shaking since the scene with Mrs Edwards. So she took a slow, restorative breath and chose to escape for a second into a sedative world of purchasing potential.

The outcome showed the same room, but she didn't recognise it at first. She remembered the website used *the learned tastes and behaviours of its users* and she could not understand it. What looked to be a spread-eagled sex worker was crying on the ottoman and another knelt between the knees of the man, her face at his groin, his hand on the back of her head. White powder dusted the TV remote control.

Eve jabbed at the screen. She hit the surface so hard, her fingers hurt. She switched off the tablet and threw it across the room. It struck, at a particular angle, a gold-plated Buddha they had only been able to fit into the sitting room by crane and by the temporary removal of the window frame. The device flickered back to life.

Fergal must have used it. He denied everything, then admitted he had used her tablet now and then, to look up a few things. She made herself view the screen again in disgust. How could this be an outcome he desired?

Harriet ran from one parent to the other, sobbing at their raised voices, lifting her arms to be picked up.

We'll play hide and seek! Eve shouted, *Hide and seek! Go!*

Harriet's grief stopped dead and she opened her mouth with a shuddering in-breath of pleasure. She hopped from foot to foot, cheeks flushed with anticipation. She ran off. Eve called:

ONE.

Fergal, coming to his senses after the Eve's ambush, yelled: *TWO.*

But Eve couldn't face being alone with him. She couldn't

make sense of the outcome, what it meant, what it mustn't mean. She left for the fair on her own.

Eve couldn't tell how long she'd been there, nodding her chin to competing beats, aiming to lose herself in the music It was deafening, as if to obliterate any thoughts of disappointment with the place, or of any thoughts at all. She welcomed it.

In an unkempt field of common land, studded with stalls for knocking down coconuts and shooting metal ducks, garishly painted rides listed into the mud, like Eve's high heels. She regretted wearing them, feeling foolish at her predicament. Here she was a mother and wife, dolled-up for exactly who, stewing on her own at a funfair built for families.

Occasionally some man would look over at her, but her expression was so hostile, so shut down, that none approached.

Feeling the need to pace, Eve trod carefully on the muddy ground. She looked at the crowds. Everyone but her had their eyes fixed on the attractions, whooping, teasing and daring each other on. She wanted to immerse herself in the moment, as they did.

She wondered if they saw what she saw, the sweat patches under the arms of the coughing litter collector, the blood on the tissue he'd used, then shoved in his sack. Or did they hear his tuneless hum and assume he was happy? The psoriasis on the hands of the candy-floss vendor, the heaving rib cage of a bony contortionist who performed in an airless Perspex box, her heart visibly pounding as if she were about to die of exhaustion.

No doubt they could see all these things, but perhaps they chose better what to focus on and what to jettison: elements which didn't fit a wished-for outcome. It had always been there. This seeing of what other, more capable people held under the skin of things.

Eve's gaze was caught by the undercarriages of the rock'n'rolla cars, their fixtures rusted almost to dilapidation, and she imagined them becoming unshackled and everyone in the cars dying.

One day they would all be dead. She and Fergal, Mrs Edwards and – there was a small black dot of an emotion - Harriet. She crushed the dot even smaller, so small she need not name or acknowledge it. Then it would be over, this accountability, the need for self-control. Nothing would matter and, being dead, Eve could let herself off the hook.

The daylight was fading and Eve was about to head back, when the sight of a horse stopped her in her tracks. This horse, this piebald wonder, without saddle or reins, ambled between the stalls. Not one person, but Eve, turned a head. She must get a photo for Harriet.

Eve followed the horse unsteadily on the uneven ground, fumbling to pull out her phone. The horse walked, sure on its path, into the dying rays of the sun, far from the riot and ruckus of the fair.

As it stepped, she hurried to catch up. She attempted and failed to match its slow, sure rhythm. The animal set its own unhurried pace, with which, as they left the crowds behind, all nearby creatures and even plants were compelled to syncopate. Crickets and dragonflies, earthworms and seditious weeds colluded and coaxed Eve in one direction only. She sensed she was getting both further from and nearer to some unknown, innate state. She tried to be ready.

Nearly at the edge of the fair, she looked back. The noise and scrum of the stalls, the spinning big wheel, were far behind.

There was a handful of people here, at the outskirts. The onlookers waited for entertainment with odd patience, not like those jostling for the rides. As she got closer they cleared a path for her. The line opened to let her in further along, until she was in second position. She craned her neck to see ahead what they queued for.

In a clearing, a hoarding was propped up against a pram. It was made of one side of a cardboard box. On it was hand-written with black marker-pen:

I GUESS YOUR AGE

A man stood behind the pram, holding its flimsy handles. He wore a tracksuit of no noticeable brand beneath a grey, wool army surplus overcoat. On his feet he wore cracked, plastic pool slides, with Lacoste on them and, underneath those, white, towelling socks, snagged and grubby at the toes. Eve tightened her grip on her bag.

In the pram was a child, abandoned to sleep. It was big to be in a pram and the seat was fully reclined. Perhaps it was disabled. Or maybe this pair was so poor, the child's pram was its bed. Its clothes were too small. Under the fingernails, dirt was compacted in lines like pencil leads. The child's mouth hung open. Its palms faced upwards, as if forced to give everything up.

Eve hid back in line behind a businessman who carried a Samsonite briefcase. He was a strange sight, in his Burberry mac, out of his natural habitat, and Eve wondered what he had followed to get here.

It was his turn. The businessman stepped forward, and gave a pound to the man, who slipped a hand inside his lapel, and dropped the coin into the inner breast pocket of his overcoat. The guesser eyed the businessman.

Fifty-four, he concluded.

I'm forty-nine! smiled the businessman. Deftly, before he could be offered his pound back, the businessman waved away any such gesture, embarrassed by what he saw was his clear superiority over the guesser. *No, no. You're all right.* The businessman left.

It was Eve's turn. Eve wavered between pity at the pathetic sight, and admiration. The guesser was an entrepreneur all right. Out of thin air, he was mining an income for himself and the child. The child. She looked away from the raided little body. She took a step back towards the fair, but the guesser said,

Please.

All right, then. Eve handed him a pound and stood to be judged, a tight, pre-emptive smile on her lips. She wanted this transaction to go well. She was the customer and he was the spectacle, so she should relax, but as he studied her, his eyes met hers in recognition and she knew they were the same and any pretences that she was better, more accomplished or stabilised by the trappings of her house, her wedding ring, her bag, fell away, revealed as talismans.

The guesser had an answer before she could prepare a response.

Nineteen.

Her expression must have shown his error.

Keep it, she said, backing away, trying to force an outcome, wanting him to see her generosity, needing him to see she was a person in a position to give. But the guesser would not hear of it. He shook his head, He was gracious. She would be refunded. His hand moved to the inside of his lapel. *No, no,* she insisted.

He drew back his coat. At first it was a beautiful sight, shimmering in the dusk, reflecting the distant coloured lights of the fair. Silverfish, hundreds, moving in waves. Her stomach clenched. She reeled back.

The man was already digging inside his breast pocket. He produced the pound. She craved to escape his too-near face, his indistinct smell she could only locate in a miasma of her earliest experiences. But the guesser stepped closer, holding up the pound. She tried what the businessman had said:

You're all right.

She looked from the hopeless child back to the guesser, who shrugged. He tossed the coin at her. She thought, nastily, *So he is giving up, the default characteristic of his type.*

Revulsion drove her from the scene, but even after she had run a long way, with her shoes in her hands, she felt she had not left revulsion behind, but that it was in her. On her approach home, she began to wonder if she had carried it inside her even before she'd left the house and that maybe she'd brought it to that man, and to that child. Maybe if she had not visited them, they would be clean and not demeaned.

She hesitated to re-enter their house, but there was Fergal, looking out for her through a ground-floor window. He opened the door to her. He was sorry. He had missed her. He ushered her in. As she passed him, she smelled his familiar Armani Code and she felt instantly back in her desired world.

Everything's all right, she thought, letting him take off her coat. She would stay here, in these surroundings, concentrate all her life on their little family. If she hadn't saved everything yet, she would do. She would try harder.

Fergal beckoned her along the hall. He'd opened the good Burgundy, a bottle they'd been saving. As she walked towards the sitting room, her feet leaving muddy clumps on the reclaimed Edwardian tiles, she smelled soap and shampoo and felt the post-bath, humid air on her face. So Fergal had done Harriet's bath time.

Relief suffused her. After the incident with Mrs Edwards, Harriet's all-seeing eyes on her would be too much.

Eve sat on the sofa, glass in hand, next to Fergal. His hair was damp. Eve imagined that Harriet must have loved that. Bath time with Daddy. The wine, on her empty stomach, softened Eve's thoughts towards him. He was a good man, a good father. Their child was lucky.

She thought of Harriet safe upstairs, in bed, clean and fresh in her new Infants of England pyjamas. Their child wasn't anything like that poor, spent thing of the far away field. Safe at home, Eve's compassion returned. She was glad she'd left without the coin and hoped that the guesser, the father, or whatever he was, would not be too proud to stoop for it.

They relaxed with more wine. After a while, Eve suggested playing some music. She hoped to get Fergal in the mood. She'd wondered recently if another baby might solve things. Harriet would have a proper playmate and Eve could work on Fergal getting rid of the dog as a failed experiment. The portrait of the dog, done in oils, that Fergal had had commissioned and which hung in pride of place over their bed, could stay, she supposed.

With muscle memory, she reached for where she often left her tablet, on the ottoman. It wasn't there. She looked at Fergal. He wouldn't have borrowed it, surely, not after their argument. Irritation gnawed at Eve. Sometimes when Eve went out or was having a bath, Fergal, to get some peace, would give Eve's tablet to Harriet to play with. This was against their rules, a three–year old being too young for screens. Harriet was very quiet. That must explain it.

Ferg, you didn't lend Harriet my screen, did you?

Maybe she took it earlier. How would I know?

You don't know?

An old rage flared inside Eve. Fergal knew the rules. She opened her mouth, but held off criticising him. She was trying to change, after all, trying to save everything. Instead, she sat back and thanked Fergal for doing Harriet's bath-time. Fergal looked up from his glass.

I didn't do Harriet's bath time. I thought she went with you.

The thought struck both of them at once. They had failed to seek Harriet. It had been hours since she'd gone to hide.

Fergal staggered to a standing position, then his knees

gave way. He recovered and blundered his way through the ground floor of the house.

Harriet. Harriet.

Opening kitchen cupboard doors, checking inside the fridge, the chest freezer in the utility room. Then up, to the top of the house. Eve heard him distantly, then his actions got louder as he tore through the house on his descent, flinging open doors, pulling beds from alcoves, wardrobes from their corners, blinds from their recesses, speakers from the walls of their home cinema.

Hearing his howl of loss, Eve pulled apart the sitting room. She broke first her nails, then her fingers. She smashed the sofa. The decorative fig trees went down, spilling their earth. An art deco drinks cabinet crashed against the Buddha, a shard of chamfered glass puncturing a goat-hide beanbag that haemorrhaged foam balls. Eve ripped apart the ottoman's deep-buttoned panels, eviscerated its main body then tried to pull off its antiqued brass castors and when they wouldn't budge, used her mouth. She fell on her knees in apology among the glass, the polystyrene, the soil, the blood, the teeth. She had known she would take the brunt.

When entry was gained to the house, one of the first items to be bagged and labelled was a tablet. The device was down to one battery bar, but still on.

The screen showed a room with yellow walls. On the settee, a crayoned horse sat with three of its five legs impossibly crossed. Above the fireplace, on an area of brick, in neon was written:

misisedwuds

Near the window, on a yellow carpet, was a huge dog. Across its torso, in places, its skin was stretched white. Objects inside

159

it parted the animal's hair with their protruding angles. Through its coat, between its ribs, shone the blue light of an activity tracker. What at first looked like a string of slobber from its mouth, the officer saw, looking closer, was a leg of tights.

The dog was hunkered down. Ears pricked, its eyes were fixed on a small shape hiding behind the curtain. A daisy chain hung around its throat. Bloody muzzle on paws, the dog waited, eager for play.

The Honey Gatherers

Gerard Woodward

DANA HAD DEVELOPED THIS new thing that he liked to do
when he and Kelly were making love. At the right moment,
just at the point of greatest release, he liked to spit into her
mouth. He also liked to make a show of force when he did
this, prizing her mouth open against her feigned resistance
and lowering a plump bead of saliva that he'd been working
up for minutes, slowly, as if by parachute, into her widened
maw. The moment felt to him like an instance of bodily
rhyming, of double release, a topping and tailing of the ecstatic
singularity. Apart from that moment of feigned resistance,
Kelly showed no sign that she found this practise distasteful. It
was, after all, only a more concentrated form of the type of
fluid exchange that happened incidentally through kissing.
Now and then he felt compelled to spell this out, even though
Kelly never made any request for such an explanation.

'It's not really any different from eating honey,' he said. By
which he meant that honey was also the product of a digestive
process. It came out of the mouths of bees.

Kelly already understood this, because she, like Dana, was
a beekeeper. Together they had been keeping bees for nearly
five years. They had an apiary of over thirty hives on the
boundary between the woods and the moors above the small

town in which they lived. In good years their bees could produce two thousand jars of honey, many of which they sold in their own shop in the town, along with honey related products – honey soap, honey chocolate, honey biscuits. By this means their bees provided them with a modest income, which had improved over the years, as it was discovered that the flowers on which their bees mainly fed - the variety of blue heron's bill that grew in abundance by the side of the moor - was believed by some to have certain unique health benefits, including aphrodisiac properties. These new claims had taken Dana and Kelly by surprise. The price of their honey doubled, then trebled, almost overnight. They were mailing their products to customers on the other side of the world. People were buying a dozen jars – a year's supply - at a time.

The National Council of Honey Gatherers had sent an inspector to monitor the hives and he was satisfied that a significant number of bees were feeding on the flowers and that there were sufficient quantities of flowers to sustain the number of hives. Having established that this was the case, Dana and Kelly were, for a while, the only producers of certified blue heron's bill honey in the country.

It wasn't long before other brands of that honey began to appear on the market. It was only to be expected. But the rarity of the flowers, their tendency to bloom individually or only in small clumps, meant that there were few places in the country that were suitable for the cultivation of blue heron's bill honey. Larger crops of the flowers, such as those that bloomed on the moorland adjacent to Dana and Kelly's hives, were extremely rare. All the same it was still a shock to discover that other beekeepers were trying to take advantage of the same food source.

Kelly was first to discover this fact, when she was walking along the margins of the moors, admiring the flowers as they stretched in a violet wave (their name was something of a misnomer) from the woodland next to their apiary, all the way up to the skyline where dark crags erupted from the heather, half a mile away.

According to the law, it was illegal to set up a commercial apiary within a kilometre of another one, and yet there they were, in a small clearing in the trees, half a dozen beehives, tall ones, active. She approached them cautiously. They formed a circle, like chairs set out for a meeting, a conclave of wooden cardinals debating some important point. As she looked at the rings of bees that were clustered around the entrance to each hive she couldn't help but see them as traitors. She could see that they were bees identical to her own bees, yet they were also unmistakably other bees, foreign bees, alien bees. If she had seen one on a flower, she believed, she would still have known it wasn't one of her bees. One or two had settled on her sleeve. She backed away, then ran back down the hill to look for Dana.

'Did you see anyone up there?' Dana asked, when they were at home that evening.

'No, there was no sign of anyone. But the hives looked well managed. And the bees were very active. They must be producing a lot of honey.'

Dana ran a hand through his golden hair, then tasted the tips of his fingers. 'We'll have to find out who's put them there. And then we'll have to ask for them to be removed.'

It proved difficult to find out who the hives belonged to. The land was common land where grazing was permitted. Under an ancient law, beekeeping was considered a form of grazing. There were no deeds to investigate, no contracts to inspect. And the next time Kelly visited the new hives, taking Dana with her, they discovered that their number had increased.

'Are you sure, Kelly? Can you be certain?'

Kelly clenched her mouth, angry with her own lack of confidence in her answer.

'I didn't count them, but I'm sure there was just one group of them. Now there are some more over there, behind the tree.'

'There's long grass over there, you could have missed them.'

There was a barely discernible track leading through the trees where a four-wheel-drive could have got through, that lead in a winding way down the hillside and back into the valley.

Dana thought that the best course of action would be to report the illegal apiary to the National Council. He had to do so by letter, as the telephone lines only connected him to a recording of an unhelpful voice. The letter that eventually came back said there was little that could be done until they knew who had put the hives there.

'What do they expect us to do, keep a permanent vigil?'

'What about the police?'

But Dana had already spoken to the local sergeant, a very unfit-looking man with a drinker's face, who said more or less the same thing. He also suggested that it would be a waste of police resources to stake out a few beehives in the middle of nowhere. If he wanted this problem dealt with the by the law, the sergeant implied, then Dana would have to do the detective work himself.

'If I had the time,' said Dana, 'then I would keep watch day and night, but we have busy lives to lead. And this is just a few hives. We can't afford to stand guard, waiting for the rogue beekeeper to make an appearance.'

It was Kelly's idea to leave a note on the beehives.

THE HONEY GATHERERS

Dear Beekeeper,

This is a polite note to draw your attention to the fact that your beehives are sited illegally. It is against the law to place beehives within a kilometre of an established apiary. We have been beekeeping in this area for many years, and your bees are within 500 meters of our own hives, which are just down the hill. You are therefore politely requested to remove your hives as soon as possible. Please call me on the number below if you would like to discuss this further.

Yours sincerely

Kelly, of Kelly and Dana's World Famous Blue Heron's Bill Honey

Kelly carried the letter up the hill to the intruding apiary and sellotaped it to the roof of the most prominent hive, so that it couldn't be missed.

And then every day she went up to the illegal hives to see if the note had been opened. For a week it stayed there, sellotaped in exactly the way she had left it.

Then one Wednesday morning, she came running down to the shed where Dana was scraping a comb, slicing the caps off with a warmed knife. The frame was nearly full, just a few cells remained open.

'It's gone,' she said, 'the note's gone. It's been taken, and read. I looked all around to make sure it just hadn't fallen off, I searched every square meter in case it had blown away, or if the beekeeper had just torn it off and chucked it – but it wasn't there. He must have taken it away to read. What do you think will happen now?'

'We can only wait and see.'

'Do you think it means he must visit on Tuesdays? I could

go up there next Tuesday, and wait. See if I can see him.'

'If you want to waste your time…'

But nothing happened. There was no phone call, and there was no visit. Nor was there any activity the following Tuesday when Kelly did make a visit to the illegal apiary.

In fact it was Dana who found the response. He brought it to the little shop they had in the valley, where Kelly usually worked in the afternoon. He put a letter down on the counter where Kelly was sitting. It was an envelope with the words 'To The Self-Righteous Bee Keeper' written on it.

'I found it taped to the roof of one of the hives. It might have been there a few days, I haven't been up there since Sunday.'

'Have you read it?'

'Yes, even though it wasn't addressed to me.' Dana laughed quietly to himself.

'What does it say?'

'Why don't you read it?'

'I'm scared.' Kelly's hands were shaking as she picked up the letter. 'Is he rude? I don't want to be abused…'

'Just read it. Reading it can't hurt you. He doesn't say much really.'

Kelly read the letter.

Dear Kelly of Kelly's world famous blah blah honey

You are talking to someone who has been keeping bees on this hillside for generations. You are the illegal one, setting up your hives just down the hill from where my father and grandfather have kept bees all their lives. I could just as well ask you to move. Your bees are stealing my nectar.

In future I will ask you to mind you own business.

A real Beekeeper.

'That can't be true can it?' said Kelly.

'What do you think,' said Dana. 'Did we go up and check out those woods up the hill when we set up? I've never been up there before, and I don't think you have before you went wandering around…'

'Don't tell me lies. We must have walked through those woods hundreds of times…'

'In that exact spot? Are you sure?'

'A million per cent. And you only have to look at the hives. They are brand new.'

They were brightly painted, it was true, but that didn't necessarily mean the hives were new.

They let things rest for a few weeks. They tried to forget about the new hives and concentrated on their own bees. The busiest time of year was approaching when the bees were at their most productive. Every day they lifted new frames from the hives, all loaded with capped cells and rich, sweet liquid that was so pale it was almost silver, the characteristic colour of their blue heron's bill honey. They had to work all day, leaving the shop in charge of their assistant Delia, so that they could fill their jars. The extractor spun in its silver cradle, the glossy liquid poured from its spout to fill bucket after bucket. Then through the filters to take out the last particles of wax, before going into jars.

Then it was out to the hives again to lift more frames. They had to make sure the frames were taken while there was still space in the hive for more honey to be laid, otherwise the bees might settle down and stop production.

As the season progressed they began to notice a change in the honey. Its colour was darkening. On top of this, production was slowing down. Whenever they checked the hives they found frames only half full that would have been full normally. The honey that oozed from the extractor now was a deeper gold, much more like heather honey, or any regular honey from mixed sources. But the heron's bill flowers were still coming into bloom and would be for several more weeks. It could only be the intrusion of the other bees.

Could a few hives really have such an impact? Were their own bees really finding it harder to obtain nectar and so were going further afield? There was no other explanation, Dana said, for both the change in colour and the slowed rate of production.

They visited the alien hives again. They were shocked to see that this time their number had unmistakably increased. They had almost doubled. A little village of weather boarded houses, each one teaming with residents.

'I don't recognise the species,' said Dana, examining a bee that had landed on Kelly's sleeve, 'They're bigger than ours. Look at its pollen sacks, the size of them. They look like they're carrying money bags into a bank.'

'They're different, Dana. They're new. They were the same as ours when I first found them, but these are new.' Kelly had been closely examining a bee that had settled on her sleeve. Suddenly she brushed it off, giving it such a violent flick it knocked the bee straight to the ground, where it seemed to stagger, dazed and muddled. Kelly put a hand to her mouth in shock. She had never in her life deliberately hurt a bee.

Later, at their apiary, Dana was helping Kelly into her protective suit, zipping her up the front, arranging her veil.

'Do you think we should write another note?' She said, from behind the gauze that made her face look soft and grey.

'What could we say that we didn't say in the first note?'

'We could threaten him with legal action.'

'But we don't know if we have any legal rights.'

'Of course we do. He is encroaching on our territory.'

'But he claims he was here first, and we can't prove otherwise.'

'Even so, we can try and call his bluff.'

And so, after they had spent an afternoon extracting more honey, Kelly wrote another letter and took it up to the intruding apiary, and fixed it to the roof of the same hive as before.

Dear 'Real' Beekeeper,

We are disappointed to find that, instead of being nice and admitting you were wrong and taking your hives away, you have gone and added some more. It is outrageous. How do you know our grandfathers weren't beekeepers as well? We might have been keeping bees since the Romans were here, for all you know. If we were the newcomers to this area, why didn't you protest about us, as you would have been entitled to? You didn't, because you weren't there. Your claims to ancient rights are false and we have informed the authorities. If your hives are not removed forthwith, legal action will be taken.

Your sincerely,

Kelly

'What does "forthwith" mean?' said Dana.

'It means "immediately",' said Kelly.

'But how does it mean it?'

'I suppose "forth" means "forward", so together it means "with forwardness".' Do you think I should just say "immediately?"'

'It's a minor point.'

'Forthwith sounds more legal.'

'Yes, like a lawyer would say.'

Customers were beginning to notice the changes in the honey.

Dear Kelly one of their mail order customers wrote – they nearly always addressed their letters to Kelly, even though Dana's name was included in the brand, *I thank you for the latest jar of honey which arrived this Tuesday, but I want to draw attention to the fact that there is something wrong with it. It looks green to me. Just a little bit. As though it has had lime added. The taste is also different. A little bit acidic, if you don't mind me saying. I can't eat it. I am sorry. And I am desperate for my favourite honey. I have never had to return a purchase before or claim a replacement. How do I go about it please, Kelly?*

More letters like this arrived. Some sent their jars straight back. Other customers complained about the green colour, though neither Dana nor Kelly could see it themselves. There had been a darkening of hue certainly, but they couldn't see any green.

Dana developed a standard letter of reply.

Dear (insert customer name),

I am sorry that you are not happy with your recent purchase. We are a small company and run a limited operation with fewer than fifty hives. Unlike bigger companies we cannot draw on different sources of honey which we could then blend together to produce a consistent and unchanging product. Our honey must vary in character with the fortunes of our bees, we cannot have full control over where they go to forage. However, we are confident that the blue heron's bill content of the honey continues to be high, though it can never be guaranteed to be a hundred per cent. If you remain dissatisfied with your purchase, we will happily replace it for you…

He then provided details of how to return the honey free of charge.

For many customers, however, it wasn't simply a matter of taste or texture. They were more concerned with the honey's medicinal properties, in particular its supposed effect on sexual health. These were people who'd sworn by the honey's powers, had told them how it had saved their marriages, had revived their or their partner's interest in sex. They were the regular customers who came into the shop every month, some every week, alone or in twos, smiling blushingly as they made their purchase, much as if they were buying condoms or sex toys. Dana and Kelly sometimes joked together about these customers, especially the ones who bought large quantities of not just pure honey but also honey chocolate, honey biscuits, honey salad dressing, basically honey everything. Did that mean their sex lives were thriving or the opposite? Did the honey abundance fuel week-long sessions of lovemaking, or did they gorge on the products in the hope of kindling a spark, but otherwise were frustrated? Some were unabashed and would state the facts quite plainly, 'My husband has never looked back since we started on your honey, I just don't know what we'd do without it, he stays firm for hours and hours, it's like a miracle.' 'My wife – I'm going to have to start rationing this stuff, I'm exhausted. Ten years of coldness in bed, now she can't keep her hands off me.'

But now they were starting to lose faith in the powers of the honey. Since it had started to turn green, some customers were complaining that it had not only lost its aphrodisiac powers, it was actually doing the opposite, and turning people off sex altogether.

One day, a lady came into the shop in tears. Her husband is leaving her, she said. He says he is moving out next Monday.

He no longer has any interest in me. It's because of the honey, since the honey has changed, he's not the same man any more.

She was the first of many. Every few days over the following weeks another customer would confide in them some sad detail of their failing love lives, how the husbands could no longer maintain their rigidity, or how wives could no longer be aroused to a sufficient level of intensity. It began to seem to Dana and Kelly that the sexual health of their community had become their sole responsibility, and when they were out in the town they began to notice a change in things. Little acts, at first. An instance of road rage. A cyclist tearing off a van's wing mirror. A busker's accordion knocked from his hands, so that it wheezed sadly at his feet.

In a local grocery store a small angry man in sunglasses was shouting at one of the managers. 'You're the reason why there's all this hysteria,' he was saying. The assistant retorted 'I am asking you to leave. And don't come back.'

They walked past their favourite baker, the little Victorian-themed establishment that sold old world baked goods – muffins (the English variety), parkin, Chelsea buns, lardy cakes. Outside there was a blackboard on which was usually chalked bargains of the day or some witty message to customers. Today the message read:

Do Not Abuse Robin
I have been baking here
For twenty three years
And never had no abuse
Before – abusif
Customers will
Not be served.

They didn't go in.

If the baker was suffering abuse from his customers, there seemed no stronger proof that something quite terrible was happening in the town.

They decided to visit the milkshake parlour that had been open for a couple of years, and which was one of their favourite places to sit and relax. They were always mildly surprised that on the vast menu of milkshakes, which seemed to offer a milkshake version of every known food substance (apple crumble milkshake, fruit pastel milkshake), that there wasn't a single honey-flavoured milkshake. They always had a little conversation about one day going up to the manager and gently suggesting such a drink. Honey, rather than sugar, should be their main sweetener. Local honey. Dana and Kelly's blue heron's bill honey. But they never did.

Dana and Kelly were sitting on the high stools that faced a little counter by the window. Their back was to the milkshake parlour and they were looking instead out onto the street. Despite this orientation, Dana felt compelled to look back over his shoulder at the interior of the parlour. Something about its stillness intrigued him. It was busy. People were filling all the available tables and many were standing in small groups, appreciating their milkshakes and talking. There were little arguments going on here and there. People's faces bore sulky expressions if they weren't actually talking. Behind the counter the manager was shouting at one of his staff for dropping a goblet of ice cream.

Dana's attention was drawn towards a young man standing near the door with two other young men. He was wearing a baseball cap and a baseball jacket. He seemed happy. Dana noticed that he was pulling a face, drawing his lips back to give himself buck teeth, and making his eyes stare bulgingly. This face was so bizarre, and so unnoticed by anyone in the parlour, that he thought for a moment he was wearing some sort of novelty mask. But in almost that instant the face disappeared, as though it had been wiped out of existence, and in that same moment the milkshake the man had been holding exploded into the hair like a glorious liquid firework, and the baseball cap also became airborne, spinning and twirling like a sycamore key up to the ceiling. The man himself was still there, but only his bodily form, which had twisted and collapsed and ended up on the floor. It had all happened with the speed of a lightbulb bursting, a moment of energy and fire, as though the man had been struck down by god himself. But it was another man who had done the work of annihilation, who had quietly entered the parlour and had landed such a blow to the side of the man's head, such a comic strip style punch that it should have been accompanied by lettering writ large across the room that said something like *KERPOW!!!* And the man on the floor who by some unexplained means had recovered possession of his face – Dana later imagined that he had somehow picked it up and put it back on – should have had a cartoon of little tweeting birds circling above his head. The event seemed to bring time to a standstill. The man on the floor sat half up, looking blearily into the space beyond him. The man who'd dealt the blow was saying something and pointing to the man on the floor, Dana paid no attention to the words but they seemed to be along the lines of a justification, a *serves you right, you got what you deserved* diatribe. Others in the parlour were looking on with shock, unable to move. The manager, who had a long brown beard, came out from behind the counter, his arms spread before him, the hands flat, as though he was wiping an invisible table top. His work of placation and calming seemed completely ignored by the aggressor, and the man on the floor was beginning to rouse himself to a state of rowdy indignation. Dana was amazed that his face bore no signs of damage other than a general blushingness. There was no blood, no broken teeth. The manager was insisting that the man who'd thrown the punch should leave, but his words seemed to bounce off the man, whose attention was fixed on the man he'd downed and who was slowly picking himself up. The aggressor seemed now to be part of a group of men, and the floored man also seemed to have acquired supporters, although Dana realised that what was probably happening was that the assault had made visible previously unseen lines of connection between the two men and their friends in the parlour. The air of the parlour itself seemed to have become thick with connection and meaning, so that to walk through it would feel like navigating currents that would draw you to one party or the other. For this reason, Dana and Kelly felt unable to leave their present positions. Also, the doorway was blocked by the aggressor and his supporters. To leave would have meant squeezing through this posse of slightly overweight men.

By this time the man on the floor seemed to have been forgotten in an argument that was beginning to swell between the manager, the posse of men, and some of the floored man's supporters. But Dana hadn't forgotten him, and he observed the way he turned over, walked on all fours a little way like a small wounded bear, then slowly picked himself up, moved to the counter and took hold of an empty food blender. He then hurled this appliance at the aggressor. The flight of the food blender across the milkshake parlour, its electrical flex trailing comet-like after it, made Dana think that he was inside a self-contained universe of non-normality that was governed by laws that were different from the more familiar universe. And from that moment the elements of the universe exploded and took on lives of their own, in which Dana and Kelly could take no part. Instead they walked like knights through a game of chess, weaving in and out of the other pieces, though unlike a chess board, the milkshake parlour had become invigorated with energy and movement as nearly every person within it began to fight for themselves.

They felt like bees in the rain who somehow manage to fly between every drop of water. Unlike the bees, though, they were moving at a slower pace than the raindrops, and their slowness was what gave them time to calculate and thus avoid the trajectories of the fighting particles in the milkshake parlour. The manager himself was now part of the struggle, his flailing swings and punches easily dodged, they transformed into a hugging competition which resulted in his sweatshirt being pulled up and bagging his head, leaving a simmering and blurrily tattooed torso exposed. While he was blinded, others took the opportunity to land fists on the wobbling midriff. The fists seemed to sink into the flesh like a baker's hands into dough.

Only having to flinch a couple of times when a fist or foot came too close, and being lightly speckled with cold splatters of milkshake, Dana and Kelly were able to work their way towards the door and leave the parlour, only to find that the fighting had already spread out into the street. It was almost as if there had been a chain reaction, that atoms of violence were breaking away from the milkshake parlour and colliding with inert atoms in other parts of the town, and releasing the potential energy stored there.

'I don't care what you say, honey,' said Kelly, 'this just doesn't happen in this town.'

They agreed that although there were always young people in the milkshake parlour, and they were always full of energy and banter, it was always good natured. They'd never seen violence in there before. It seemed such a strange thing to see. It was like going into a field of lambs and seeing the lambs biting each other, eating each other. That's what it was like.

It was a disconcerting thing to find that, a few days later, the fight in the milkshake parlour had been filmed and put online.

The milkshake parlour had CCTV, and the manager had placed the footage on the web in the hope of identifying some of the protagonists in the brawl. Dana discovered it as he was browsing through his social media, and was about to tell Kelly but decided to watch the clip alone first. It was odd to see what had seemed so full of noise and fury reduced to something so small and compact and silent – there was no soundtrack. In this version the initial assault looked like nothing more than someone being pushed over rather roughly. You didn't hear the smack of the fist in the face, and you didn't hear the smash of glass or splatter of milkshake, or the shocked silence that followed. And from the camera's high vantage point you didn't see people's faces very clearly. Dana and Kelly were out of shot at the beginning. It took Dana a moment to work out the orientation of what he was seeing, but gradually he realised that he and Kelly were sitting beneath the lower frame of the shot, the tops of their heads must have just been a few inches out of sight. He called to Kelly to come and see the clip.

'It's the fight,' he said as she came over, 'it's been recorded on camera.' He clicked on the picture so that it would start playing from the beginning.

'Oh – I'm not sure if I want to see it again. Why are you watching it?'

'They're appealing for anyone who can identify the people who were fighting.'

'Well we already know we didn't know any of the people in there, don't we?'

She was standing behind him as he sat at the table, his laptop in front of him. She watched over his shoulder, apparently as drawn in by the spectacle as he had been.

'It looks so different. Where are we?'

'We're down here.' Dana pointed to empty space below the table, 'off screen. We'll come into shot later.'

'It's so weird. Not like I remember it at all.'

On the screen the fight looked as though it was something acted out and choreographed, and not the spontaneous and chaotic event they remembered. They watched the movements of individuals within the mayhem, some moving rapidly, twirling and spinning like tops, others static and moving carefully to avoid the others or keeping out of the way of a swinging fist.

'That's your head,' said Kelly, as the bald spot in the centre of Dana's golden hair came into view at the bottom of the screen. The natural tonsure seemed to glow in the camera's over exposed image.

'And there's yours.'

Dana and Kelly watched themselves moving through the fighting crowd, they couldn't help smiling at how carefully they trod, as though walking through a living maze. At one point they became separated, and Kelly was at the door first, and was then through the door and outside. At this point Dana was still inside, and there was a brief lull in the fighting.

What happened next on the screen left both Dana and Kelly lost for words. The video clearly showed that Dana threw a punch at a man with a beard who at the moment was arguing with another man, but otherwise was standing still and passively by one of the tables. Dana's punch was thrown from behind the man the victim was talking to, so to him it must have felt that the fist had appeared from nowhere. He was knocked straight backwards onto the table where he rolled over and fell on the floor.

'My God,' said Kelly finally. 'Was that you who did that?'

'I don't think so.'

'But it's there, I just saw it – you whacked that guy in the side of the face.'

'I never whacked anyone in my life.'

There could hardly be any doubt about the veracity of the

film, though it was true that the film only showed Dana from behind and above. The bald spot and hair colour were his, and the white T-shirt. Was there the slightest chance that he had a double in the parlour that afternoon?

'It's you, Dana. You hit that man. Why did you do it?'

'It looks like me. I can't explain, Kelly. I didn't hit anyone. It's got to be a mistake. Or a trick. They can do things with videos now.'

Kelly was replaying the video, pausing it, examining it frame by frame.

'It's you, Dana. There's no mistake. And you can tell it's not faked. It couldn't be. You just lashed out at someone, punched them when they weren't looking, really sneaky.'

Dana could say nothing but shake his head in disbelief. The way the victim went down, stiff as a board, toppling onto the table then rolling onto the floor. Like the original victim he seemed to have his life wiped out of him for a moment, as though his face, his identity, his humanness had been detached from his body in a single swipe, and the unconscious lumber was all that was left. They watched the video to the end, long after Dana had exited the scene, and were relieved and grateful to see that the figure on the floor soon began to stir, he was unconscious for only a matter of seconds, and by the end of the video was on his feet and walking around with a drink in his hand.

Just like the men who'd been hit and had, for a moment, been detached from themselves, and just like the majority of people in the milkshake parlour who had undressed themselves of their social identities and thrown the clothes in a collective heap, so Dana, he supposed, had for a moment ceased to be Dana, and had become the body of Dana. It was his body that had thrown the punch, operating without conscious intervention. The spirit of the milkshake parlour had sucked his consciousness from his body and left it to do what it pleased. And what pleased the body were simple physical things. This was the only way he could explain what had happened.

Kelly rolled her eyes at this explanation and said, 'I never thought I'd be in bed with a thug.'

They drove up to check the hives that afternoon. Walking through the village of white bureaus, each with their busy little population, they could sense immediately that something was wrong here as well. It wasn't that the bees were being aggressive or irritable in any way, it was just something about their movements. There was less of the flow and smooth rhythm of flight that one sees in a contented colony, but instead the flight of the bees seemed jerky and stilted, almost as if they were blind and might fly face first into things. Then they saw that one of the hives was lying in the grass, that it had fallen sideways and, like a maiden who'd fainted, was supine and dishevelled. Dana and Kelly couldn't go immediately to the aid of this fallen hive but had to put on their bee clothes first, in case the bees were still alive, in which case they might be angry.

'So I knew something would be wrong.'

'It's just the wind, I suppose.'

'You think so? It hasn't been windy for days. Not windy enough to turn a hive over.'

They had never had a hive fall over before, and weren't sure what to do. Some of the boxes had come apart. It all depended on whether the queen had survived. And it depended on how long the hive had been lying there on the ground. It had only been a couple of days since they had last visited, but they supposed even that was enough time for damage to have been done.

They approached the hive cautiously, Dana with a smoke gun, as gingerly as they might have approached a discovered body. As they got nearer they could see bee activity. A little crowd had formed around and opening between the boxes. The bees had gathered as if for a meeting, or a demonstration, or they were like people who'd gathered outside an entrance when a fire alarm goes off and are unsure whether to stay where they are, go back inside, or wander off somewhere else. Dana squirted small puffs of smoke into the hive. There were bees everywhere, in the grass, clinging to edges of the wooden structure, some had clustered around a gap, thinking it was the entrance. Slowly the two beekeepers managed to press the boxes back together and then lift them as one piece back into the upright. It was a difficult thing to do, though the smoke had sent many of the bees into a dream, the danger of collapse and the frames falling out was always very real. Finally they righted the structure and were able to inspect some of the frames. In some of these the bees clung to their cells like figures at the windows of an office block on fire.

'Someone has pushed this hive over,' said Dana. 'Deliberately,' he added, because Kelly had looked at him blankly, her mouth a little open. Through the wider bee keeping community they had heard about occasional attacks on apiaries. Bees were in the same class of vulnerable animals as horses in lonely paddocks, who now and then fell victim to a sadist with a knife. Dana had often wondered about that impulse that existed in certain human beings, to deliberately inflict physical suffering on something as solid and as large as a horse. That must have been part of the thrill, he supposed, to harm something so obviously sentient but that wasn't human. If you fantasised about killing a person, to enact it upon a horse was probably the closest thing. But bees? Who wanted to be cruel to bees? He imagined that the hive vandals probably thought the bees would just go off and live somewhere else, it was the hives themselves they wanted to destroy, for the sake of causing hurt to people, the beekeepers.

They may not have realised how destroying a hive might lead to thousands of deaths. Hives *are* bees.

'I think we should visit those hives up the hill.'

Kelly didn't agree.

'Don't jump to conclusions sweetheart, anyone could have done this.'

'Not anyone. Do you think anyone would come all the way up here, above the farms and above the fields, miles from a proper road, deep in the woods, just to turn over one beehive out of forty?'

Dana thought the time was right and went straight away, walking through the little style in the stone wall at the edge of the trees and following the moorland edge up hill towards the rocks. The heron's bill flowers were still in bloom, though there were many that had faded. The flowers came in successive waves throughout the spring and early summer months. They still presented a beautiful sight, little purple tufts, tiny explosions of life on the brown peaty earth.

They came to the alien apiary.

'What are you going to do, Dana?'

He went up to one of the hives.

'Look, there are more.'

'You're not going to push one of them over are you? Please tell me you're not going to do that.'

Dana didn't say anything.

'What about getting stung?' Kelly said, 'have you thought about that?'

They had taken off their bee suits and left them back at their own hives. Dana didn't seem to care. Kelly could see that he was thinking about which hive to pick as he walked among them.

'What are you, twelve years old?' Kelly said, as Dana found his hive and prepared to turn it over. 'Think what you're doing.'

A hive was a city. What Dana was doing would be like dropping a nuclear bomb, or instigating a major earthquake. And he pushed. Just as if he was pushing over a piece of furniture. Kelly cried out in shock, unable until the last moment to believe that he would do it, and the hive keeled over as if in slow motion. Kelly was reminded of videos she'd seen of tower blocks and power stations being demolished, a crack of explosives takes away the base support and the structure starts to topple, but for a certain amount of time retains its form – so the beehive remained a beehive until suspended between the upright and the horizontal – it seemed to pause before coming apart. Boxes clattered, frames fell out.

They ran, conscious of being at the centre of a moving cloud of rage. Kelly felt bees thread their legs into her hair, she looked down and saw tiny bodies clinging to her, she brushed them off. Then a needlepoint of pain in her arm, another on one of her legs. Something was crawling into her collar, she had to unbutton her shirt as she ran, seeing to the side of her that Dana was in trouble as well, he was running at the same time as trying to brush the bees from his hair and his clothes. By the time they reached their own apiary they had divested themselves of most of their outer coverings and were in their underwear. They made for their Land Rover and climbed in, slamming the doors shut.

Now what are we to do? Kelly thought, and in fact she spoke these thoughts aloud. Do you realise what you've done, Dana?

'I have redressed the balance,' was all he would say.

'What you have done is invited retaliation. That's how it works. Do you think our friend up the hill will think – oh, fair enough. I got my just deserts. Now I'll pack up my bees and leave. No, that's not what will happen. What will happen is that our friend up the hill will pay our bees another visit, and perhaps this time he'll fell two hives. Or all of them.'

'Then I'll keep watch. I'll camp up here all night if I have to.'

'Will you really? Can't you see that's mad? Who lives out with their bees? It might be days and days before he retaliates. And so it will escalate, until neither of you have any bees left.'

Dana had hoped by the time they got home that evening and into bed that he had done enough to convey to Kelly how sorry he was for what he'd done. They had eaten at home, fearing that the violence they had seen in the milkshake bar and elsewhere in the town might be repeated in a different setting, so they ate steak and drank red wine at their own table, while Dana expressed sadness about the bee hive he'd turned over.

'I was angry,' was all he could say, by way of explanation.

'It wasn't the bees' fault,' said Kelly.

'I know that.'

'And it wasn't that man's fault. What had he done to you?'

She meant the man in the milkshake parlour. The one Dana had punched.

'I've told you, I don't know. I don't even remember doing it.'

'You knocked him down, just like the beehive.'

'Maybe I thought he was the beekeeper.'

Kelly looked disbelieving, as though she was unsure if a joke was being made.

'I think that's a sick thing to say.'

By the time they were getting ready for bed, they had each calmed a little. When Kelly was undressing Dana saw the marks on her body. Little red circles with a black speck in the middle, like volcanoes seen from space. There weren't many, but enough to make it seem as though her body had been marked up as if for something much more destructive later on.

But it was as if Kelly hadn't noticed them. Only when

Dana drew her attention to them did she feel them.

'How come you weren't stung?' she said to him, a little offended. Then, to his surprise, he found that he had been. There were stings, identical to Kelly's in their colour and size, all over his body – not a great quantity, he counted five that he could see. They didn't feel painful either, at least not until he noticed them, and then, rather than a stinging sensation, a sort of dull ache, as though something was pressing its thumbs into his body.

With a sort of concentrated indifference, they made love, and it was only when their naked bodies came together, front to front like the recto and verso of a book, that they realised the pattern of stings on their bodies matched, sting came to rest against sting and in so doing seemed, by some unknown process, to neutralise each other. But even so their lovemaking could not progress beyond this full-body touching, and when Dana tried to indulge his favourite thing at the moment of spitting into Kelly's mouth, she regarded the forming bolus of saliva on Dana's lips with a horror that his own eyes were reluctant to register. This many-windowed pearl that, as if by means of a silver line, began to abseil the gulf between them, seemed suddenly to her the agent of some all-reaching ever-self-replicating disease, and she closed her mouth and turned her head in disgust to feel the spit land on the side of her face instead.

'For God's sake why do you have to do that thing?'

She had thrown Dana off and he had toppled sideways onto the bed. Kelly was wiping her face.

'What thing?'

'You know what thing, you were doing it again.'

'I thought you didn't mind.'

'Well I do.'

By now she was walking with as much indignation as she could manage in the absence of clothing, to the bathroom.

Dana could do nothing by way of argument to save the situation. You can't reason with a feeling of disgust. His stings began to hurt again. When Kelly came out of the bathroom, robed like a Roman queen in fluffy folds of whiteness she looked set to ignore him. He asked her if there was anything he could put on his stings. She told him that yes, there was something, and they spent twenty minutes applying an antiseptic cream. It troubled them both that in all their years of bee keeping they had never suffered stings before. It was something they liked to tell people, a matter of pride at how skilfully they managed their bees that they had never before stirred one to hostility or anger. But Dana thought to himself, he had still not been stung by his own bees. They still trusted him.

Adobo

Paul Theroux

FROM THE LANAI AT my house in the woods that night, I looked for the wild pigs that often gathered after sunset, their dark hairy bodies like tarnished silver in the moonlight. They were fat bulky things propped up on dainty trotters, but they moved without a sound, and in the darkness seemed to glide, spiriting themselves across the grass, hardly touching the earth. Feral pigs, people called them; but I thought of them as friendly familiar shadows, keeping me company. Where were they tonight?

I sat there reflecting on the send-off for me in town that had just ended. I had taken early retirement from my job in the welding division at Pearl Harbor naval shipyard – I had risen to supervisor – and my men decided to celebrate my leaving at a Korean bar – beer and karaoke. The mama-san pushed a skinny girl at me, saying, 'You go with her – she very nice!' I knew what that meant.

'No thanks,' I said. 'I'm good.'

Some of the men mocked me, but my buddy Rick said, 'Harry, I'm impressed. You're a real decent guy. You should find yourself a decent woman.'

He knew I'd been divorced for years, that I'd have plenty of free time as a retiree, living alone on a hill on the North

Shore, and that I was not yet sixty.

'Someone like Bing,' Rick said.

Bing was his Filipina wife, much younger, hard-working, good gardener, great cook, and tough: for their first year in Hawaii they'd lived in a shipping container Rick had welded into a simple habitation; but on a hot day like an oven. No complaints from Bing.

'No thanks,' I said.

'She has lots of friends back home.'

'I'm good, Rick.'

But on my lanai later that night I considered my situation. For the first time since high school I would not have to go to work the next day, which was a Monday. I wondered what I'd do – some errands, I supposed, and then? The nights I could manage – beer, sleep, dreams – but the days ahead looked empty.

And that's when I saw the shadows on the moonlit grass. A stranger would take them for dogs, but they were too fat for dogs, and didn't sniff and mutter like dogs; utterly silent, shifting on the large sloping lawn, six or eight of them. Usually they headed for the tree. It was a Java plum. The ripe fruit plopped onto the grass, and the pigs ate them.

But this was not the Java plum season – the small plums were just swelling and would not drop for a month or more. It was as though the pigs knew I had nothing to do and was harmless and needed consolation. Noted for their intelligence and resourcefulness, they smelled loneliness. I pitied myself for feeling grateful for their companionship, the way I'd once felt for my family's ritual consolation.

They were dark silhouettes, tame and two-dimensional at night. But in daylight they looked much bigger and mean, lumpy and feral and usually muddy, with stiff black hair, a spiky ridge of it rising like in a wiry comb down their spine, and a way of standing still and watchful, the big boar always up front, the others gathered behind him, the sow, the smaller ones, sometimes a clutch of hairy piglets.

I said out loud, 'I know why you're here.'

My voice did not spook them, but when I got to my feet (slightly drunk) to repeat it I heard that snore-like piggy honk from the big boar. He looked up, narrowing his eyes at me. They did not run; they melted away into the darkness.

That was my future, the company of wild pigs, the brotherhood of the boar. The next day I called Rick.

He told me what I knew already, that he'd fixed up other guys from our welding unit, and mentioned that they were very happy. It is not unusual to find older haoles married to young Filipinas. And the men know what they sign up for: a kind of dowry at the outset, regular payments to the family back home, money for educating a brother, or to support a relative. That prospect did not daunt me – it made me feel less lonely.

Within a few weeks I was in Manila, interviewing candidates – all of them Bing's friends - to be Mrs Harry Lappin. They were young, friendly, eager to please. One was a nurse – a plus for an older man. Another a sales clerk in a department store – cosmetics counter, very prettily made up, lip-gloss and long lashes. A third was chaperoned ('my uncle and auntie') and said she was a trained masseuse. If I gave her uncle and aunt some money to get a taxi home, she would stay and massage me.

Many women think a guy is an easy mark for being a predictable male, not hard to find the right buttons to push, simple to switch on, getting him to say yes, dear. But I wasn't looking for sex. I wanted a good companion – a female buddy – which is a more difficult assignment.

The last candidate was Josie, from Bing's distant hometown. At once, I knew she was the one. She was older than the others, mid-thirties, but was still way younger than me. The kicker was, 'I live in the village.' No big city manners, no make-up, no ploys; a plain speaker, and practical. She'd taken an overnight bus from Ilocos Norte, where she worked on the family farm with her widowed mother. They raised pigs, they harvested bamboo, they had fruit trees. She was sturdy, unlike the others, a farm girl who did not yearn for expensive shoes and manicures – her hands were toughened from hard work. She had the shoulders of a welder, and that same squat stance too, someone I would have hired on the spot.

In the course of our talking about work, she said, 'You know why Filipino people work hard?'

'No. What's the secret?'

'Because we so poor.'

I said, 'I want to take you to Hawaii.'

She agreed, with conditions, to marry me. I knew the conditions: dowry, presents, payments, airfare for her mother to visit, the ticket bought in advance. Her mother came to the wedding, planned by Josie's uncle and some of Bing's friends, a priest officiating. It was held at a hotel function room – hastily arranged, the priest, the food, the flowers; simply a matter of money.

Just before the ceremony began, sitting in the front row of folding chairs, with her mother beside me, the old woman turned to me, I thought to congratulate me, welcome me to the family, saying 'Good luck, Harry!' But she looked fierce, her lips parted, her bony teeth clamped together.

'You not beat my daughter!' she hissed through her teeth.

I was startled, but managed to say, 'She's safe with me.'

The reception afterwards was a buffet, a table of platters and pots, the biggest a bubbling stew in a tureen.

'Adobo!' one of the guests said, a woman poking her fingers at her smiling mouth, indicating 'tasty!'

I looked in and saw meat and bones, the sort of density that retained the look of the carcass it was made from, a still recognisable remnant of the live thing it had been, except that the aroma was of soy sauce and vinegar.

'You eat! Adobo is tradition!'

But I couldn't. It looked more like a hacked-apart animal – probably a pig - than a pot of food. My sour expression was noticed. People judge you by your reaction to their food. Afterwards, I thought: next time I'll say yes to adobo.

We flew to Honolulu together. Josie got a temporary visa, and I applied for her residency, which would lead to a Green Card and - after the usual probationary period – citizenship.

Having a young wife in Hawaii – a woman from a far-off place – was a thrill. The simplest pleasures delighted her – a movie, an ice cream in Waikiki, a picnic on the beach, a drive around the island in my car, listening to music on the radio. Meeting Rick's wife Bing after so long was a relief for her, talking excitedly in their own language. She had a supportive friend.

Rick said, 'What did I tell you?'

And one night coming back late from a movie, sitting on the lanai, we saw the pigs. They were less obvious – not much moon – but Josie saw them clearly. She said she was used to such sights in her village. The creatures prowled without a sound, and because we were so quiet ourselves they lay on the grass, flopped sideways, six of them tonight, the biggest one who usually stood guard looking upward, his head cocked at an inquiring angle, looking at me and then at Josie, as though I'd spurned him for her.

Josie touched my leg and leaned, her whisper hot in my ear: 'Adobo.'

She spoke softly but in the juicy salivating way of someone very hungry. Yet before I could say anything – I was about to say, 'They're kind of my friends' – she pressed my thigh again, letting her hand warm me, a fond gesture, the more loving for being spontaneous and casual, as though that's where her hand was happiest.

As she led me into the house I glanced back and saw the pigs on the lawn, ranged together standing, the moon glow lighting their eyes, staring at Josie and me – or was I imagining it? That night, and the nights that followed, were bliss – Josie in my arms – I blessed my luck.

She was, to my delight, frugal and old-fashioned. It was her farming background. She did not use the dishwasher – she washed the dishes in the sink, then dried them and put them away. She fashioned a clothesline at the edge of the lawn, from the Java plum tree to the monkey pod, and hung the laundry, instead of using the dryer.

'My mother used to do that.'

And she ironed the clothes, as my mother had once done.

She found guava and lilikoi in the woods, and one day said, 'Lomboi' – indicating the swelling fruit on the Java plum tree – and promised to make jam with the fruit when it was ripe.

I said, 'Not if the pigs get there first!'

The pigs were more frequent, always seeming to appear when we were together on the lanai, looking out at the sunset and the sea beyond the treetops. I'd be smiling at the last of the light and my eye would be drawn to the shadows on the grass; and I'd see them, the big boar, the fat sow, the four smaller ones, all of them standing still, silent and insulted.

Whenever Josie saw the pigs she said, 'Adobo.'

And I laughed, thinking how I'd looked at the meat and the bones in the tureen at my wedding reception in Manila, and walked away, while the guests clucked disapprovingly.

One evening, Rick called me and after inquiring about how I was getting along – 'Never better,' I said – he asked, 'Josie told Bing you want to use my rifle – is that so?'

'I don't know anything about it.'

'Something about your pigs.'

'The wild pigs? They've been around so long they're like part of the family.'

'Anyway, if you want to smoke one of those pigs, let me know.'

Something I have not mentioned so far. Josie could not read, her English was passable, yet she always seemed to know what was going on – what I was saying, even what I was thinking. It would be silly to call it animal cunning. I saw it as her having developed keen observation, as a compensation for her poor English. She must have been listening in another part of the house, because she hurried into the room where I'd been talking to Rick and she raised both arms as though aiming a weapon and said – like a kid with a toy gun - 'Pah! Pah!'

She knew we'd been talking about Rick's rifle.

Still in the gun firing posture, she smiled and said, 'Adobo.'

'Not me,' I said.

'Me. I do it,' she said, smacking her chest with the flat of her hand.

I hate guns, I think they're magnets for violence, but I saw her eagerness. This was Josie's element, probably the reason she was so happy – the wild pigs, the Java plums, a gun: a little bit of Ilocos Norte here on the North Shore of Oahu.

It was a black 9mm carbine, wickedly sleek and quite new. Rick handed it over saying, 'Regular ammo won't do the job, so I'm giving you a box of hollow point shells. They sort of swell and mushroom on impact. Go for the heart.'

Josie took the rifle from me and fiddled with it. What a strange experience to see someone I loved, but did not know well, expertly work the safety lever, click the sights into position, and use her thumb to push bullets between the steel lips of the magazine, all the while seated with the weapon on her lap.

I say 'strange,' but I mean like a different person, dangerously so, well armed with this black rifle: a hunter, her finger tickling the trigger. She looked alert – more than alert, wired, poised to shoot, a potential sniper.

Disturbed, unsettled by the new demeanor of my wife, I went inside, leaving her on the lanai. After a long while, an hour or more, I called out.

'See anything?'

She shushed me furiously, a scolding reaction that I hated. And so I avoided her, that night and for some nights thereafter, whenever she was holding the rifle and watching the lawn for the pigs.

This business seemed to cast a shadow over us, as she reverted from being the placid picture bride to the gun savvy farm girl, awaiting her prey.

And so I joined her, and that very day, late afternoon, as we sat together on the lanai, the pigs appeared from beyond the Java plum tree and the clothesline flapping with laundry. It was as though they were reassured by my presence, but questioning it too. The piglets as usual wandered near the flower garden in front of the house, while the big boar watched, and the plump-bellied pig dug beneath the flowers, unearthing roots and allowing the smaller pigs access to them. I was fascinated, because I recognised the procedure of a hen scratching the soil so that her chicks can peck at ants. It was mothering – the big pig was the sow.

I was studying this when I heard the bang, a noise that almost toppled me from my chair, that rang in my ears. And then I saw the fat sow knocked flat, its hind legs kicking slowly, but the creature silent in its suffering. Another bang and blood gushed from beneath its chest, not red in the bad light, but black, like motor oil flowing among the flowers.

Josie put the rifle down, she laughed a little, she said, 'Adobo.'

And she said she'd skin and gut the pig in the morning. Her mother had taught her, she went on. Her mother had a good knife and was expert with the knife – Josie slashed, as though demonstrating the gutting and disemboweling of a pig, looking murderous as she did so.

But in the morning I called my Hawaiian neighbours, the Kailana family, and told them what had happened – they had heard the gunshots, they said. They sent over twelve-year-old Chelsea and ten-year-old Nalu, with a wheelbarrow. They hosed the dirt and blood off the dead pig and wheeled it up the road. Old man Kailana set up a table outside his house and gutted the pig, and smoked it. They gave us a bundle of meat a few days later.

Josie shrugged in a superior way. 'My mother have a better knife.'

She made the smoked pig meat into adobo, in a cast iron stew pot, and insisted I help her – I passed her the onions, the vinegar, the soy sauce. And when she was done I looked in and was reminded of seeing the tureen in Manila at our wedding reception, the still recognizable portions of the carcass – meat and bones.

She made so much of it I brought a container of it to the Kailana family. Chelsea was at the door, wide eyed, looking offended. She took the container from me and whispered sorrowfully, 'She had babies - was pregnant!'

'Was the sow,' old man Kailana said. 'Plenny keiki.'

The boy Nalu said, 'You never see those pigs again. They real smart. They get scared away.'

But that very night, after delivering the adobo, walking back to my house I saw the shadows, lurking near the Java plum – not eating, not rooting in the flower bed, but watching in a way that unnerved me, silently, with a stubborn look – unnerved me because all they were doing was staring, the big boar rigid, severe in his gaze.

I mentioned this to Josie. She said quickly, 'Where the gun?'

'I gave it back to Rick.'

'Adobo,' she said in a tone of complaint, as though I was denying her this meal.

'We've got plenty.' I did not add that I found adobo gamey and repellent, not just for the sharp taste of the soy sauce and vinegar, but for the look of it, the meat and bones.

'Gun,' Josie said, insisting.

Rick said he'd been surprised that Josie had succeeded with one shot in taking down the big sow. He also cautioned me. The police would not make a fuss about one dead pig, but it was a different matter with the Department of Land and Natural Resources. For them you needed a hunting license to shoot an animal, even a wild pig or a mongoose on your property. Rick didn't want to get into trouble by loaning his gun, perhaps losing his firearms permit.

I told this to Josie. She didn't like hearing it. And when I said she'd have to be careful after dark hanging clothes on the line, or walking around the property at any hour, she scoffed.

'Wild pigs,' I said.

'Adobo,' she replied.

This was another side of my wife I had not seen before: defiant, willful, mocking what she took to be my soft-heartedness. It was annoying, but I reminded myself that these were the qualities that had made her self-sufficient on the farm. And still the pigs appeared most evenings, not eating, but watching – vigilant shadows, staring upward at me. I thought of Chelsea's sorrowful, *She had babies.*

Rick called. He had become a sort of interpreter. His wife's English was better than Josie's, so he reported on what was on Josie's mind.

'Bing says that Josie wants you to get a hunting license, so that you can bag a few more pigs, legally. She's pretty keen on more adobo. Reminds her of home. But I can't let you use my gun unless you get a license.'

'I looked online. It takes ages – a long application, red tape, a waiting period.'

'It's in a good cause. And it seems you still have a pig problem.'

'I never saw the pigs as a problem,' I said. 'And Rick, don't tell Bing, but I hate adobo.'

He laughed. He said, 'You want a happy wife?'

It was forty miles into Honolulu to the office of the DNLR, to start the process of applying for the hunting license I did not really want. On the long drive I reflected on the four months of my marriage, the little pleasures of ice cream and movies, the occasional evenings of passion. I realised that in those four months Josie and I had not been apart – always together, in the house, in the car, on the beach, on the lawn. So this drive into town was odd for the freedom I felt, my old self, the silence, the empty seat beside me. The mood of facing the friendly family of pigs that first night of my retirement party.

I found the office at Punchbowl Street, and took a number, and when my number was called I went to the window and submitted my application, showed my ID and paid the fee.

'How long before I get the license?' I spoke into the hole in the glass.

'Try wait,' the smiling man said in the Hawaiian way.

On my return home I called out, 'Josie!' There was no reply. It was late afternoon, failing light, the distortion of shadows on the grass – and that was when I saw her. But it was not Josie, it was the rags of her torn clothes, my poor dear wife twisted and mauled on the grass, almost unrecognizable, just meat and bones.

Frantic, I called the police, I called Rick, and I asked Bing to break the news to her family, saying that I would have her cremated and bring her remains back as soon as I could.

A week later – a week of misery - the coroner at the morgue asked me to sit, and his expression was of a great sadness that matched mine, which somewhat consoled me. Then he said, 'Did you know your wife was pregnant?'

At home, grieving, I was sitting on the lanai and saw the shadow – just one, the big boar, Josie's killer, staring upward at me, and there was just enough light for me to see Josie's blood caked on the stiff bristles of his snout. The telephone rang, and yet the pig was undisturbed by the ringing, but only kept staring.

'Hello?'

'Me Josie mother.'

'I'm so sorry,' I said. 'I'm planning to fly to Manila, maybe next week. Where are you?'

'Me here.'

On Monkeys Without Tails

Mike Nelson

WORDS HAVE ALWAYS EXISTED akin to physical things to me, however sitting here incarcerated in my decaying body I recall the day I cast aside material sculpture for text, and now lament the entrapment of words unto the same fate as my beloved objects thirty years ago. As a young man I had celebrated the aura of the things that I hunted and found – the unloved and discarded – I basked in their radiant provenance, imbibing their histories and living out their mythologies in my imagination.

My studio is still the same pastel blue it was when I bought the long lease shortly after the death of my father, a moment indelibly etched on my psyche as a marker of the mortality of middle age. The row of shops built onto the backs of a Victorian terrace that fronts onto a parallel street behind still remain, however most are residential now, gone are the junk shops I once nestled amongst. This street was once full of them, the kind that unloaded their miscellaneous goods each morning onto the wide pavement and brought them in again in the evening. An ebbing tide of matter built up of people's lost lives and the histories that they had witnessed, the spectacle brought onlookers and those with more things to sell and barter – spring tides came and went as did more spartan periods but the flow remained constant. The space previously had been occupied by a PR man to some of the more obscure music festivals across Britain, and before that a sound system shop – the legacy of which had left the heavily fortified mesh on the windows and a depiction of a roaring lion's head rendered in vinyl and centred in the top left window. Superstition had drawn me to it – a crude rendition of my astrological sign it became a moniker of my confused ideologies. Before that, it had a life as a neon sign shop – a collection of lettering I kept and still remains, the kind that would have adorned the likes of an Angus Steak House in the 1970s; their gaudy red and gold livery struck dumb in the darkness under the floorboards, a silent anagram waiting to be unearthed.

Various other histories have been suggested for this lowly building, amongst these were a pirate radio station, a sex dungeon, and a puritanical ghost that put pay to an affair whose elicit meetings were conducted in the basement. These theories were revealed through chance meetings – a pirate DJ at a flea market, two passers-by on the street curiously staring through my open front door one day, and a musician at a dinner party. The space has been adapted to allow my ailing body to pass through it, navigating the encumbrance of the staircases through a series of ingenious devices both structural and prosthetic, giving the building a sense of absence... of a phantom, that of myself. Aside from these, the basic architecture remains the same as does the furniture and many of the objects that occupy it.

I had renovated the building when I moved in, even though to some I had retarded the process, adding old floors with hidden trapdoors hinged on nineteenth-century ironmongery, and obscuring the shop windows with wired glass – a municipal aesthetic, curiously called 'Georgian', popular in the 1950s and 60s but out of kilter with the twenty-first century. To enter the building you had to pass under a small portico that I had weatherproofed with lead, and step down into a low ceilinged atrium which sat below a mezzanine supported by four columns; these would not have looked out of place from the interior of a seventeenth-century ship had the paint concealed wood as opposed to concrete. To the right as you entered, I had installed a kitchen constructed from the remnants of a photographic darkroom, the sink and hardwood tops redolent of the chemicals that had developed the images of disease-ravaged bones and distorted skulls. The yellowed photographic prints I had found within the same building as the dismembered laboratory that had formed part of the Royal Orthopaedic Hospital in Fitzrovia, now demolished. These were the remains of a project that never came to fruition, its spoils sitting restlessly in my shop, now akin to an archivist's tomb, my own, a burial mound of my own making. Further into the space and the scale changed, a large square room resembling a Welsh chapel in miniature provided relief after the cave-like entrance. The Edwardian lamps overhead also heralded from the hospital. Slung on chains, their glowing globes made their way to various hooks fixed into the ceiling to allow their movement to facilitate a clear passage for projections onto the back wall, but also evoking the high ceilings of their former life in the institution of a past now only remembered in imagery.

One such object that had washed up on the shores of Chapel Street was an old bureau. The desk remained unchanged from the day I purchased it, missing a door and the sliding glass panels from the upper section, the object had given up any hope of restoration. However I still harboured a belief in its completion, a metaphor for a multitude of things in life that I was blind to, and that accompanies many of us to our end. These appendages that

201

chaperone us through life now only exist to be passed on, akin to a baton-like humerus bone in a macabre relay race of the dismounted four horsemen, on and on from one unsuspecting optimist to the next. As a piece of furniture it was handsome, in a brutish way, its solidity of form only surpassed by its weight. The proprietor of a neighbouring shop, from whence it came, had helped me manhandle the three sections into the building – two block-like stands that supported the third; the main bureau. The design was simple and modern, in keeping with the fashion of the early-to-mid part of the last century, however what made it peculiar was its handmade construction from a dense tropical hardwood, inappropriate both for the design and the technique of construction, and yet it was this that first drew me to it. When at last the desk was set in place and my chair drawn up – as it is today – with its hinged writing surface lowered, the secret to this object's peculiarity was revealed. The small drawer positioned centrally in front of me bore an inscription rendered by hand in gold paint upon its underside:

BUILD BY MR. DUTT OFF CALCUTA, INDIA. FOR
L.E.NAPIER 1930.

An afternoon of research had later revealed the mystery of the desk's provenance: Lionel Everard Napier was a doctor of tropical medicine who specialised in research into the transmission of parasitic diseases via the sand fly. This was a hypothesis that he had helped to prove, and, in some small part, was responsible for the acceleration of an area of research that would eventually come to preoccupy the world. A world where infection circumnavigated the earth at the advancing speed of growing populations and their movements. Whilst working at the school of tropical medicine in Calcutta, Napier must have employed Mr Dutt to construct the piece of furniture, supplying him with images of fashionable items from his native land. I can only imagine Mr Dutt's horror at the simple lines of its construction, with no decorative surface to distract or hide the difficulties that the material and the tools to hand would conjure. I harbour great respect for this craftsman who through his desire to please, or fear of displeasing, created this remarkable object at which Dr Napier pursued his line of enquiry. At certain moments I try to envisage its past lives, the rooms it once occupied, the objects that adorned it, the books that sat behind the now absent glass doors. Sometimes I catch sight of something imagined, at others a sound or smell, the invoked apparitions of an object's journey. I would often wonder if the nature of these momentary 'glitches', for it is the only way I can describe them, were traceable to the second owner of the desk, and in many ways it was he that intrigued me more.

John Russell Napier inherited the bureau from his father; the new owner was a primatologist whose specialism in taxonomy led him to the classification of great apes – living, extinct and imagined. His scientific credentials merged with the subculture of pseudoscience in his investigations, which were often public, into the Sasquatch or Bigfoot, and its supposed relative, the Yeti. These mythic creatures were part of the indigenous folklore of the peoples that populated such remote places, the colonists adopted their tales – imagining them, seeing them, wanting to possess them. Napier was part of this lineage – his television appearances a precursor to the woven complexity of stories that abound upon the internet. As this mythic entity occupied more space – both in the minds of humans and the technological space that surrounds them – its reality or actuality diminished or at least became redundant in meaning. It mirrored my fears, that somehow these creatures in their absence could draw into their silhouette such a mass of words and images that could negate their possible existence still further. Here indeed was not only the end of my belief in matter but the beginnings of the erosion of my faith in words themselves. For if an excess of words can obliterate a myth, then the tangible has no hope.

So here, in a single object, were the histories which would come to preoccupy or even occupy me. Primarily the transmission of hitherto obscure medical conditions across the world, for it is this that you can see physically manifest within me. These, we would come to see, were ultimately instigated through the empirical exploitation of finite resources, and its rewarding of greed as a societal structure. The spectre that haunts me is both unseen and real, as is the condition that ravages my body, its undisclosed point of entry somewhere on the coast just outside Hong Kong island in 2023. The similarity of my destiny to the fated creatures of John Russell Napier's investigations seems unavoidable. My attempts to exist, to mean something, through matter, word and ultimately myth as an artist has come to a similar conclusion. Existing in fractured form, my entity is disseminated across the ether – captured by the holding structure that has overtaken us but is also of our own making. Only now can we see the wisdom of those that we colonised as they refused to have their photographic image taken, the camera a device of incarceration of what we would once have understood as the soul, not the liberation of the individual. The conversations about a mythic creature's identity that abounded in the late twentieth century, those that suggested lost tribes of Neanderthal or Homo-erectus seem less preposterous now as I teeter on the edge of extinction myself.

In the drawers to my right remain a collection of objects that seem steeped in pertinence to this shift in human-being.

Old headphones, their trailing wires and jacks ready to transmit sound to the physical body, their design cumbersome in their imaginings of our anatomy. Light meters, tripod heads, shutter release cables and dust blowers – the language of an epoch where to capture an image was a skill as rarified as the hunter of old, the alchemy of chance the deciding factor, as matter and motive discussed their possible collaboration. Amongst these relics of the analogue era, the beginnings of another – cables with an evolutionary array of connecting heads herald the historic shift to what we once called the digital. The idiosyncrasies of these were once dictated by our need to communicate, and to do so more clearly, but now overridden by the drive to consume – and the forced redundancy of existing systems purely for the economic benefit of those that superseded it. I reflect upon the twisted analogy to the early British colonisers of the seventeenth century on their arrival in what we once called Australia. Here, an excess of five hundred languages existed on the landmass, within three centuries there was to all extent and purpose only one – the one I pen this text in today. The difference, or twist, is that it is the status of complexity which is reversed; the motive remains the same – to exploit, as does the effect – to destroy. This desk to which I am now tethered has become my barometer. The object was imbued with warnings and possible solutions but I did not heed them. I came to it too late, its voice only audible as I offer my last remaining organ intact to its comprehension – my brain, yet the language is not written but empathetic. The desk, the surrounding objects and space have taught me this.

So it seems I am now returned to the status of matter, back to dust in a biblical sense and yet I still live. Humanity with its proud, self-defining categorisation – as civilised or being 'guided by reason' – has no reason to exist. So I write this story to add words, to add pages to the book you hold in your hands, a final object of such decorative impotence I cannot start to explain. Perhaps it's all I can do, so that the book can sit behind the absent glass doors of this bureau. Extinction beckons, but that would imply that someone or thing cares. It doesn't, we will just slip away without even the ability to render our departure meaningfully in words.

Let this be my headstone, my goodbye.

The Room Peels

Alan Beard

MARK LEFT HIS WIFE. He left his son. He had to live somewhere, so he came here: within his range. It *was* a bit of a squeeze. The last tenant showing him around: 'Only enough for one really, glorified bedsit. No cat swinging. Door to the street sticks,' he was informed and shown the shoulder and key twist technique needed. She then stood back against the sink, a bit out of breath, one stout leg behind the other.

She kicked him out, actually, his wife, ex-wife, gone wife Lucy. He was *womanising* again: he was with Belinda, after Rachel, Trudy, Mary and Sue. Met Belinda via work, where he was security man/receptionist/handy man at a small firm. On one works drink night Belinda showed up, a friend of an admin clerk he chatted with in the back office. Thinking back now, it probably was a set up. But, he liked. The tumbling hair and a whipish body. He thought enough of himself then to move closer, move in. Where had that confidence gone? He had had it drained. Belinda and her 'brother', Darren's lack of texts. The years going by. The room: it closed in on him and wouldn't let go.

Funny though, Darren liked the flat at first. It being above the cafe, where Mark sometimes bought him not-very-frothy milkshakes, and Darren made friends with the owner's son, as children that age – 9 – do. His son liked the stairs up to it, narrow and wonky. The uneven floors, the place as though squeezed under the eaves – people ducked when they moved about it, unnecessarily. The bed that folded up into a wardrobe and when down took up most of the available space and they had to edge round it. When Darren was 9 and 10 he laughed here, he ran around the place opening the cupboards and getting the pillows out and piling them up by the sofa to jump on; hiding from Mark the monster. It was only later – 12 and 13 - he sat, on his phone, his head down. Shooting armies coming at him, grunting. Even when he won, grunting. All to be expected Mark supposed. But what a chore then to connect with him. 'Darren, Darren, are you listening?'

Others at work told jokes their kids told them, his son didn't tell him any. He told him the ones he heard at work, tidied up, and Darren didn't even politely laugh.

Still he'd give everything to have him back here, sit and talk to him again, even if grunts were all he got in return. They'd had good moments. On this brown corduroy worn-to-a-nub sofa, beating him at Simpsons Road Rage. That's how long ago it was. He'd bought a PlayStation to keep Darren happy (Darren was appalled he didn't have Sky Sports). Mark lost and lost, the controls making new grooves in his thumbs and fingers, and he was happy to lose, he was keeping Darren close. And then one long Saturday afternoon after innumerable losses he swerved the right way, he accelerated when he should and, instead of crashing into the Springfield sidewalk, he won. He shrieked: 'First time ever!' 'Last time ever,' his son said.

He could see himself in Darren, his Markism. He wanted him here, if only to question him about Richard, Darren's stepdad to be, who luckily Darren seemed to dislike too. Mark saw it as having a bitch as if they were colleagues in an office. Bants. Rich listened to folk music. 'And psychedelia, I bet,'

Mark said. How did he know? 'Just a guess,' he said, 'I bet he goes to Glastonbury.' Darren confirmed – he'd got it all planned, went on the website early to get the tickets. Mark could imagine Luce lapping all that shit up, after nothing of the sort from him.

★

Belinda was a regular visitor for a couple of years too. Although she always said there was something weird about the room, like it was listening in to their sexual shenanigans. They shared a love of drugs – cannabis, ecstasy, ketamine, cocaine, acid – and sex. Although there wasn't always sex towards the end. Sometimes nothing but crying and beating his chest. Sometimes long rambling stories, sagas of shopping incidents – what was she thinking talking to Marie at the bakers' who was a slut and a bugger and stole her cigarettes when she used to smoke – she was smoking as she said it. Very rarely a meal, but he did bring Balti takeaways to the flat, still hot, and they ate them quickly before she asked him to tie her up. Tight as fuck.

A tame leftover from when she was with someone who was into S&M. She liked it, encouraged it. But then it was just the same and it got too intense. 'Boring, don't you think, intensity?' She said it was hard breaking up with that one. He hung around on corners, she saw him when she came out of work. Had to get her brother on him to shake him off. Her brother was in the army. Mark imagined him on manoeuvres crawling on his front holding a rifle. 'A few on the trot after that,' she said, 'like you, but *I* wasn't married.' She was now, to a Manchester United fan, she went to Mark on matchdays.

Night he knew he was in love with her was European Cup Final Night 1999. Apparently. Loverboy off to see the game with pals, to Spain or somewhere. He imagined them in sombreros with beer foam moustaches, while she shared stuff with him, then handed herself slyly to him while they sat on the sofa sniffing, in a deep buzz. He remembered, replayed, when the room let him, each scene as it had played out that night. The words she said, the moves they made. Started with his hand on her warm hip, sticking up from her jeans. She snuggled closer, smiled up in his face. Everything flowed as it should, he watched her, them, change, shed years, take on colours. At one point she separated from him and flew like a bird round the room, a flow and shake of colours, a few feathers dropping. She glided and swooped.

She said in his ear wasn't he the guy at that do so many years ago? Didn't they end up in some shed round the back of a building? Refugees from the party in next door's shed and weren't they dishevelled and disturbed by a cat, didn't a cat jump with claws out into their intertwined bodies, forcing them apart? Weren't they once all jumbled up in each other? He let her think so. He let her ramble. Later they danced, to the Chemical Brothers, 'Setting Sun', pushed themselves up off the sofa, and held each other up as they swayed. 'I dig his friends,' she said. He could remember her breath breaking on him, her whole slippery body up against his. They weren't quite naked, she had a T-shirt which she pulled up over her breasts in mock strip, he was in his socks. 'Like the tattoo', he said. She had a tiny rearing horse by her hip ('Got the idea from a sports firm logo,' she said). In those days quite new.

These moments, scenes, had happened on this same sofa, in this same room. He hadn't been able to move on, a few encounters in the years following, but they felt half-hearted, no one was a match for Belinda. Maybe it was so good, so sharply recalled because she was only ever there overnight or for a couple of days even after she left her husband and the *family home* (though they had no kids). She got herself a flat that had a mezzanine floor well across town, and although Mark helped her, driving the hired truck with furniture and boxes, and afterwards they sweatily christened the place on the stairs amongst stuff piled around them, he was never invited to stop over there, let alone move in. Her brother returned from the army and had nowhere to stay so she put him up.

★

The noises began well after Darren and Belinda had gone. Years after. Started as sounds that were piped through tiny apertures in the fabric of the room, the room trying to communicate, to get him to listen. It pushed sounds to his ear, and then bored through to the brain, and became there little sticky sentences she'd said to him in the height of passion, or Lucy's admonishment of his appetites, his lack of respect, his estrangement from his kid, or Darren grunting, saying, 'spose so, spose so.'

There seemed to be a whole army of invisible soldiers in the room, the size of those on Darren's phone screen, coming through the wall with their fixed grins to nick him with bayonets or shout commands in his ears to get him to do press ups or confess to acts of terror visited on his son and wife; or berate him for disgusting habits; his inability to walk properly.

His stoop his squint his smell his narrowness his repetition.

One of them sounded like his dead father alive again, the low hissed voice saying he was a bully at school and a lazy fucker out of it.

He'd come to hate the thing in him, the room round him, but worse outside, the talk down the shops, the people in front of him, the angles of buildings. The pavements and properties covered in scaffolding, he always thought he'd bump his head (he wasn't tall) or scrape his hand on the metal poles bolted together. Drills and endless lorries, trucks and builders' vans.

Outside was harsh, abrasive. He was losing skin and thoughts to the wind and rain. He began to want to only be indoors, inside his room. When he left it called him back, it sent out snares, invisible ropes and strings to snag him, it wanted to torture and pamper him at the same time, to mix him up and send him backwards. Sometimes he did end up lying upside down on the sofa, as he'd seen Darren doing, years ago, in imitation of Bart Simpson.

★

Belinda said this room was where you came to pay for your sins. 'That's what I'm doing here. Being punished.' 'You like being punished,' he said but they'd gone well past that stage now. Everything was her brother now, her brother this and her brother that. Feats accomplished; bombs defused in deserts. Mark met him twice. First time, in her new flat, he witnessed them banter and talk about music, 90s dance of course, the new millennium's stuff not up to scratch. Crap. The three of them smoked, but when they put on tunes the siblings danced together, mirroring each other's movements: he knew somehow his time was up.

He told Belinda and Darren and anybody else who would listen (no one) he was only here temporarily, just to get himself sorted out, find a better job, look for somewhere else to live. He never did look, nor did he get another job.

He lived alone, unhindered by visitors. Didn't answer the door. Nobody knocked anyway, not even for rent or to canvass his opinion. A lone child, often left by his parents for long periods, he went back to his lone-ness.

Downstairs, finally, the café went, he missed looking down at the café customers, so familiar with the tops of their heads; Darren leaning out and shouting and then withdrawing, ducking below the sill, or Belinda at the window remarking on the hair twisted up, absent, parted, sticky, dry. Gone.

The little block he lived in was closing down from either end. All the businesses, corner shop (not on the corner), Balti, hairdressers & wig shop, a second-hand place that seemed to only sell pieces of machinery, closed one by one. Across the road the properties now seemed to be being demolished rather than renovated. One by one, gaps. On boards a new community had been promised — people walking in twos and threes and smiling at each other, sitting outside under parasols by a fountain - but the years had faded that depiction and behind the boards now were the tops of piles of rubble, empty space. From his window he could see the wasteland, the acres of mud and puddle between dumped concrete.

He kept things of Belinda's, strands of her hair, a shoe, her snot in a tissue stuck together, her voice on his phone, the photos he sneaked, a piece of her, smell of her, the sight of someone like her. He'd stopped stalking now, like her old sadist lover, he'd stopped going to the streets where she lived. It took more time to stop looking for her on local TV news bulletins that came from the city centre. He scanned the crowd going by in the background. (Wasn't that her? Her hair, her walk.) He was too far gone now, could hardly lift himself off the bed, the room pinned him there with the voices and soldiers it sent out. Sometimes he worked himself, with drugs and attitude, into getting up, freeing himself from the room's command, and play music, often the same track, Modjo's 'Lady', she loved that track. Belinda would come then from the past, the 90s, to this room, the dance music hanging around her, haloing her and announcing and glorifying her.

Once he bumped into the previous tenant, recognised her stout thighs first, every muscle visible in black tight leggings. 'Christ, must be over ten years,' she said, taking a while to see who it was, 'You still up there? I thought everyone had gone, now the development's stopped.' She gestured around her, 'There's kids looting these buildings now.'

After that there seemed fewer and fewer people about when he did go out, and nobody he recognised, apart from the old bent Sikh with the walking stick. He stopped him to talk and ask what was going on, chat about the former residents, the café, and the Sikh waited, stroking his long beard, but the words didn't come.

★

He came out in boils and rashes. He tried to cut them off with a knife but even his best kitchen one was too blunt. His hands were against him, wouldn't do as he wanted, wouldn't open her left behind book (*Memoirs of a Survivor*), a jar, move a chair or hold his cock. No one else ever would.

What was he supposed to do? He stopped going out for one. It got harder to get out anyway, the door to the street seemed to get tighter and tighter in its frame. When out the activity, the traffic, noise, exhaust, mud, bitter bits of flesh and hair the passing people shed, gave off a taste of sick and metal, he coughed, squirmed, kept his head down when he went to get provisions, food, booze, rizla. A gang of kids shouted to each other across the road and blocked him and others as he tried to get past. Back he was safe. When the room didn't interfere with him, let him be a while, there was just him and his memories: eight-year-old Darren as goalkeeper diving to save from him, sofa the goal, booting the ball he'd bought about until it smashed a cup; Belinda winking, her little foot up on the chair next to him as she took off a shoe, undid a strap, the music blaring, drugs coursing through them both.

One day he got down the stairs and couldn't get the street door open at all. It felt final, so he retreated. Now music, when he could play it, went backwards, when he sang the lyrics went backwards into his mouth. Words would come out of the walls, dangle for a bit then withdraw back in with a slurp. Impossible that anyone should talk to one another and be understood; impossible.

He should have stayed with Lucy, if he wanted to see his son grow up, he knew, but at the time his homelife was just an added boredom, on top of his days at work. He knew he should have tried harder. Tried not to argue, at least, in front of the child. As Lucy found out, one by one, of his affairs, some live, some not – after the fact, she said, hands on hips – there would be the same argument and sulking. The quiet times were worst he felt, things unsaid washing around the house, around Darren.

When his boy stayed here (only twice) he'd leave the bed down and Darren said it was his kingdom and Mark would be the giant unable to get on the bed, because it was magic, instead he flailed at its end, roaring at the boy prince, magician and hero able to laugh at him, safe. Darren slept on the sofa, the two times, Mark in the bed next to him, so close as to see the small frown on his brow, the puckered lips, as if he were slowly working something out.

It was unbearable. What he realised in his sofa-and-bed prison, in his jaundiced eye, was that there were unbearable things weighing you down, but you had to bear them. Every day you had to get up and bear them. Darren now living with his new hipster dad, gone with Lucy to a town far away; the new set of people he'd grow up with he would never know and never know their motives and intentions. At least Darren would have left home by now, probably. Been in work for years, or maybe he finished university first. The lack of texts or interest in him told the story he knew was true. Darren was bored indifferent in his presence finally, particularly towards the end when he tried to give him advice on bullies – Mark saw signs: withdrawal, how he never looked him in the eye. He had other things to do, grown out of indoor football, he had another dad, a better dad and friends to look out for him.

★

The toilet's porcelain yellowed; dust balls wheeled across the floor; the corners grew grit and mould; the curtains stained. The room shifted course in the night, in the day, when he turned around, all to get back on him for his stupid disastrous life, for his pointlessness. It wasn't enough, it was never enough. Belinda, the only one he'd ever wanted to stay, was after something beyond him. Even when they embraced, and her flesh was next to his something in her felt far away. Looking back she was soon over their heady days that he often tried to recreate with her. And later without her.

The window at the end showed a lump of black air. There seemed to be no streetlights, the view of the far city had long since disappeared. His breath slid to the floor, fetid and dry breath, and the voices drew back and then surged, commenting on him, his uselessness, his fartiness, his seediness, how he treated women, how he boasted to his mates, how he didn't have any mates, he used to have workmates before he left work didn't he? As if he would have mates, the state of him, let himself go, let his beard grow and fluff out horribly, his nails not cut, his wrinkles wrinkling, his smell worsening. He was wasting away like he should, not worth the paper he was written on. All the air wasted oxygenating him, keeping him going and him interfering with the world in a bad way, a wasteful way, a poor way, the opposite of as advertised.

★

He ran out of food, ran out of coffee, succumbed to the voices in the wall that both pampered and tortured him, pinned him. When able he inspected the floors and skirting, the walls and ceiling for signs of entry. He rambled round the room mumbling to himself, talk like a digesting belly, answering the voices, the tiny conversations creeping about him and scattering words underfoot.

For her last visit, Belinda came round here with her brother, and accused him of not only breaking her heart – as if – but stealing her stuff. Jewellery, drugs. £20 notes missing from her purse. Her brother who looked nothing like her got even by pinching Mark's stash, his collection of pills. He'd just bought an ounce. Brother smoked a bit here to test the quality and complimented him on the skunk: Lemon Haze. The smoke curled round the room, seeking its corners and heights, but he didn't offer Mark the spliff. She was at a distance, by the door, went away and came back.

People could get out then. Now they couldn't, at least he couldn't: he tried but couldn't shift the door, after breathless attempts which hurt him, winded him, he gave up trying.

His boy was turned from the phone-obsessed teenager he saw last to a man's voice, on a message he finally heard days later. Sounded like Darren was a smoker too, twenty a day at least. 'Happy birthday Dad' – he'd forgotten it was his birthday – must be a big one for Darren to call. 50th. That's what he said. Mark found he didn't have a voice, words, to call him back. He wanted to tell him not to be like him. Maybe you're more like your mother he was going to say, he hoped so. He would meet him somewhere, he would travel to wherever Darren wanted, he would have a pint with his son at his favourite pub, did he have a favourite pub? Did people still go to pubs? They could discuss his job and wife to be, the grandkids he might get. But he didn't, couldn't, call back.

★

Phrases came chopped with long silences. Infantile. Bubbly but thin enough to get into his systems. Darren's baby and young voice distorted with fuzz, like an effect on a dance record. 'Spi–der', 'comin' up', 'sun kill'. The words made the deepest sense to him, seemed to sum him up and prophesy some end.

He lay on the now never-put-away bed, splayed across it for the room to inspect and manipulate, insert the words.

It was so damp, matches wouldn't light, the electrics fizzed. In the shower and toilet room plaster slid to the floor. The doors buckled; walls bulged. He sank in. He couldn't seem to move, his limbs hurt. When he could he was discussing and playing the room at strategy, promising new behaviours, more contrition. He promised to obey and salute, to distract it from hurting. It would ease up a little, breaks like you'd have at work, half hour or so.

Dust and dregs accumulated; the room peeled its layers. The room's sounds had crept into him and stayed there. Up and down the flesh now from the inside and the outside he was hurting: burning and scarring. His mind went. It broke like a dam and the release was heaven. The smiles of Lucy and Belinda mixed; green drenched trees; music that might save him but didn't; Darren telling a joke.

He slid down, off the bed, not quite dead, a trace of his mind, voices and noises, in the stained air when the kids broke in.

For Joel Lane, RIP.

O Death

Mark Haddon

MY MOTHER MENTIONED IT in passing, between complaints about changes in the post office opening hours and the neighbours' unruly hedge.

Hang on. Rewind.

He fell down the stairs and banged his head.

He's in hospital on his own?

I had to call an ambulance.

And Terry…? Forget it. Rhetorical question.

You have a lot of blood vessels in your scalp, apparently, that's what the woman from the ambulance said.

Once upon a time I could picture it in my head: Northampton; Corby; Kettering; Leicester. Nowadays it was a series of indistinguishable dual carriageways and roundabouts, satnav country, because God forbid you open a map and choose a scenic route where corporations can't fleece you. I stopped for petrol and a strong black coffee at a featureless BP + M&S Food To Go. Gulls overhead, which meant a storm over the North Sea, or so I'd been told as a child, though we were fed a great deal of misinformation as children. All those poor kids who died from turning lights on with wet hands.

Night was coming down. Warehouses and distribution hubs, the countryside flatlining, the towns getting smaller in every sense. For a long time I'd harboured a fantasy that maps lied, that the world was in truth much smaller than we realised, long journeys looping back to reuse locations for a second, third, fourth time, Scooby-Doo chases on a global scale.

My father was in the early stages of dementia. He couldn't draw a pentagon or remember Mr Brown of Sea View, Brighton who'd been mentioned at the beginning of the conversation. *Your father's never even been to Brighton.* Though I suspect I'd fail the same test if I watched daytime television and lunched at the garden centre every Wednesday.

Tents of orange light stood under the floodlights in the near-empty car park. I pulled up by the ticket machine, turned off *Rinaldo* (the Bartoli/Daniels/Hogwood 2000 recording on Decca) and was fleeced for a minimum stay of three hours.

I have never liked hospitals: the obesity; the tattoos; the ugliness of the ill; the graphic confirmation that poverty and poor health walk hand in hand. There was a machine selling crisps, chocolates and fizzy drinks in the A & E waiting room to make sure customers kept coming back. A drunken man was swaying to and fro on his green plastic seat as if the building were a galleon rounding the Cape, his bleeding hand wrapped with what looked like a pair of underpants. A small child was racing back and forth pretending to be a motorcycle, with convincing sound effects. The receptionist directed me to bay 13 and gave a little shiver which might or might not have meant *Unlucky thirteen! Prepare for a terrifying surprise!*

My father was reclining on a raised stretcher, holding a spouted, translucent beaker of milky tea and wearing a bandage round his head which made him look like a cartoon of a man with a bandage round his head. His bald pate shone in the artificial light and a bruise of many colours was starting to bloom on his right elbow. There was a ghastly photo-mural of otters.

Hello, Carol.

I'm never sure which irks me most, the lack of gratitude or the presumption that I will materialise in times of need. I have learnt not to bring the subject up. Footnote: Terry can't help because he has 'problems of his own', problems caused largely by a life in which he has never been asked to help anyone do anything.

You've been in the wars.

I broke the phone table.

The phone table is not important. How's your head?

Apparently you have a lot of blood vessels in your scalp.

The inside of your head.

He was dressed in a flimsy pink gown which exposed not just his scrawny, hairless shanks but toes with which something seemed to have gone terribly wrong – crusted, flaky skin, the nails long, cracked and discoloured. Was this the reason he'd been having trouble walking recently, the reason he'd lost his footing?

They gave me a lovely scan. He was, I think, on strong painkillers.

A very lucky chap in the circumstances, said a short, plump, cheerful doctor who could have been the landlord of a Dickensian coaching inn if Dickens had come from Chennai or Hyderabad. *You will be very sore tomorrow, but your spinal column is in one piece and we could see nothing of concern up top.* He tapped his own head. *Cuts and bumps and bruises only.*

I left my father in a borrowed wheelchair under the entrance awning and jogged through the drizzle to retrieve the car. On the way home he regaled me with injury-themed tales from his childhood, one of which was actually new to me. *And that's why you don't wear a tie in a factory.* He didn't ask about my life – neither of my parents did, ever. Occasionally

I would offer a piece of interesting news (*Only two performances and we get a free week in Aix-en-Provence*) forgetting that the limpness of their response was always more aggravating than their failure to ask in the first place.

We passed the muddy swings where Keith Blackshaw had burnt a live frog with a magnifying glass, we passed the boarded-up dentist surgery where Megan Kirk had been abused while under anaesthetic, we passed places where nothing had happened in the entire span of human history. I could still feel that same low thrum of anxiety despite the fact that it was no longer home.

Terry's van was, of course, parked outside when we arrived, confirming that he hadn't been *tied up at work*, though quite how a boarding kennels might tie anyone up had never been made clear. *Dog Day's* on the side of the van in comic sans with a paw print rising behind it like the sun. Seven years and the apostrophe had lost none of its power to aggravate.

The bloodstain on the hall carpet lived up to its billing, a big, off-centre splodge with a pointed spout like Antarctica. The constituent parts of the broken phone table were stacked under the coats. My mother appeared in the over-sized bubblegum-pink tracksuit trousers she had begun wearing lately, took my father's elbow and guided him into the living room. *I hope you had the heater on in the car.*

And thank you for driving all this way, Carol.

There's no need to be sarcastic.

Terry saluted me with a neatly cut sandwich which Mum must have made for him despite it being past midnight. *Sis.* There was egg mayonnaise on his Hotel California T-shirt.

Terry.

An episode of *The Last of the Summer Wine* was churning away on one of the re-run channels. That weird colour palette old TV programmes have, canned laughter as punctuation. My father picked up the cat and dumped it into his lap as if it were a hot water bottle. The cat had a name so infantile I cannot bring myself to repeat it.

I'll get myself a coffee then.

Don't make a mess. My mother plumped a cushion and wedged it behind my father.

I'll pay for any damage.

It is, I believe, an immutable law that if your parents treat you as the twelve-year-old you once were, then you will behave like the twelve-year-old you once were and this phenomenon ends only with the death of either party. *Also, Dad has only superficial wounds. No brain damage. In case anyone was interested.*

Not that we'd notice. Terry chuckled to himself as he followed me into the kitchen.

Seriously. How's Dad doing these days? I said quietly so that our parents wouldn't hear. *I mean, apart from falling down the stairs.*

Absolutely gaga. He took a bite of sandwich.

I excavated a bag from the box of Twinings Earl Grey. *Any hot news in the dog business?*

Funny you should say that...

One thing I'll say for Terry is that he can be set going like a wind-up toy and thereafter requires only nods and ums, unlike certain members of the family. While the bag was steeping in the I Heart Norwich mug I glanced at the wall clock. 1:23am. Christ. Head off to a Premier Inn and I wouldn't hear the end of it. I'd have no choice but to bed down in my old room with the Leaning Tower of Suitcases and porcelain chimney sweep.

You all right, Caz?

I was finding it hard to breathe. *I'm just tired. It was a long drive.* The framed picture of that fucking windmill above the fridge. You forget the panic, the desperation, then it all comes flooding back. I silently counted to ten, loosened my grip on the Formica worksurface and exhaled slowly. I removed the teabag, dropped it into the pedal bin and returned to the lounge.

There's a coaster on the mantlepiece, Carol.

I placed the coaster under the mug to prevent the house collapsing and burying us alive.

If it's all the same to you, Mrs Pegden, I went through that style when I were four year old.

I felt sure I'd seen the episode before, though everything in the house had the same déjà vu horror to it: the anti-macassars; the salt and pepper carpet. *Have you seen Dad's toenails?*

I'm sitting right here, you do know that?

Horrible, said my mother, holding up her hands in self-defence. *Don't even talk about them.*

Shouldn't you do something?

There's nothing wrong with my toes.

You're having trouble walking, Dad.

Terry was surprisingly knowledgeable about the dangers of amateur chiropody performed on elderly men with poor circulation. *If the wound gets infected you have to amputate.*

I think the drugs are wearing off. My father was rubbing his knee.

I'll fetch some Nurofen.

You get a bag of frozen peas, said my mother, lest I take charge of the situation. *I'll get the Nurofen.*

I went through the door on the far side of the kitchen, closed it behind me and stood in the chilly, soothing dark of the garage. Creosote and WD40, the acoustic of a room without furniture. They were still there, the splintery planks we used to make ramps over which we rode bicycles at thrilling speeds until Rosie Barclay lost her teeth. God alone knew where she was now. Given what I recalled about the rest of her family, prison was not entirely out of the question.

I pulled the cord and the single fluorescent tube buzzed reluctantly into life. Peas acquired, I was about to drop the lid of the chest freezer when I saw the corner of a distressed cardboard box. I wiggled it free. *Birds Eye. 12 Crispy Cod Fries, All Fish – in Special Batter.* They were two decades old, if not three. *Like Howard Carter opening the tomb of Tutankhamun with Lord Carnarvon at my shoulder.* It was a good joke but one I would have to save for my return to civilisation. I was working out how I might dispose of the box and thereby prevent my parents dying of listeria when I saw, in the frosty nook uncovered by their removal, a hand.

Well, Carol, I said to myself, *This is something of a turn-up for the books.* Talking to myself being an old person's habit I picked up when visiting my parents' house. *A cup of tea, I think... Now where did I put that magazine...?*

Perhaps it belonged to a very large doll, or to some kind of garden statue, though why either of those things should be in my parents' freezer was a mystery. I thumped aside a concreted bag of oven-ready chips. The hand was attached to an arm, the arm to a shoulder, the shoulder to a head.

My mother called from the living room. *Carol...?*

I balled the sleeve of my sweater round my fist and brushed away the fuzz of tiny, white stalactites from the face. *You'll never guess what I found in my parents' chest freezer.*

Carol...? What in God's name are you doing in there?

I would later discover a large bruise on my shoulder but at the time I was aware only of coming round to find myself sitting on the garage floor, waiting for the world to swim back into my ken. It took three attempts to get to my feet. I stepped forward just far enough to see over the rim of the open freezer. It was a small dead child. I stepped backwards and felt briefly very unwell indeed.

Carol! A loud snap this time, as if my mother were calling a badly behaved dog back from the far side of a park.

Concentrate. I walked back into the kitchen, steadying myself on the door frame and silently rehearsing my announcement. *There's a dead child in the freezer.* The idea was preposterous. There couldn't be a dead child in my parents' freezer. I had made a mistake. I had briefly lost my mind. I was about to make a fool of myself and confirm all my parents' most exasperating prejudices. I paused in the centre of the kitchen. I had to be absolutely certain that there was a dead child in the freezer. I walked back into the garage and looked at the big open box spilling white light onto the ceiling. I couldn't bring myself to get any closer. There was very definitely a dead child in the freezer. I had seen it with my own eyes. I had touched it. I said this out loud. *I touched the dead child.* I wanted to wash my hand in very hot, very soapy water, but there were more important things to think about. I walked into the living room. *There's a dead child in the freezer.*

Don't be ridiculous. It was my mother's standard response, always uttered before she had processed the content of what I was saying.

I am not being ridiculous. I said it more slowly this time. *There is a dead... child... in... the freezer.*

Oh, said my mother, *It's probably something to do with your father.*

He laughed, *She blames me for everything.*

Terry pointed a half-eaten chocolate digestive in my direction. *You're having us on.*

Is anyone actually listening to me?

How old is it? asked Terry.

What? It doesn't matter how old it is.

I mean, is it, like, a baby or is it a teenager? One's really small, one's really big.

Jesus Christ.

There's no need to use language like that, said my mother.

Terry brushed the crumbs off his hands and spoke through a mouthful of biscuit. *Let's have a look-see.*

He wandered into the kitchen, then I heard the echoey scrape of his shoes on the concrete floor of the garage. Mum poured herself a generous sherry. Terry reappeared.

Well, well, well. You're not as stupid as you look. She's not as stupid as she looks. There is a dead child in the freezer.

Do you know anything about this, Geoff?

About what? My father's habit of zoning out had become more pronounced since his diagnosis.

About the child in the freezer.

My father shook his head. *I haven't the foggiest.*

It's a boy. Terry picked up another biscuit from the plate on the draining board. *One year old? Eighteen months? It's not really my department.*

Anyway, said my mother, *it's none of your business why we have a child in the freezer.*

Of course it's my business, this is my family.

Well, you don't act like it, you act like we're an embarrassment.

I drove four hours through the fucking night to pick my father up from… No. Stop. It doesn't matter whether you're my family or not. You killed a child.

Maybe it just died, said Terry.

Or it died and you hid the body. Or someone else hid the body. None of this is in any way good or normal or legal or… I'm going to ring the police

I wouldn't do that, Carol, said Terry. *I really wouldn't.*

Are you threatening me?

You're blowing everything out of proportion, as per usual. My mother picked up the remote and turned off the TV to show that she was serious. *You shove your nose into other people's lives and stir things up. We were doing absolutely fine, thank you very much, until you swanned in here with your hoity-toity singing and your I-don't-want-any-children.*

Bloody hell, said Terry. *She's really off on one now.*

Asking all these questions when you know your brother's got his problems…

I'm pretty sure Terry winked at me at this point.

And your father's got his dementia.

I haven't got dementia.

You always forget. He always forgets.

Which is quite funny, said Terry. *You know, in the circumstances.*

What has happened to you people? For a moment I forgot about the dead child, which is some measure of the strength of my feelings. *You are so fixated on sticky rollers to get cat hair off the furniture, and how the moss wouldn't have built up on that fucking conservatory roof if the builders had added three or four degrees to the angle of rake, that you have totally lost your moral compass.*

Nice return, said Terry.

My mother put her sherry down. *You have no idea of the hours your father has spent cleaning that roof.*

There's a dead body in the freezer and none of you are surprised. Only now was the truth dawning on me. *You knew it was there, didn't you. I'm calling the police.*

Except I didn't call the police because the cat leapt to its feet and snarled. The cat never snarled. The cat had lived its entire life one step away from a coma. Its fur stood on end in a big, tabby-coloured mohawk. Terry, my mother and I turned instinctively towards the kitchen. For a couple of seconds there was absolute silence. Then we heard the freezer lid shutting, that breathy *whomp* as the two long rectangles of rubber seal bumped against one another. The cat let out a noise like a skidding car, pinballed off the front window then scaled the dresser, dislodging a small carriage clock which clanged and shattered as it hit the carpet.

Goodness me, said my father.

A naked, frost-covered toddler was standing in the kitchen doorway. The dying clock ticked off-kilter from behind the sofa. The child waddled across the rug and wrapped its arms round my knee. I could neither speak nor move. I felt the cold of its body and the wetness soaking through my jeans. Its way now clear, the cat erupted from the top of the dresser, arced over my father's head in the most athletic feat of its life and exited through the kitchen to the garden, tearing the cat-flap from its hinges by the sound of it.

The child pressed its head against my thigh.

See, said Terry, *I told you it was nothing to do with us.*

The child looked up at me. The child was shivering.

My parents still had an electric bar fire with plastic coals; little metal fans rotating in the heat of the hidden bulbs to create a wholly unconvincing fire-effect. Working entirely on autopilot, I stepped forward, leant down and flicked the switch on the side of the heater. The child let go of my leg and spread his hands in front of the elements as they started to glow orange in their silvered housing. There was an expanding patch of dark, damp carpet around his feet and the frost-fur which had covered him in the freezer was rapidly disappearing.

Then, very softly, he began to sing.

Lascia ch'io pianga
mia cruda sorte,
e che sospiri
la libertà.

Let me weep over my cruel fate. Almirena's aria from Act Two. The one Cecilia Bartoli had been singing two hours ago in the car. For a few moments the world went fuzzed and staticky as if someone hadn't tuned it in properly.

Is it a foreign child, asked my mother?

Il duolo infranga
queste ritorte…

Blimey, said my father.

I was still incapable of forming words.

The child turned and gripped the leg of my damp jeans in his little fist and tugged at me, trying to pull me in the direction of the hallway.

He wants you to take him home, chuckled Terry.

You're welcome to him, frankly, said my mother.

When I refused to move, the child let go and tottered out into the hallway by himself. I heard something shatter but I didn't work out what it was until the latch clicked and, after a few moments, a cool breeze blew into the room.

Has he gone now? asked Dad.

There was a *boop-boop* from outside and a faint double flash of indicator orange through the thin curtains.

He's got my car keys. I was finally able to talk. *He's got my fucking car keys.* I ran into the hallway. The door stood open and the key bowl lay in pieces on the bloodstained carpet. I stepped outside. I was too late. The child was opening the passenger door of the Fiat and climbing in. *Shit.* I stood, paralysed on the crazy paving. *Shitting shit.* A red light tracked slowly across the night sky. A drunken cyclist with no lights weaved past the house. Somewhere a cat yowled.

The child was dead, then he wasn't dead. He knew I'd been listening to *Rinaldo*. It seemed entirely possible that he had other powers at his disposal which had not yet been revealed. God forbid I left him here and he made his way to Clapham. I marched over to the car, slammed the passenger door and climbed into the driver's seat.

He gave me the keys and struggled for a few moments with the seatbelt. I leant round and strapped the lower part over his stomach, leaving the upper part flat against the seat behind his head. He seemed very pleased with this arrangement. I put the key into the ignition, lined up the rear-view mirror and saw Terry marching towards us carrying what I would later realise was my leather bag containing my wallet, phone and apartment keys which would have to be couriered to London at great expense. I inserted the first CD of the Harnoncourt *Clemenza* and put the car into gear and pulled out of the drive.

Drizzle became rain. We reached the ring-road and headed south, wipers on max, the oncoming headlights flaring wetly then whipping by. Warehouses and distribution hubs. I stared into the dark. I did not look at the child.

Just south of Peterborough we reached the end of the first CD. I ejected it, and glanced briefly at him while I slipped it back into the case. He had a forlorn look on his face. He knew what I was thinking. He knew it before I had even properly formulated the thought in my own mind. It seemed unavoidable now. What other options did I have?

He started to cry.

Seriously, I wouldn't waste your energy. There are forty-five reasons I decided not to have children, and that noise is pretty much number one.

The crying became sobbing. The self-pity, that was the straw which broke the camel's back. I was lucky the layby was there, or I would have pulled over onto the muddy verge and been forced to dispatch him with the hazard warning lights on and lorries honking and swerving through the rainy dark.

The sobbing became a wail.

I leant into the back and grabbed the chequered picnic rug, got out, walked round and opened the passenger door. I threw the rug over him to avoid any flesh-to-flesh contact, grabbed his head and hauled him into the driving rain. He was entirely defrosted by this stage so there were no hard bits left. I'll spare you the details. Suffice to say that Schuh Black Tempest boots are both sturdy and easy to clean, just like they said in the shop. Fortuitously there was a storm drain whose grating lifted easily. I stamped him into the shaft then put the grating back. I shoved the soiled rug into a waste bin and used up the entire pack of wet wipes from the glove compartment.

Being keyless I was forced to ring the bell. Raul let me in as if it were teatime and didn't ask for an explanation as to why I was soaking wet or why I'd driven through the night to get away from my family. He'd met them.

Your father?
You have a lot of blood vessels in your scalp, apparently.
You can tell me everything in the morning.

The consort performed at St Saviour's a couple of days later. A tiny venue but a full audience and wonderful acoustics. No Hotel California T-shirts, no bubblegum pink tracksuit trousers, just serious people who wanted to listen to something so beautifully crafted that it could mainline your heart four hundred and fifty years later.

A couple of *In Nomines* by Tye and Mundy, *A Song called Trumpets,* then I was on my feet. The feeling that never quite goes away, the prickle of fear dissolving as the viols rise under me and bear me aloft into that great stone space. Singing at first, then being sung by something larger and older than me, something larger and older than all of us.

> *O death, O death, rock me asleep,*
> *Bring me to quiet rest;*
> *Let pass my weary, guiltless ghost*
> *Out of my careful breast.*
> *Toll on the passing bell*
> *Ring out the doleful knell,*
> *let the sound my death tell.*
> *Death doth draw nigh.*
> *Sound my death dolefully, for now I die.*

Wretched

Lucie McKnight Hardy

IT'S THE GROWLING IN my stomach that makes my finger twitch on the trigger. I steady myself and readjust the angle of the tripod. The screen shows three of them, standing in a huddle. They're garbed in the semi-official uniform of the Wretched: filthy anoraks over woollen sweaters and tatty jeans, and each one is holding a lumpen bundle of bedding and possessions. I zoom in on the one on the left first: male, white. A beanie hat pulled down low over his forehead and an unkempt beard make it difficult to ascertain his age, but that's not my job. The red dot appears on my screen, and I swipe my finger and thumb across the touchpad to enlarge it, so that the whole of his face is covered by a pulsing circle.

I'm about to pull the trigger when he jerks his head to the side, and I have to readjust the bloody laser again. From the camera's vantage point on the second floor of the multi-storey car park I have a sweeping view across the ring road and down to the canal. It's late in the afternoon, and the concrete walls of the flyover merge with the sky.

I'm distracted, and I force myself to refocus the sight on the Wretched. Once I am sure he's not going to make any sudden movements, I squeeze. On my screen, his image is frozen, caught in the red circle. I quickly move the sight to the other two and *bam, ba*m, pick them off in quick succession. I double click on the touchpad and then hit *transmit*.

*

When I get home, I'm surprised to see that Cassie is up and about and has already made a start on dinner. She's standing at the sink, but she doesn't turn around when I open the door, even though, from the way her back stiffens, I know she's heard me. I stand for a moment, drinking her in. She's thinner than ever, and her shoulder blades point at me, sharp, through her thin cardigan.

There is protein frying on the hob. It's the usual smell: sweet, but with something sharp that clings to the back of the throat. They say it's from hanging it – like they do with beef – to tenderise it and make it more palatable. It took me a while to get my head around the idea of eating it, and at first Cassie refused to touch it. She said she'd decided to go vegetarian, and I'd gone along with it, and watched her getting thinner and thinner. She'd tried to grow vegetables on the window sill of the flat, but there wasn't enough natural light and the seeds hadn't even sprouted. After a couple of months she'd had to start eating the stuff or she would have starved, just like her sister. Sometimes, there's only so far your principles will get you.

Finally, she turns around and acknowledges me with a nod. Her skin is sallow and greasy, and pimples are sprouting on her forehead and chin. I get that pain in my chest when I see how sharp her cheekbones are, how hollow her eye sockets have become. She's still beautiful, though.

'How was work?' she asks, and I shrug.

'Fine.' I say. 'I got three targets, so that's good.' She winces and looks away. I go over and put a hand round her and when it settles on her back, I can count the notches of her spine with my fingers. She looks up at me and all of a sudden, I'm pleading with her.

'We need money to eat, Cass. Look at you. You're wasting away.' I notice that her hair is thinner, and there's the first sign of a bald patch on one temple. She sees me looking and puts up a hand to cover it. The movement is frail and childlike and I feel myself crumbling. 'It's not like I'm hurting them, Cass.' I'm begging now. 'I'm not the one rounding them up. I'm just collecting their data for the cops. They're the ones doing the bad stuff.'

She turns back to the sink and neither of us speaks for several minutes. I lay the table and slice the cooked protein. It oozes blood onto the chopping board: paler than beef, darker than pork. Cassie pours two glasses of water from the tap. I haven't eaten yet today and despite myself, my mouth is watering, and there is an acute tension in the underside of my jaw. We sit in silence and stare at our plates, hers with barely a few slices, mine with more.

'Bon appétit,' I say, in an attempt to lighten the mood. She keeps her eyes on her plate and stabs. Raises the fork to her mouth and chews, hard. The tendons in her neck stick out like ropes.

*

The next day is a Sunday – my day off – and I get up early and walk along the canal into town. Even though there's a fair wind, the sky is overcast and the stagnant water throws back flat, grey cloud. The towpath used to be a hotbed for the Wretched, but they seem to have moved on in the last few weeks, since the crackdown. In all honesty, it's unusual to see them out in daylight these days, so I'm feeling pretty smug about the ones I bagged yesterday.

My walk takes me past the Waitrose on Commercial

Street, but the barriers are still up after the raids last week, and there are armed guards at either side of the entrance, their machine guns slung across their chests like monstrous musical instruments. I keep my head down and try not to make eye contact.

I cross the river over the old bridge and there's Giggsy, standing outside the Bull and Flag, his dented mountain bike propped against the pebble-dashed wall. He gives me a grin, all brown teeth and cold sores.

'Alright, mate?' His voice is nasal and there's a trail of slime running down his upper lip. He must see me looking because he swipes at it with the back of his hand.

Giggsy's got a mate who works at the Waitrose. Not a fluffer or a shuffler or anything fancy like that. He's a van man, and so he's not meant to have access to the produce, but he's found a way of pilfering items from the pallets as they're unloading and he, in turn, unloads them onto Giggsy.

'What have you got, then, eh?' I'm trying to act cool, but really I'm shitting myself; I could go straight back inside for breaching my parole like this. Giggsy lets out a little high-pitched giggle.

'I-got-cake-I-got-cheese-I-got-bro-cco-li.' He sings this, rather than saying it, and I know he's taking the piss.

'How much?' I ask.

'Fifty for the lot,' he says, in his whiny voice, and he takes a rollie from behind his ear and puts it in his mouth.

'Christ, mate, that's a bit steep isn't it?' He takes the rollie back out of his mouth and jabs it in the air at me.

'If you want it, you pay, alright? Simple as. I got other customers, you know.'

I take out my wallet and turn around so he can't see as I peel off two twenties and a tenner. I got paid last night at the end of my shift and there's a fold of notes in there but it's not enough, not really, not if we're going to make up the rent this week. I hand over the money. Giggsy picks up the knapsack that's slung over the handlebars of his bike and hands me a paper bag from it. It's a lot smaller than I was expecting. He knows what I'm thinking, because he swings one leg over the bike and pushes himself off. He sets off over the bridge, and I think I can hear him shout, 'Loser,' but I can't be sure, as it's lost on the wind.

I hide the bag under my coat and head back towards home, looking forward to showing my loot to Cassie. I stop to turn up my collar against the wind and realise that I'm opposite the Waitrose. I risk a glance up. There's a woman in a designer jacket and high heels, her hair piled up in a manner even I know to be expensive. I guess that on the Value Index she'd be somewhere around a B65 or a C70. It's a game Cassie and I play – or used to play – whenever we were out: to try to guess from someone's appearance where they score on the Val-In.

From a patent leather handbag the woman takes out a purse, and from that she removes a card. The guard takes one hand off his machine gun and inspects the card closely. It's not quite the level of scrutiny you get at passport control, but it's still fairly rigorous. He even lets go of the machine gun and lets it hang from the strap around his shoulder, and uses a finger to rub at the surface of the card, making sure it's not a forgery. Finally, he takes a hand scanner from his back pocket and points it at the card, then he angles the scanner at the woman's face. She lifts her chin and looks straight ahead. He looks at the screen on the scanner and then nods and the woman walks into the store. Before she moves out of sight, I see her stoop to pick up a basket. The guard resumes his position, the machine gun hoisted across his midriff, and I'm aware of the rustling of the paper bag under my jacket as I turn onto the towpath.

The canal hasn't been used in years, and the water is still and oily and home only to empty drinks cans and bags for life.

There's a billboard high up on the side of an old factory on the other side. It's just one massive Union Jack, with a single sentence superimposed in stark black text:

MAKING OUR STREETS SAFE AGAIN.

It's ironic, really. That's the government's latest slogan, but hardly anyone risks going out at night these days, unless it's to do bad stuff or to go to work. They can say anything they like, though: all the billboards are owned by one company now. It happened fairly quickly. One firm bought out all its competitors, or forced them out of the market, and just kept expanding, while reinforcing the government message. Cassie said it was like a vaccine: by dripping minuscule amounts of poison into the public's consciousness via the billboards, society was being immunised against the realisation of what the government was doing. The same company that owns the billboards was also given the contracts to run the trains and the prisons, and then the hospitals.

I'm halfway along the towpath when I spot a pack of about a dozen masks twenty metres or so ahead. They're standing at the entrance to a building site, waiting for the foreman to arrive, I guess. I wonder about turning back and going the long way round, past the multi-storey, but they seem more afraid of me that I am of them, and they shrink back as I approach. I stop and take a good look at them, each one indistinguishable from the next, other than in height and build: black jeans, black hoodies, and a grey, moulded-plastic face mask. The only thing that sets them apart from one another is the QR codes tattooed on the backs of their hands, and even they all look the same to the untrained eye.

The general election had resulted in another landslide, and it wasn't long after that the first steps were taken towards the Initiative. Of course, no one knew what it was all about then. There was a big publicity campaign, inviting people to come forward to have their faces mapped by computers, and a 3D model was produced which, the company behind it announced, was the representation of the aggregated features of the volunteers – a literal portrait of British society. At first, it was claimed, an enormous sculpture would be produced – The Face of Britain – which would be displayed on the fourth plinth at Trafalgar Square, a kind of coming-together of all the different people who make up British society, a celebration of diversity. When this failed to materialise, the delays were put down to technical issues to do with the sculpting process, and then it was reported that some of the people involved had changed their minds about having their faces used in this way. One of the anti-government websites stuck its neck out and claimed that the data was being used to produce visors: twelve thousand identical grey moulded-plastic face shields. At the time this was neither confirmed nor denied, but not long afterwards the masks started to appear on the streets.

They're cowering away from me now, shrinking into the chain-link fence, and not for the first time I wonder if the rumours about what has been done to their faces are true.

*

When I get back Cassie is in bed, the curtains still closed, even though it's eleven o'clock. There's a pale light filtering through the thin curtains and it renders her fragile and vulnerable, like a fledgeling abandoned in a nest. I stand there, just watching her for a moment. She moves her legs under the covers and groans. I draw back the curtains and she rolls over, away from me.

'Look, Cass, look what I got us.' It's the rustle of the paper bag that makes her turn back round, and she opens her eyes and allows herself a smile when I empty the bag onto the bed and she sees the yellowing broccoli, the stale cake, the rubbery cheese. She reaches out and touches the bag, and then she places her hand on the back of mine and I know it's going to be alright.

*

When Cassie and I first got together I'd just been let out of prison. I'd been dumped, along with a dozen other ex-cons, under the railway arches, with just a sleeping bag and a couple of quid. A few of the others knew of an illicit charity that worked out of an empty shop on the ring road and ran a foodbank and I tagged along with them. Cassie was volunteering there and we got chatting. She wasn't that friendly at first, and kept herself to herself unless she had to organise the other volunteers or talk to customers: she'd stand at the back of the shop with a couple of the other helpers – a tall, bearded guy called Gav and a small, dumpy woman they just called AJ – and they'd be whispering furiously, or showing each other stuff on their phones. I started calling in every day just to see her, and eventually, when she did look up, she'd acknowledge me with a nod, and then a smile. Gav would give me the evils though, and it was obvious that he fancied her. With hindsight, I think it was the threat of competition from Gav that made me ask Cassie out so quickly, but even then it took a few weeks to persuade her to go for a coffee with me.

We'd agreed to meet at a café on the High Street. It was one of those perfect summer's days, the sky a brilliant, cloudless blue and the heat from the sun gentle and welcome, rather than harsh and oppressive. We sat at a table on the pavement and ordered iced coffees. I remember how Cassie wouldn't quite look at me at first, she just swirled her drink, looking down at the table, smiling. That was when I noticed the tattoo on her inner forearm, up near her elbow. It looked like the outline of a wave, a curve that rose up and curled over itself before flattening out again. It reminded me of a poster one of my cell mates used to have – a famous Japanese woodcutting he'd said, and he'd told me the artist's name, but I'd forgotten it. I was going to mention this to Cassie, and ask her about her tattoo, but she looked up and saw me staring. She pulled her sleeve down to cover it and went back to stirring her coffee.

I realised then that she was actually quite shy, that the person she was at the food bank – organising and instructing people, advising and directing – wasn't really her. There was a softness to her, an ethereal, waif-like quality that was at odds with the blurred, dark blue ink of the tattoo. It seemed incongruous - violent, even - against the faintly translucent flesh of her forearm.

'What was it like inside?' Her question surprised me. We'd been making small talk up until then – discussing our families and where we'd grown up – and it took me a couple of seconds to answer her.

'Not bad, I suppose,' I said eventually. 'Could have been worse. I just kept my head down and got on with it. As long as you don't get yourself into trouble, the time passes soon enough.' She nodded and went back to stirring her coffee.

'What were you in for?'

'Just a couple of bits of joyriding, graffiti, that sort of thing. It just all added up, and the last time was the straw that broke the camel's back, I guess. I got six months.' She nodded again, as though she was satisfied with the answer.

'What about you?' I asked. 'What do you do when you're not at the food bank?' She looked around her, at the other customers and the waitress and down at the pavement, as if she was trying to decide what to say. After a few moments, she looked back at me and opened her mouth to speak, but then, all of a sudden, she was grinning and looking over my shoulder. I turned to see that a tiny bird had landed on the back of the spare chair next to me, just a couple of feet away. Small and brown, it had flashes of paler brown on its wings and around its eyes. Cassie was beaming.

'A wren,' she said. 'I haven't seen one of those since I was a kid.' She was the happiest I'd seen anyone look in ages; her whole face had lit up, and her pleasure was contagious. I found myself laughing, and then she started, too. The bird looked at us as if we were nuts and flew off, but it had sparked something.

★

On Monday I'm on the late shift. Before I leave, I make Cassie a cup of tea and I've got the radio on because sometimes the silence of the flat is too much. She's having a lie down, which I know will merge with bedtime and she'll just doze on and off until I get back tomorrow. Something comes on the radio about a 25% reduction in the number of Wretched, and a corresponding increase in the number of Treated (the official term for masks). They interview the Social and Moral Justice Minister, who says that if it continues along these lines, the country will have eradicated the Wretched by 2030. Then someone from the opposition comes on, but they aren't really given a chance to respond. They just about manage to mention the escapes from the treatment centres, and the four Interims that are on the run, before the presenter cuts them off.

Cassie's asleep when I take in her tea, so I leave it on the nightstand with the last chunk of cake and give her a kiss on the forehead. There's a sheen of sweat there and she feels hot. I double lock the door on my way out.

★

After that first date at the café, Cassie and I started spending more time together. Nothing fancy, just a walk in the park, or meeting for a coffee. I suggested that maybe I should volunteer at the food bank, so we could see more of each other, but she didn't seem keen, and said I should concentrate on getting a paying job. Gav still looked daggers at me whenever I called in to walk Cassie home after she'd finished her shift, and even though she never said anything, I got the impression they might have had history. He always tried to act the hard man around me, puffing his chest out and pushing his shoulders back, all textbook tough guy stuff. It amused me, really - I think he felt threatened by my ex-con status. One afternoon, when Cassie was late because she was drawing up the inventory, Gav came out and did the classic thing of rolling up his shirt sleeves when he saw me, and that's when I saw his tattoo: a dark blue wave shape, curving up and over. The same design as Cassie's.

After we'd been seeing each other for about six months, she asked me to move in to her flat, and we had a bit of a celebration. Our Value Index had gone from an H12 (me: ex-con) and an E25 (Cassie: graduate, good employment prospects) to a collective E37 (part of the Val-In was aggregated for a couple who were co-habiting: the government thought it increased stability which led to greater productivity and thus value). We took our newly-issued Val-In card and spent a small fortune – by our standards – in the Tesco on the ring road, and gorged ourselves on fresh fruit and vegetables until there was juice running down our chins and our bellies were straining. I remember thinking at the time that it was Cassie who had got me here. She saved me. I was a hair's breadth from being like all the other ex-cons. Wretched.

At weekends, we'd go on protests together. It wasn't hardcore stuff, and certainly nothing illegal: the conditions of my parole meant I'd be chucked back inside straight away if I put a foot wrong. It was just waving placards as we wandered up and down the High Street along with Cassie's mates, or writing letters to our MP asking awkward questions about government policy – which were never answered. It wasn't much, but it was something, and we needed to feel that we were fighting back. Cassie, in particular, would get really angry that not enough people were doing anything. She said it was as though a collective apathy had blanketed the country, like a layer of ash had been deposited on everyone from a previously extinct volcano and rendered everyone immobile. Fossilised indifference, she called it.

*

A woman from the agency called on a Friday morning while Cassie was at the food bank. They had a job for me. She described the set-up at the flat, said that training would be provided to use the gear, and mentioned a wage that was peanuts. I knew immediately that Cassie would hate it, of course, and so I tried to tell the woman that I'd wait to see what else came along. She reminded me in a bored voice that accepting the first job I was offered, no matter what, was one of the conditions of my parole. Shit.

I met Cassie at work that afternoon and suggested a walk in the park; I didn't want to be confined to the flat when I told her about the job. It was one of those overcast winter's days, with the branches hanging low and leafless and a dampness in the air that wasn't rain, but would still saturate your clothes and your hair. Cassie had on a long, thick woollen coat and a huge grey knitted scarf, and she looked tiny and vulnerable in the enormous layers. I waited until we were standing at the duck pond, her favourite place in the park, even though there were no ducks left there anymore. The water was clouded with the green scum of algae.

At first she looked incredulous when I told her, and then she went ballistic.

'For fuck's sake. You'll be a part of the Initiative, don't you see? You'll be one of them.' She started pacing up and down the edge of the pond, hands clenched and eyes flashing. I was terrified she was going to dump me, ask me to move out. I'd been worrying about it all day.

'It's not my fault.' I started to recite the speech I'd prepared, even though I knew it sounded weak, pathetic. 'I have to take it or–'

'Yes, I know, they'll chuck you back inside,' she shouted. She stopped walking and turned away to stare out over the pond. The light was starting to fade by then and the water was flat and blank, reflecting an empty sky. She stood there for ages, completely still, and then after a while her shoulders started to shake. When she turned around, her eyes were wet. 'Well, I suppose we have no choice. You'll have to take it.' There was a bitterness in her voice I hadn't heard before, even when she was on one of her rants. I reached out to her, tried to put my hand on her shoulder but she pushed me away and ran off. I considered following her, then thought it was best if I left her to calm down.

I walked back to the flat along the High Street, conscious that it was almost dark and that Cassie was out on her own. By the time I got home I'd phoned her half a dozen times, and each time it had gone straight to voicemail. I hung my coat up and fried up some protein and ate it leaning against the kitchen worktop, feeling my jaw working mechanically against the spongy resistance. There was a bottle of tequila on top of the fridge that I'd got off Giggsy and we were saving for a special occasion, but I felt suddenly reckless and unscrewed the cap and downed a mouthful, and then another. Fuck her, I thought. It wasn't my fault. I had no choice in the matter: I had to take the job. Anyway, I didn't need to worry about Cassie – she'd be out with her mates from the food bank: fat AJ and that lanky twat Gav. Gav with the tattoo.

I grabbed a tumbler from the draining board and half filled it with tequila, then I sat at the kitchen table and picked up my phone. I didn't mean to snoop on her. I'd asked her a couple of times about her tattoo, but she'd always change the subject, fob me off. I'd never really pushed it, always felt that if she wanted to tell me she would. Now felt like a good time to do some research.

I spent a couple of hours on a reverse image search, drilling down through the vestiges of defunct websites, following dead links and getting lost down worm holes, all the time with half an eye out for a notification to tell me that Cassie had messaged me. By the time I found something, my eyes were raw and the tequila bottle was half empty.

It was a pretty inconclusive result, even I had to admit. It was a news site that hadn't been updated for a year or so, which seemed to consist mainly of articles about activists and what they'd done – a sort of fan club for anti-government disruptors. There was one article about the Reprieve hack, which rang a faint bell, and as I read on I found out why. When I was inside a group had hacked into the systems at the Ministry for Social and Moral Justice and taken down their databases, resulting in thousands of prisoners' records being wiped. It had been all that anyone had spoken about for weeks, all the cons wondering if their criminal records had been destroyed. The news site claimed that a group called Insurgency was behind the hack, but gave very little information about the group itself. It said that their main objective had been to disrupt the government's tech: hack into websites, force databases to crash, basically anything that would enable 'a tidal wave to rise up against the threat to democracy'. Its logo was a wave.

★

It was the snick of the front door closing that woke me. I was still sitting at the kitchen table, slumped forward, my neck twisted at an awkward angle, and I only just managed to sit upright when Cassie walked into the living room. My head felt heavy and sodden, and I couldn't remember if I should be angry or compliant. I decided the best policy was to let Cassie speak first.

She'd taken her coat and scarf off and looked fragile in her leggings and enormous boots. Her mascara was half-way down her cheeks. She didn't say anything for ages, and then she came over and slid onto my lap. I pushed the chair back from the table to make more room and she wrapped her arms around my neck and pushed her chin in under my ear.

'I'm sorry,' she said. 'I know it's not your fault.' I ran a hand through my hair and could feel how much I was sweating.

'I'm glad you're home, I said. 'I was worried about you.'

'I'm fine. I went to AJ's.' She sniffed. 'Have you been drinking?'

'Yeah, sorry. I fucked up.'

She smiled. 'It's OK. I never really liked tequila much, anyway.' She brought her arms back round and laid her hands in her lap. Her sleeve had ridden up and her tattoo was just visible, peeking out from the edge of the fabric. I reached out and touched it with the back of my finger, just lightly, a moth's touch. She flinched, and frowned slightly, but she didn't say anything or pull away.

Nothing else was mentioned about the argument, that night or the next day. There was a truce, an unspoken agreement. In fact the only trace of it ever having happened was my blistering hangover.

A few months after that evening Cassie got ill and had to stop working at the food bank, and quickly went downhill, day after day. Eventually, she couldn't leave the house and had to stop going out to meet her mates as well. The first thing we knew about being downgraded to a G15 on the Val-In was when the new card arrived in the post, along with directions to the processing centre and instructions for downloading the Protein Voucher app.

★

There's a café over the road from the tower block where the control room is, and if I'm on the late shift I always go there first and make my cup of tea last an hour. That way, I've done the walk through town while it's still light, and it's just a quick dash across the estate in time to start work. It's the usual guy behind the counter, and even though we've never made conversation, he'll start to pour the cuppa when he sees me come in. He seems nervous tonight, and his eyes keep flitting behind me to the door.

I'm blowing the steam off the top of my tea when my phone buzzes. It's Kenny, my supervisor.

LADS. TRIPLE PAY FOR ANYONE WHO NABS ONE OF THEM INTERIMS TONIGHT. GO FOR THE QR.

I sit up straight in my chair. I think of the vegetables and fruit I could buy for Cassie. Salad, even, and milk. If I was careful and didn't have any myself, she wouldn't have to eat protein for weeks. She might even get well again.

★

Some days, I find it difficult to remember what it was like before the Initiative was introduced. It seemed to come in gradually, the country being drip-fed new information in the weeks and months after the election. The first real sign of it was the early release of prisoners with less than a year to go on their sentences, in a bid, the government said, to ease over-crowding. No one seemed to be concerned about why so many ex-cons were let out all at once, at least not until it transpired that there were no support systems in place and they were just being dumped on the streets. As crime levels rose, so did the country's indignation. Some places adopted semi-official curfews, and for a while there was wide scale moral outrage. Eyebrows were raised in the press when the company that ran the prisons was given the job of turning the empty ones into treatment centres, but that, like everything else, didn't last long and was quickly subsumed into the national consciousness. And then there were the rumours, of course, about what went on in these places.

One of the left-wing websites published an exposé, alleging that there was intelligence profiling, with those at the higher end of the scale immediately deemed unsuitable for treatment; they would be sent directly to the processing centres. It was claimed that the Interims were dealt with in an appallingly demeaning fashion in order to break their will, in much the same way as wild horses would be 'broken' to make them more pliable: they needed to be made suitable for institutionalised work after they were released. There were rumours about what was done to them physically, to dehumanise them, but even the left-wing outlets wouldn't report on that.

*

The control room is in a flat in a derelict tower block next to the ring road. After I'd come to terms with the fact I had to take the job, I allowed myself to entertain the idea that it might be interesting – exciting even – and I had visions of being given a night scope camera and stalking my prey through all kinds of terrain, like a real-life assassin. Of course, I knew I'd never actually be killing anyone, and remembering these expectations makes me feel embarrassed as I let myself into the flat on the fourth floor. I'm sweating after walking up all the piss-stinking stairs because the piss-stinking lift doesn't work. My gear – a screen equipped with a laser sight and transmitter – is all set up in the bedroom of the flat. The bed is still there, a pink candlewick bedspread wrinkled over the surface. Not the hideout of a world-renowned assassin.

The camera I control is only half a mile away, but the signal from it is encrypted, and then bounced around the world, from one VPN to another, to make it more difficult for the sabs to intercept. On slow days, I like to imagine the footage ricocheting around the world, from one city to the next, before ending up here, in the control room, a blink of an eye later. I'm paid to sit on the bed (there's no chair) and just watch the screen until I see movement. The flat's been derelict for years and I open the window onto the tiny balcony to try to clear some of the smell. I settle down and wait.

I've been there for about twenty minutes, and I'm thinking about having a nap, when there's movement at the bottom left of the screen. I zoom the camera in using the touchpad, and the image on the screen is enlarged, but it turns out just to be a pair of cops. They're looking at their scanners, and I'm guessing they've just had a report of a sighting. They'll have access to a map, which will show the area in the immediate vicinity. Overlaid onto the map will be the locations of the Wretched that have just been sent in by people like me – people sat in grotty flats in derelict tower blocks all over the city, paid peanuts to monitor cameras and scan faces. The data we capture is logged onto the Initiative's main database at the same time as the facial recognition info is sent to the cops along with the location of the Wretched.

It's easy to round them up after that. Like shooting fish in a barrel.

The police move out of view of the camera, and I lie back on the bed, but it's only a matter of seconds before there's movement again, and a figure peels itself out of the shadows, as if it was waiting for the cops to go. It has the usual dark clothing and pale face of a mask, and I'm wondering whether to grass it up for being out after curfew when something makes me sit up. It's the face.

The face is not the grey moulded-plastic I've got used to seeing on the ones I've passed working on building sites or waiting to be let into factories. It's like flesh, but at the same time, it's not. I zoom the camera in and, on the screen, the face is suddenly magnified, massively enlarged, and my stomach heaves. There is no mask but it is no longer identifiable as an individual, or even as a human. And suddenly I realise that all the rumours about what goes on in the treatment centres are true. When some people said that the treatment involved cosmetic surgery to remove any identifying features from the faces of the Wretched, they were telling the truth. But it's worse than that. The eyes are merely two black holes in a flat space. Two nostrils remain but there is no nose, and it looks as though the lips have been cut away: there is only a hole, a black hole that should show teeth, but I suspect those have been removed as well. There is no blood – the wounds have healed – and as I zoom in even closer, what is left of the face appears on the high-def screen like melted wax.

I'm off the bed and I grab the scope. I'm thinking of the triple pay as I focus in on the Interim. The red dot lands squarely on its chest and I move it downwards until I find the back of its hand and I rest the laser on the QR code. I use the tracker pad to enlarge the dot until the red circle covers the entire code. I pull the trigger, and the image is frozen on the screen, capturing the data. I just have to double click and press *transmit* and the details will be sent to the police. The cops will be there in a matter of seconds. The Interim will be arrested and detained, not at the treatment centre – his escape has proven that he has the wrong personality profile for a mask. He'll be taken to the processing centre.

I'm trying to decide what to do, when there's movement in my peripheral vision, and I turn from the screen to the open door and the balcony.

There's a bird. It's landed on the metal balustrade, and it's watching me, its head at an angle. It's weird, because it's dark, and surely birds only come out in the day time? It's a tiny thing, fragile and delicate. Defenceless. It fluffs up its feathers, and hops from one foot to another, and that's when I recognise it as a wren.

My finger hovers over the touchpad.

Out of the Blue

David Constantine

1

AND THE BEST THING about this house, said Ronald, is the garden. And the best thing about the garden is that it's not overlooked. So saying, he took off his clothes and stretched out, face up, on the sun-lounger. Ten minutes front, he said. Ten minutes back. And then...

Still biddable, though less so than the time before, Angela likewise, but saying nothing, undressed, lay down within arm's reach on the second lounger and closed her eyes under the blue south-London sky.

Rami's still in Freetown, Ronald continued. Coming back tomorrow, in case you were wondering. Always gives me the key. Make yourself at home, he says. Very good of him, don't you think? If I'd had the breaks he's had, I'd have a place like this by now. He's off again next week: Dubai or Seattle or somewhere of the sort. So that's another opportunity. We're luckier than many in our situation, wouldn't you say?

Angela made no answer, which did not trouble Ronald. He mused softly upwards towards the heavens. Then he was silent. Must have dropped off, she thought. And he hasn't turned over though it's certainly ten minutes we've been facing up.

2

To the best of my knowledge, said Superintendent Malik, this is the first instance of a falling human body striking and killing a fellow mortal on the ground. But I am very much afraid it will not be the last. It was a tragedy waiting to happen. Since the Millennium, over London alone, a dozen persons have been reported as having fallen out of the sky. And very likely, in my view, there will have been others whose arrivals over woodland and wasteland have gone unreported. I shall leave to the experts a proper discussion of the how and the why of these enterprises, but it is common knowledge that more and more very desperate people, mostly young men, will, when all other means have failed, stow themselves away in the wheel-well of transcontinental airliners in the uncertain hope of making a safe landing and being granted asylum in a land they believe will be kinder than their own. A few, extremely brave and extremely lucky, have succeeded. Two brothers risked it in Kuala Lumpur in 2012. One lived and, I am reliably informed, now runs a small funeral parlour in the West Country. But the odds are stacked against you. You have a far better chance of survival putting out in a leaking and overcrowded dinghy in darkness and foul weather. In the undercarriage of a Boeing 787 there is very little room. You risk crushing by the wheels when they retract. You must make yourself small. You are starved of oxygen, you become unconscious. The temperature drops to around -60. You freeze, you are a block of ice when the trapdoor opens and over the land of your dreams you are evicted. As to the sunbather, for all the difference it would have made, he might as well have been hit by an asteroid as by a frozen asylum-seeker travelling with a terminal speed of about 120 mph.

In conclusion, said Superintendent Malik, I am well aware that there is a good deal of local interest in this event and some speculation that there might be more to it than meets the eye. Questions are being asked which I am not yet able, or at liberty, to answer. Enquiries are ongoing. But at the heart of the affair, he said, there lies a human tragedy. One man seeking to escape harm has died and, dead, has innocently slain a citizen of the land in which he hoped for sanctuary. The identity of the sunbather has been established by documents found among his clothes which were lying nearby. It will be announced in due course. All I shall say now is that he is not the householder. Very likely the asylum-seeker will never be identified. The airline has said it will pay for, and help with, the clean-up.

3

Angela had not been looking forward to sex with Ronald. The allure of it had not lasted, disappointment was setting in, and the beginnings of sadness (the bid had failed) and of remorse (she had done wrong, it had not really been what her body and soul wanted). Still, not to put the blame on him, not to hurt his feelings, she would have gone through with it one last time. But when she heard him holding forth into the sky and when he fell silent and seemed to have gone to sleep and to have forgotten that he should by now have been sunning his back, it had seemed to her this was the moment and she must very quietly gather up her clothes, get dressed indoors and make her escape. She would text him an excuse and an apology, and in a week or so end the affair, if possible without hard feelings. She felt she would be able to look him in the eye and say that much at least, should he ever ask her to explain herself, as well he might. But then came the thing beyond all likelihood or imagining. A frozen black young man fell out of the sky and with terrible speed and force measured his length on Ronald's pinkish nakedness. Smashed into him face to face. And neither was given even a split second's vision of the other before they merged.

4

That garden is indeed a private place. And besides, in that neighbourhood there is a good deal of buying and selling and multi-occupancy, people come and go and on the whole don't know much about who lives next door. A man might one day turn out to be a terrorist and the neighbours will say on television how amazed they are, he seemed a nice enough person, always said hello and smiled at the children. And a few streets away only last year an old lady lay dead in her bedroom best part of a fortnight and nobody knew. That sort of thing. Which says nothing bad about the local population and doesn't depreciate the house prices. Rami at No. 11, where the asylum-seeker fell to earth, the most anyone could have said about him was that he wasn't often there.

So far as people on the ground were concerned the stowaway in the Boeing Dreamliner had been falling for 3000 feet or so in total silence. Perhaps only at the very end was his coming audible and even then would anyone have been able to say what he was? This is London 2019, not London 1940 or 1944. The impact itself did of course make a noise, but not of breaking glass or the shattering of, say, a trellis. One neighbour, a Mr Suresh, new to the area, said he thought he heard a woman scream. But it was a while before two or three men together, curious to know, went round to the back fence and took a look. Unsure, they climbed over and took a closer look. Jesus, said the Englishman of the three. The only certain thing was the blood, a vast amount of it. The rest (its source) was a muddle.

Angela had gone. At the arrival and impact she had screamed, but then a great swipe of blood had drenched and silenced her. She could make no sense of the event. And as though it were not finished, as though she might still be in mortal danger, she gathered up her clothes, that lay in the lee of herself on the lounger, and ran naked and soiled indoors with them to the bathroom. Her comprehension lagged far behind; her thinking had halted at the decision to leave Ronald while he slept and text him on the bus that things henceforth would have to be different between them. She stood ice-cold in the shower and from top to toe sluiced herself clean with cold water. Her blue sundress was spattered, but not too obviously. It would do to get home in. She dressed, dried her hair, looked at herself in Rami's mirror. She could not fathom the she looking back at her. I'll do what I said I'd do, she said to it. And let herself out on to the street just as the emergency services were being directed towards the back entrance into the garden. Nobody accosted her. On the bus she composed the text to Ronald already decided in her head, and had almost pressed Send when two thoughts occurred to her: the first, he is dead; the second, I don't want them to know I was there. She deleted the message and in present time on an ordinary slow London bus felt perhaps what in very ancient times she would have felt as a wrongdoer or unlucky mortal whom the fiends and furies that inhabit the darkness below the earth's thin crust have elected to invade.

5

After school a couple of times a month, on the days when Angela saw Ronald (or before Ronald, in her bid for some happiness or consolation, one or other of his few predecessors), her son Michael, aged nine, whose father had left home soon after the birth, was collected by a friend to play with her boy for an hour or so. Angela would do the same for her, of course. Neither woman ever asked the other what she did with the free time, yet they were quite close friends. On the afternoon of the terrible event − which, she knew, had caused a rift through her life − Angela practised some everyday looks, gestures and phrases in the mirror, and when they were as lifelike as she could make them she left the house. What I can't tell, she said to herself, is whether it is obvious. But even if is, she thought, nobody can possibly know *what* it is. Fran may already have heard the news, of course. But she can't have any reason to connect it with me.

Yes, Fran had heard the news. So Angela said that she had heard it too. The boys haven't, Fran added, but I suppose they will soon enough. Yes, said Angela, it's always everywhere. My mum, said Fran, when she could still read the newspaper, she was forever looking up and saying, Aren't there some terrible things happen abroad? And she'd shake her head, in wonder and pity. But now, as you say, it's here, there and everywhere. Then Angela did look deep into her friend's eyes, but only in agreement, in a generalised horror and sorrow, and not in any plea to be allowed to confide and be comforted. I shan't ever confide, I shan't ever be comforted, she thought, as she walked home hand in hand with Michael, asking him what he had done at school and what he and T. J. had played at.

That night she drank some wine and took a sleeping tablet. The desolating thought that she would never be comforted mixed with the dread that she would be found out and would be known for ever as the woman who had been *there*, to commit adultery. And Michael at school would be known as the child of that woman. Would that be bearable? Would they not have to leave home and every familiar face and seek asylum among complete strangers? She allowed herself three nights of dosing and oblivion. Then she was a week devising ways and means of self-defence and self-assertion. Whatever else she was doing she was doing that. Like post-natal depression. Michael and I were on our own then too, she said. And the self in the mirror answered, This is worse. The crash-landing of a fugitive, the flesh and blood of him and of another man, in broad daylight, a yard away. My thorough soiling. And then like an identical twin sister, a naked woman screamed once and got to her feet and seized her clothes and ran indoors and cleansed herself from head to toe in icy water and went out like a normal citizen and caught a 49 bus and walked along a sunny street to the house of her friend who had been looking after her son and they chatted and she kept her secret. And in the days that followed, the sun still shone and she stood at the school gates with others who liked that part of the day when they stood chatting and watching out for the appearance of their young children. She asked herself would this twin sister do it all for her? Would she act out the part of a woman of thirty-three, a single mother, life at the best of times never easy, but doing bravely? Angela dearly hoped so. She hoped this twin of hers would see it through.

Then, three weeks into her new life, Angela received an email-letter from Ronald Elton's widow. It read: Dear Angela, I don't know whether this is a good thing I am doing or not. I've worried about it for a week and in the end I feel it might help. Will you meet me? I'll suggest somewhere if you say yes. Nice Superintendent Malik came round with the two things he could give me of Ron's belongings – one was his wallet and the other was his phone. I don't know whether the police looked at the phone. I doubt it. Mr Malik assured me that there's no criminal enquiry. Why should there be? He said it was 'an act of God'. So I trusted him when he told me that as far as the police are concerned, the matter is closed. I know it's not closed for you, Mrs Elton, he said. For which I thanked him. They won't be making any more statements and they won't speak to the press. So I feel sure that even if he did look at the phone he won't get in touch with any of Ron's contacts. So really I'm the only person who knows. I hope you will be brave enough to meet. I do feel it would help both of us. With my good wishes. Yours, Mercy Elton.

Angela read the letter again, and replied at once, without caution, as though something vital but fleeting were being offered her and she must prove her faith not just in the woman offering it but also, perhaps more, in herself, as fit for helping, able and willing to be helped. She wrote, Oh, Mercy, please, please, let's meet. I work three mornings a week when I've taken Michael to school but I could come somewhere on one of those days from, say 2, till about 4.30 because a friend will collect him to play with her little boy if I ask her in good time. And on the days when I don't work, which are Tuesday and Friday, I'd be free between about 9.30 and 2.30, without asking her. Where do you live? I'm in Kensington, in the bad part, not far from the horrible tower. Say where and when and I'll come. Do, please. Angela. She dispatched this answer, faster than a heart-beat. Then for the first time since Death smacked down beside her in the private garden she wept with abandon, uncontrollably.

Five minutes later the meeting was fixed. Angela washed her face and set off to fetch Michael, and T. J. with him for an hour or so.

6

It's a lovely name, Angela said. I don't know anyone else called Mercy. – I hated it myself, said Mercy. At school I wouldn't answer to it. I told everyone I was called Alice. My parents were Gospel people and changing my name was part of me saying no to them. They called my little brother Standfast. But I feel alright about it now. It says what we need from one another. Were you in love with Ronald? – I thought I was, Angela replied. I haven't been sure of my feelings, except for Michael, since his father left. But I thought I ought to keep trying. Now I don't think I will anymore. One thing nobody else could tell you, Mercy, is that Ronald fell asleep a couple of minutes before it happened. He was talking, to himself really, and then he went quiet and he was asleep. And in the short time left I decided I would get dressed and leave the house and text him from the bus to say I was very sorry but I couldn't continue with him the way it had been. And then the poor asylum-seeker fell out of the sky and killed him and covered me with blood and I grabbed my clothes and ran into the house. – Yes, said Mercy, that's another thing I decided not to tell you, not till we were face to face. I was afraid it would frighten you and you wouldn't come. Forgive me that dishonesty. – You spared me something. What was it? – That the police found blood on the second sun-lounger and footprints going into the house and in the hall and on the stairs and in the bathroom. So they knew that someone, probably a woman, had been in the garden with Ron. – I became an automaton, moving very quickly, Angela said. A sort of other self did what it had decided to do. On the bus I even wrote the text saying our relationship had to change. I only didn't send it because I remembered that he was dead. Also I didn't want anybody to know I had been there. How strange of me to think I could continue my life! But I couldn't think what else to do. – Mercy nodded. Then she said, When Superintendent Malik came to my house to give me Ron's few belongings, he told me they had seen the footprints and the blood inside the house. He looked me fully in the eyes when he said that. And he added, it made no difference, the case was closed, no crime had been committed, it was an act of God. – I had blood in my eyes, Mercy, and in my hair and in my mouth and up my nose, I swallowed it. Saying that, staring into Mercy's face, Angela began to shake. It was hot, I wanted to be freezing cold, the water in the shower wasn't cold enough. Her teeth chattered. Mercy pushed a glass of water across the table-top into her hands. Drink, she said. And put your feet flat on the floor. Keep them flat on the floor while you drink. Feel them firm on the floor. You are OK. We are here. This is a good place. See how people are smiling at one another and having conversations. They enjoy being here. And outside it is still sunny and under a blue sky the flowers and the trees are flourishing. Feel your feet on the floor in this café which is firm on the ground on the earth. We are in a safe place. You will be OK. Drink, it will pass, it is passing. See now: you are properly here again with someone who is your friend.

After a while Mercy said, Trauma is not the same as memory. When you remember something your brain has processed it and put it away. It has a sort of date-stamp on it. When you fetch it from that place, if it is an unhappy memory, of course you will suffer, but not so *presently*, it is past, it is at a little distance. But an event that traumatises you has not been processed, it has not been date-stamped and put into the past, it is there in you, alive, all the time, at any moment, by influences beyond your control, you may be seized back into it, in its full strength, as it was when the thing first wounded you. What work do you do, Angela? – Cleaning, Angela replied. First I was with an agency but now I just have a few people I work for and like and they seem to like me and trust me. Some of them are people I first went to when Michael was a baby and I had him with me in a sling while I worked and laid him down for a sleep when it was time and they were nice to him. Believe it or not, I like cleaning. It is quite satisfying when I leave a place looking better than I found it. Even though it will soon all need doing again. How did you come to marry Ronald? – I think he liked me for being black, Mercy replied. Or perhaps he liked the *idea* of me being black. We were fond of each other, we got on. Partly I still wanted to show my mother and father I was different from them. Much to their chagrin, it was some years before we married. And when we did I didn't quite know why. I think that at heart Ron, like a lot of men, was always rather frightened. He lived *serially*. I wonder if you noticed that? I mean he always needed to know, and even to tell somebody else, what he would be doing next and then next after that. Did you notice that? Angela admitted that almost the last words Ronald said to her as he took off his clothes and stretched out, face up, on the sun-lounger, were, Ten minutes front, ten minutes back, and then … 'Then' being sex, I suppose, said Mercy. I suppose it was, said Angela. – The spaces between doing things filled him with dread, said Mercy. Fortunately, he went to sleep at once after sex. – On the occasion in question he went to sleep without it, Angela said. Then she asked, What sort of people do you see and help them with their trauma? – People like the man who killed Ron, funnily enough. Even if against all the odds he had clung on and landed at Heathrow and been taken straight to hospital, he would have been traumatised, very likely by what he had endured at home, and then by the flight. I see people like him. So very many there are like him. When Superintendent Malik visited me with his sincere condolences he told me how little room there is in the wheel-well of even the biggest planes. The stowaway must curl for many hours in the foetal position. Mostly when the doors open he is unconscious or already dead and out he drops, like a stone. Yes, said kind Mr Malik, a grown man hides in there like a babe in the womb and as a stillbirth he is evicted. Then the Superintendent was embarrassed. I am forgetting myself, he said. Forgive me. I do not forget your bereavement. Then Mercy said, Will you let me try to help you, Angela? I want you to be my friend. Angela nodded. Since it happened I have felt myself to be bottomless pit of fear. I doubt I will become a very good friend but at least I will make you believe that I do want to be.

When I was six, said Mercy after a silence, my mother dressed me in a frilly white dress with white ankle socks and a white bow in my hair and put me in a choir with other girls my age and a bit older and in front of the congregation we had to sing 'Are you washed in the blood of the Lamb?', every single verse, and the congregation coming in for the refrain. All the mothers of the little girls were in tears and got congratulated. I thought I was chosen and it would be safe to die because I would certainly go straight to Heaven and be with Jesus. And I went around the house singing it for weeks until my dad said if I didn't shut up he'd belt me. Pretty soon I felt it was quite the most disgusting song any child could be made to sing and I added it to the list of things I swore I'd never forgive my Gospel parents. – But you did forgive them in the end. – Yes, I did and I accepted being called Mercy. But I still think 'Washed in the blood of the Lamb' is a pile of puke. – I'm not very religious either, said Angela. Excuse me a minute. And she stood up. – It's over there on the right, said Mercy.

When Angela came back, Mercy was looking away through the window. Angela thought she had never seen such sadness in a woman's face before. She sat down at the table and touched her hand. The funeral was three days ago, said Mercy.

The Coroner 'released the bodies', as they say, and there was a decent cremation of the two of them. The pathologist, so I heard, said it was impossible to be absolutely sure which was which and to separate one from the other. I asked could the ashes be scattered together and to my surprise the Director of the crem agreed. If that is what you wish, Mrs Elton, then of course, he said. So many thoroughly decent, kind and compassionate people I come across, Angela. And in this passage of my life more than ever. You will meet me again, won't you? We don't live really very far away. Do you have a photo of Michael you could show me? – Angela touched the screen of her phone. This is just a couple of months ago, she said. On his birthday in fact. Mercy studied it close and for a good while. He has a smile that might heal the world, she said. I don't give up hope of having a child of my own one day. I guess I'm about your age. Not old. I talk to women who have watched their children die of starvation and disease, or seen them killed by shrapnel, sniper-fire, falling masonry. We're not made to withstand what we do to one another. Shall we walk across the park to the tube station? I'm due back at work and you have to collect Michael from your friend's house. I do hope I will meet him before long.

Walking across the rather parched grass, Mercy continued talking, quite softly, as though to herself. It wasn't *meant* to be, she said. Angela leaned close, listening. Nothing is ever meant to be. Everything is always more or less an accident, for good or ill. Her tone was matter-of-fact, resigned. But here we are, said Angela. For months, even years, before the man fell out of the sky, I wasn't in my right life. I was becoming ashamed of myself. Then a thing happened that nobody could have imagined happening and a great crack went through my life causing it to have a before and after. And you will help me? I know better already, having been with you, what my life is like and also what it might be like.

You will teach me. I should like to be useful. Cleaning is *very* useful, said Mercy. I suppose it is, said Angela, More useful, then. And perhaps there are things I can give you in return.

The two women descended together into the underground, embraced, made promises, said, Goodbye for now, and into throngs of fellow-humans went their separate ways.

Extending the Family

Ramsey Campbell

'Is this Mr Lasky?'

'No, it's Cliff.'

'May I have a word with Mr Lasky?'

'Who's after him?'

'The name is Kenneth Trent. I'm looking at his house, or one of them.'

'Sounds like you've got a buyer, Mr L.'

Cliff's voice gives way to another. 'Sid Lasky.'

'Mr Lasky, Kenneth Trent. Could we talk about the property you meant to renovate?'

'Cliff tells me you're looking to buy.'

'I'm afraid that isn't me. I overlook your house. I don't suppose you could be letting anybody live there while it's in that state.'

'What's my house to do with you?'

'We met in the street once, don't you recall? You wanted an eye kept on it. That's why I have your number.'

'So what do you think you're seeing?'

'A baby and a little boy and presumably the father, except he doesn't look nearly old enough. You'll agree nobody like that should be in there.'

'I don't know anything about them, and I wonder if you

realise how hard squatters are to shift.'

'You'll need to, though, won't you? For the sake of your property if not for their sakes.'

'I'll be looking into it.'

'Better soon. I don't like how the father is behaving. Yes, you're being discussed.'

The last remark is aimed at the youth in the room Trent is looking down on. He would have expected Lasky to grasp this, but the old man demands 'With whom?'

'With you, Mr Lasky. We're talking about him.'

'I'm quite aware who's who. I'll do what's required in my own time and without seeking your approval, Mr whatever your name is.'

'Trent,' Trent says, but he's talking to himself. The youth at the window across the back yards – the closer one spread with rugs of turf that flank a flagged path to the alley, the other cluttered with rubble – has just finished mouthing at him, so that Trent could imagine the phone has been dubbing his voice, however imperfectly synchronised. On the far side of the room scattered with takeaway cartons, the baby in a spavined crib next to a drooping patch of wallpaper starts to wail as though it has been waiting for its father to fall silent. As the youth tramps to the crib he shouts 'Shut the curtains, Billy. Some old twat thinks we're his show to watch.'

Dropping his phone, on which Trent assumes he has been playing a game, the boy trudges to the window. His unhealthily pale face is a shrunken version of his father's – small reddish eyes, sharp nose and cheekbones, a pallid slash of a mouth. Why does it seem familiar? Was the father a pupil at one of the schools to which Trent was supplied in the last years of his career? As Billy stares up at him the boy's lips twist into a grimace Trent imagines him giving a teacher. The boy grabs one of the curtains that lend the window a gloomy penumbra and drags it across the glass, swinging monkey-like on it as it stutters halfway. The rail can't support even his meagre weight, and crashes to the floor.

'What did you do now, you little shit?' The father darts across the room to deal his fallen son a vicious kick. 'You shut up, Colum, or you'll get some too,' he tells the baby in his arms as it adds to the sounds of woe, and then he glares at Trent. 'Don't feel left out, you old twat. Got some for you as well.'

Trent won't be the first to look away. The youth needs to understand he's being watched, but this doesn't prevent him from turning on the boy, who has dodged out of reach. 'Give it a hug,' the youth tells him.

Trent thinks he's entrusting the baby to his son until the boy slouches to fetch a nippled bottle, which he fills from a carton of milk on the floor. As Billy sets about warming the bottle by pressing it against his chest the father says 'I'll be cleaning up the mucky little bastard.'

An April wind chills Trent's fingertips as he inches the sash of the window up to help him eavesdrop for the children's sake. He hears the baby's cries beyond the frosted glass of a bathroom window while water falters down a drain. Is there any hot water in that house? The transom of the frosted window jerks open, and a hand flings a soiled plastic nappy into the yard. The father dumps the baby in the cot while he finds a nappy somewhere out of sight, and pins the infant down with one hand on its chest until he succeeds in positioning the plastic. 'Give us the bottle,' he shouts, having fixed the adhesive tags.

Trent is afraid the milk may fail to quell the baby, but its silence lingers when the youth deposits his burden in the cot. 'Got to feed you too, have I?' he complains. 'You're not getting curry. Don't want you farting when I've got to have you in the bed.'

He types an order on his phone, and Trent feels as if the family he's compelled to watch has stolen his appetite. He mustn't starve himself, and he calls the Darling Dhal to deliver his dinner. When a doorbell rings he can't tell which building it's in. Perhaps it was both, because on returning to his apartment he sees dinner has arrived opposite as well. He dines out of cartons at a table near the window while the youth and his son sit gobbling on the floor, and comes back from binning the remains to find the father yelling at the boy for abandoning his meal. Trent is surrounded by shelves of books he has been meaning to find time to read at last, but now he feels unequal to any that might make demands on him. He falls back on a detective novel, only to be dogged by a fancy that Roger Ackroyd's doctor keeps uttering a word the father opposite appears unable to do without, a monotonous monosyllabic repetition that puts Trent in mind of the tuneless thumping of a stereo. Though he's reluctant to forsake his vigil, it eventually drives him to seek his bed.

His bedroom faces the other house, and he raises the window an inch. In the night he hears the boy's cries, which set off the younger brother's and provoke shouts of virtually inarticulate rage. Trent stumbles to the window but can see nothing in the unlit room across the yards. His pulse takes even longer to subside than the uproar does, and sleep stays clear of him long after the baby's wails have been exhausted. By the time he rises red-eyed he knows he has to make a call.

It oughtn't to be up to him to contact the authorities, and he recalls the last number he called. A voice answers almost at once – speaks, at any rate. 'It's your Mr Trent again.'

'That's who I am and no mistake. Mr Lasky, please.'

'He's not available right now.'

'Then who were you just talking to? Kindly put him on at once.'

'Don't worry, Cliff, I'll deal with him.' In a moment Lasky says 'What's your problem this time, Mr Trent?'

'I was wondering how soon you'll be looking into the situation we discussed.'

'When it suits me. In my own time. I thought I'd made that plain.'

Trent has stayed clear of the window so as not to be seen phoning, but ventures to it now. Just Billy is visible in the dilapidated room. Though the boy is intent on his phone, he glances up at once. 'The old twat's there again,' he shouts.

'That's an example of how your tenants are behaving, Mr Lasky.'

'I've not the least idea what you mean. They're no tenants of mine and not a thing to do with me.'

The father has come to his window, displaying the baby like a trophy if not a challenge. 'They're in your rooms,' Trent insists. 'That's not how anyone should live, let alone children. I believe the social services would agree.'

'If you're so concerned, why don't you pester them instead.'

'I should have thought you might want to talk to them yourself.'

Trent is distracted by a grotesque fancy that the youth is mouthing his words. The boy's lips and the baby's are moving as well, but he hears only his own voice until Lasky says 'You thought wrong.'

He's gone before Trent can speak again. The boy and his father are smirking as if they heard the call prove useless. The youth is still brandishing the baby, which makes Trent wary of worsening its situation, and he moves out of sight before he searches his phone for a number. The council switchboard makes him jab several keys as a requirement of rewarding him with a less artificial voice. 'I want to report a family in danger,' Trent says at once.

'Do you have a name and address for me?'

'I can tell you the address.' Trent gives it and says 'There's a boy about seven called Billy and a baby by the name of Colum, and a father too young for them.'

'It sounds like the Williams family again.' This isn't said to Trent, but she informs him 'We believe they're known to us.'

'You aren't telling me you've seen how they're living.'

'How are you saying that is, Mr...'

'Trent. Kenneth Trent. You wouldn't keep a dog in there. I can see it all from where I am.'

'When did Maggie visit them?' A hand muffles a discussion, and then the woman says 'Their worker happens to be in your area. We'll see if she has time to look in.'

'Do more than see,' Trent retorts, but only to himself. Surely he has time to use the bathroom while he awaits the intervention. Afterwards he's dressing in the bedroom when he hears a harsh shrill cry across the yards: 'Give me it now.' When it's repeated with exactly the same cadence he gathers it's the first line of a piece of music, though it doesn't sound much like one to him, and doing duty as a ringtone. He hears Williams answer the phone with a respectful attitude bordering on mockery, but he can't make out any words.

He's breakfasting on coffee and a bagel from which he had to scrape a tinge of greenish mould when a doorbell shrills. He sees Williams clutch the baby to his chest and shove his son out of the room, and then they appear beyond the frosted glass. Are they hiding from the social worker? They've grown so still that Trent could imagine he's staring at an impressionistic daub of a family group. He's willing them to betray some movement when his apartment doorbell summons him, and he stumps down the corpulently carpeted stairs to the front door. A woman is retreating across the concrete car park that used to be a garden. 'Can I assist you?' Trent calls.

She turns like a mime of reluctance. She's large-boned with a wide flat face suggestive of a poster for concern, and her plumpness may be designed to look maternal. 'Mr Trent?'

'Guilty as charged.'

'Maggie Renfrew.' She bustles to the doorstep before adding 'I understand you were in touch with us.'

'If you're the social people I was. I hope you're planning to take a good look at the situation I reported.'

'Just now the client's with his children in the park.'

'Is that what he told you when you rang to warn him you were visiting?' As her face grows professionally blank Trent says 'Come up and look.'

'I don't want to be late for my next service user.'

'It won't take a minute,' Trent pleads. 'Someone besides me needs to see.'

He's hoping the Williams family may have emerged from concealment, but the main room opposite is deserted. 'They're hiding in the bathroom,' he insists, 'keeping the baby quiet somehow.'

He strains his stinging eyes until they bring him hints of figures that can only be the lurkers in the bathroom. The social worker has already turned to him. 'I'm not sure what you're expecting me to see.'

'Look at the room they're all living in.' Trent jabs a finger at it, only to realise the angle of the sunlight has rendered the window as opaque as a screen awaiting a projection. 'Wait till the light goes,' he urges. 'You'll see what he's reduced his family to.'

'Approved accommodation will be found for them.' She's scrutinising Trent rather than the apartment opposite. 'And I've seen a young man trying to do his best for his family against very considerable odds,' she says. 'We can't all enjoy your advantages.'

'We must be thinking of two different people. If you trust

him that much, why did you go to the house when he'd told you he wasn't there?' As her face renews its blankness Trent says 'And do you know what happened to the mother, assuming there's only one?'

'There was, yes. I'm very much afraid she died.'

'Of what, if you don't mind my asking?'

'We don't give out that kind of information.'

'Then I'm guessing an overdose.'

'I can't spend any more time on this, Mr Trent. Please be advised the situation is in hand.'

She's making for the door when Trent glimpses movement beyond the frosted glass. 'I think they're coming out,' he cries. 'Watch and you may see them.'

She strides to the window and almost instantly away from it. 'There's nothing to see, Mr Trent,' she says and gives the room a longer look. 'Maybe you should keep your imagination for your books.'

'This has nothing to do with my imagination.'

'Then maybe it should have. Try imagining what it must be like to be Mr Williams and his family.'

'I had to do enough along those lines when I was teaching.'

On the stairs she offers him an afterthought. 'Maybe now it's time for you to learn.'

'I don't need to learn how to deal with his kind,' Trent tells the slam of the front door. The sunlight has unveiled the window opposite. Williams looks poised to dump or even drop the baby in the cot, but glances warily about and lays the infant down. When he meets Trent's eyes he utters several words Trent would never have permitted in a classroom, and then appears to mouth 'Give me it now.' It's his phone, and the screen or the caller's name lights up his face.

He mutters at the phone and then rounds on his son. 'Just going up the road. You stay with Colum,' he says, miming a backhand slap that makes the boy flinch. 'You can do whatever needs doing. About time you learned.'

Trent thinks he sounds too much like the social worker. The boy should be learning, but at school. Trent doesn't look away or even blink while he backs across the room as if he's imitating Williams and gropes behind him for an armchair. When he grasps its fat arms he finds it too cumbersome to drag, and has to dodge around it to shove it to the window. He sidles onto it and plants his fists on the windowsill, and sees Billy staring at him.

For a while the boy lets fly words he may well have learned from his father. Trent feels as if he has been trapped into competing not to blink. He has no idea how long they remain in their stance like tomcats paralysed by a confrontation, but eventually the baby starts to wail. The boy sneers at Trent before making for the cot, where he fumbles at the trousers of his grubby grey track suit. Trent lurches to his feet, hauling the window all the way up. 'Don't do that,' he shouts, 'you wretched creature.'

Perhaps he should have kept the last phrase to himself. He would have done his best in any classroom. The boy swings around, preceded by his flailing penis, and swaggers to the window while the baby continues to wail. Having forced the sash up, he directs an unhealthily orange stream in Trent's direction and waves the emptied member at him, then yanks up his trousers and sprawls on the floor with his phone, leaving the baby to howl.

While Trent dreads how the father may react, he's at least equally afraid to see the boy deal with the infant. Should he offer help? Even if this weren't met with contempt or worse, the boy would never let him in. He can only watch until his eyes smart and the images of boy and baby flicker like imperfect simulations – like the figure that throws the door open and grimaces savagely at the howls from the cot. 'Told you to fix him,' he shouts and deals the boy a kick that lifts him off the floor. Over the chorus of cries, Williams snatches the baby out of the cot and stomps with him to the bathroom.

He reappears with a used nappy in one of the hands that are holding the child. Having deposited the infant in the cot, he flings the nappy out of the window with such force that it lands in the yard of Trent's house. Soon clouds of smoke from offstage make the purpose of his recent outing clear. 'You're getting none,' he tells his elder son, who responds with a pitiful sniff. Smoke gathers over the cot, and an intense smell of cannabis seems to soften and expand Trent's skull. What may it be doing to the youngsters in the room? He keeps his phone out of sight while he jabs the emergency icon and asks for the police.

'I want to report a cannabis user.'

The voice representing the law sounds unimpressed. 'What were they doing?'

'He is right now. I can smell how much.'

'You need to be careful it doesn't affect you.' With little increase in enthusiasm she says 'What is the address?'

'His, you mean, obviously.' Trent supplies it and adds 'The name's Williams.'

'Not yours.'

'Of course not mine. I don't know the rest of it, but there's a small son Billy and a baby Colum.'

'We'll send someone as soon as we can. Please be aware the number you called is reserved for emergencies.'

'I'm looking at one. He's smoking in front of the children. If it can affect me as you suggest, it must be affecting them.'

'Have you contacted social services?'

'They were worse than useless. I'm hoping you won't be.'

Might this antagonise her? It doesn't matter so long as the police do their job. He rings off before she can ask for his details and grips the windowsill while he watches the apartment opposite. Extravagant masses of smoke drift over supine Billy's head to settle on the cot, and Trent has begun to feel time has slowed to the pace of the smoke when he hears a doorbell. Williams darts to the window, stubbing a fat cigarette out on his tongue before swallowing the remnant, and wafts at the air. He snarls at Billy as he almost trips over him on the way to stowing a plump translucent greenish package under the baby's mattress, and then he makes at not much speed to answer a protracted outburst of the doorbell.

The baby hasn't stirred by the time Williams reappears with a pair of police a good deal closer to his age than to Trent's. He looks so resolutely deferential that Trent is sure they'll see through the pretence, but they halt in the doorway while Williams indicates the cot, then loiter as he beckons to his son. Whatever they ask the boy, it makes everyone look at Trent. 'It was me all right,' he declares just as the police turn their backs to him. 'The cot,' he shouts, 'it's under there,' but they leave the apartment, taking Williams with them.

If they're arresting him, what will become of the children? The boy has fallen flat again to play on his phone, and the baby isn't moving. When the door opens Trent is ready to imagine his concern for them has brought someone to look after them, but the door lets Williams in. He stalks to the window to offer Trent a gesture to go with the words he sends, and then retrieves his prize from the cot. He's rolling another cigarette for Trent to see when they both hear a doorbell. It's in Trent's house.

As Trent opens the front door the police step forward in unison. 'We understand you called us,' the woman says.

'Mr Williams said so, did he? Then he told the truth for once. Couldn't you smell what he was up to? Why didn't you go in?'

'Because the youngest child isn't well,' her colleague says. 'We made the decision to let it sleep.'

Their superficial efficiency reminds Trent of head teachers of their age, quite a few of whom dismissed his experience. 'That was a ruse to keep you away. Didn't you hear me saying that was where he hid his drugs?'

'We saw no evidence of drug abuse.' As Trent makes to protest the policewoman says 'Is there some reason you haven't asked us in?'

'None whatsoever unless you object to books.'

'That would depend what kind they are.'

'What kind would they have to be?'

As though she has abandoned the subject she tells him 'Mr Williams says you made the allegation before he could contact us.'

'Why is anyone like him going to want you?' When she confines reproof to her eyes Trent says 'Contact you about what?'

'About your behaviour.' It's the policeman's turn to speak. 'He says you exposed yourself to his son.'

'Why, the lying little –' Trent manages to regain enough control to say 'I don't know which of them is lying, but the boy showed himself to me.' He's sure he senses contempt, which provokes him to demand 'Did Williams say he saw me? Then he's a bigger liar than I thought. He wasn't even there.'

Could they mistake this for an admission? Trent can't judge as the policewoman says 'We'll need your name.'

'Kenneth Trent, and I don't care who knows it. Maybe I should have all of theirs.'

'That isn't necessary,' the policeman says, adding a cautionary look. 'We may want to see you again.'

'I'm not the one you should be seeing,' Trent says, slamming the door with such force that he's afraid he may have roused the baby and the father's rage at it. Of course, he's thinking of the wrong house, though he can't recall who else lives in his. He hurries upstairs to find the entire Williams family waiting for him.

The boy is at the window with his father, who is holding up the baby like a doll. The sight leaves Trent barely able to think. Lasky should be faced with it, not him. He stubs a wincing finger on his phone as he drops into the chair. 'Speaking for Sid Lasky,' a voice informs him.

'I wonder if that means you're him.'

'This is Mr Lasky's phone. He isn't here right now.'

'You're Cliff again, are you? Just let him know I've called the social workers and the police. I imagine he'd rather they weren't seen at his house.'

Silence is the answer. Williams and Billy have been mouthing every one of his words, and their lips didn't stop moving even when his did. Throughout the conversation the father pumped the baby's arms up and down, causing its mouth to take ventriloquial shapes in its sleep. Why hasn't this wakened it? His fears for it prompt Trent to make another call. 'Can I speak to Maggie Renfrew urgently, please.'

'She's out visiting all day.'

Surely the woman isn't her, however similar she sounds. 'Then can you contact her? It's about the Williams case.'

'Did you phone earlier? It's Mr Trent, isn't it? Maggie has already made a visit.'

'Yes, to me. She didn't bother seeing them. I'm telling you those children are terribly at risk.' The family is imitating him again, another reason he's enraged. 'I can tell you who owns the property,' he says. 'Sid Lasky's the name. Surely if you people speak to him he'll have to help.'

'I don't know if that's likely.'

'You've had dealings with him too, have you? I rang his office earlier but I couldn't tell you if I reached him. His secretary, if that's who I spoke to, he's something of an obstructive type.'

'His secretary.'

'He calls himself Cliff. I did wonder if it could have been Lasky putting on a performance.'

'Mr Trent, Cliff is Mr Lasky's carer. Mr Lasky doesn't have an office any longer. He's in a home.'

Is she trying to confuse Trent? Certainly the figures mouthing at the edge of his vision are. 'It's being left to me, is it?' he says in a rage so intense it seems to blot out his surroundings. 'Don't anybody think I'm less than equal to it. I had to be the police and the social services even though they were never my job.'

He could almost fancy the watchers are mouthing his words before he utters them, forcing him to speak. The impression aggravates his fury, and as he shoves the chair backwards he feels the carpet rip. 'You did that, you wretches,' he cries and marches out of the house.

An alley leads alongside the suppressed garden and the nine-foot wall of the back yard opposite. The far half is carpeted with litter, and there are holes suggestive of embrasures in the yard wall. He hears Williams urging 'Come on' but has no idea whether this is aimed at him. The cracked concrete of the front garden of the other house is strewn with so many obstacles – the charred remains of a plastic bin, a child's deconstructed tricycle, oily fragments of at least one car – that they might be intended to deter intruders. He nearly trips up more than once as he limps to the front door.

Its rusty digits lie on the fractured doorstep. They've left their outlines on the scaly paint, and the house has the same number as his. None of the metal slots beside the grimy doorbells contain names. He would rather not ring any, but how else can he gain entry? Perhaps somebody other than Williams may let him in. He fumbles with his keys as if they're some kind of charm while he tries to decide which bells are least likely to belong to the apartment opposite his. How senile has he grown? Without thinking he's slipped his front-door key into the dislocated lock. Of course it won't work – but the unhinged door stumbles inwards.

Trent pads across the gloomy hall strewn with brown official envelopes and tiptoes rapidly up the splintered carpetless stairs. As he sets a cautious foot on the first-floor landing, which is barely lit by a dusty skylight, he hears Williams beyond the door ahead of him. 'He's here.'

He dashes across the landing to fling the door wide. 'Yes, I'm –'

His challenge peters out, because the room is empty – not just utterly bare but deserted. He reels towards the bathroom, which contains nothing but fixtures, all of them perilously damaged. A greasy kitchen is bereft of utensils apart from a pan brimming with scummy water. A loose board clatters underfoot as he totters across the main room. He's on his bewildered way out when he hears a series of sprawling thuds beyond the window. The Williams family is in his room.

As the father hurls handfuls of books at the floor Billy clambers up the shelves, on one of which the baby is pulling a paperback apart. 'Get out of there,' Trent shouts. 'Leave those alone.' When nobody even glances at him he flounders out of the room.

The stairs feel capable of collapsing beneath him, and so does the world. Dodging obstacles outside the house almost throws him on his face. At his front door he's seized by a fear that his key won't work. It admits him, and he struggles up the stairs to hear what he could imagine is a belated echo. 'He's here.'

'You won't escape me this time,' he vows, snatching out his phone. He'll take photographs of the intruders before he calls the police. He throws his door open, but the phone he's raising to capture the miscreants almost falls out of his unsteady hand. While the floor of his room is a mass of broken books, nobody is to be seen.

The bathroom and the kitchen are equally unoccupied. He picks his enraged way between the vandalised books to the window, but the apartment opposite is as empty as before. 'I'll find you,' he cries, only to stare at the task that surrounds him. He's stooping to retrieve a relatively undamaged volume when he catches sight of a solitary page on the floor.

It isn't from any of the books, unless it was hidden inside one. It has been torn out of a diary. Although the date printed at the top is more than sixty years old, he recognises the teenage handwriting all too well, and the aggressively adolescent style of the entry. *smoked too much weed today – remembered stuff i must have wanted to forget – had to keep an eye on little cousin Gus – needed to pee so much i nearly did on him because he was a pain – peed out of window instead and neighbour saw, so i peed at him – see if more dope lets me forget again –*

He tries to be dismayed just by the immaturity of the handwriting. Perhaps that was caused by the drug. The thought can't fend off the shame of what he read, and he can only hope it leaves him again soon. The inside of his head feels as if it's sliding into a dark pit, and he's barely able to waver over to the chair. He slumps in it, clutching his phone while he gropes at a number on the screen. 'Cliff,' he pleads. 'Come and take me where I have to live.'

About the Authors

Bernardine Bishop (1939-2013) was an English novelist, teacher and psychotherapist. In 1960 she was the youngest witness in the Lady Chatterley Trial. Her first novel, *Perspectives*, was published by Hutchinson in 1961, and her second *Playing House* in 1963. During a half-century break between publishing her first two novels and her third, the 2013 Costa prize-nominated *Unexpected Lessons In Love*, she brought up a family, taught, and practised as a psychotherapist.

Alan Beard writes stories and flash fiction. He has published two collections, *Taking Doreen Out of the Sky* (Picador, 1999) and *You Don't Have to Say* (Tindal Street Press, 2010). He won the Tom-Gallon award for best short story, and his work has been broadcast on BBC Radio 4 and appeared in *Best British Short Stories 2011* (Salt), *Best Short Stories* (Heinemann, 1991), and *The Book of Birmingham* (Comma, 2018), as well as in numerous UK, US and Canadian magazines.

David Constantine has published several volumes of poetry, and two novels (most recently *The Life-Writer*) as well as five short story collections: *Back at the Spike* (1994), the highly acclaimed *Under the Dam* (2005), *The Shieling* (2009), *Tea at the Midland* (2012), and *The Dressing-Up Box* (2019), as well as *In Another Country: Selected Stories* (2015), the title story of which was adapted by Andrew Haigh into *45 Years* – an Oscar-nominated film, and starring Tom Courtenay and Charlotte

Rampling. He is the winner of the BBC National Short Story Award (2010) and the Frank O'Connor International Short Story Award (2013). He is also translator of Hölderlin, Brecht, Goethe, Kleist, Michaux and Jaccottet. He lives in Oxford.

Ramsey Campbell is described by the Oxford Companion to English Literature as 'Britain's most respected living horror writer'. He is the author of over 30 novels (most recently *The Way of the Worm* (2018) and *The Wise Friend* (2020), six novellas, and hundreds of short stories, many of them widely considered classics in the field and winners of multiple literary awards.

Margaret Drabble was born in 1939 in Sheffield and educated at Newnham College, Cambridge. She had a very brief career as an actor with the Royal Shakespeare Company, before taking to fiction. Her first novel, *A Summer Birdcage,* was published in 1963, and her nineteenth and most recent, *The Dark Flood Rises,* in 2016. She also edited two editions of *The Oxford Companion to English Literature* (1985, 2000). She is married to the biographer Michael Holroyd and lives in London and Somerset.

Karen Featherstone is a screenwriter and playwright, as well as a prose writer. She has written storylines for *Coronation Street* and *Emmerdale* and her work has been featured at the National Theatre Studio and broadcast by Channel 4. A Northern Writers' Award winner, her stories have been published by Retreat West Books, Mslexia and Otranto House.

Saleem Haddad (born 1983) is the author of the novel, *Guapa* (2016), which won the 2017 Polari Prize and was awarded a Stonewall Honour. His essays have appeared in

Slate, The Daily Beast, LitHub, The Baffler and the *LARB*, among other places, and his short fiction in *Palestine + 100* (Comma, 2019). He lives between Lisbon and Beirut.

Mark Haddon's first novel for adults was the multi-award-winning *The Curious Incident of the Dog in the Night-Time* (2003), which was later adapted by Simon Stephens into a prize-winning play. His subsequent novels include *A Spot of Bother* (2006) and *The Red House* (2012). He has written for TV and radio and published one collection of poetry, *The Talking Horse, the Sad Girl and the Village Under the Sea*. His play, *Polar Bears*, was produced at the Donmar in 2010. His short stories have been shortlisted for the Sunday Times EFG Short Story Award, the O'Henry Prize, and the BBC National Short Story Award. *The Pier Falls*, his first collection of short stories, was published by Cape in 2016.

Gaia Holmes is a freelance writer and creative writing tutor who works with schools, universities, libraries and other community groups throughout the West Yorkshire region. She runs 'Igniting The Spark', a weekly writing workshop at Dean Clough, Halifax, and is the co-host of 'MUSE-LI', an online writing group. She has had three full length poetry collections published by Comma Press: *Dr James Graham's Celestial Bed* (2006) *Lifting The Piano With One Hand* (2013), *Where The Road Runs Out* (2018) and *Tales from the Tachograph*, a collaborative work with Winston Plowes (Calder Valley Poetry, 2017). She is currently turning her attention towards writing short stories.

Matthew Holness is a writer, director and actor. He created and starred in *Garth Marenghi's Darkplace* for Channel 4 and his short films include *A Gun For George*, *The Snipist* and *Smutch*. His stories have appeared in *Phobic, The New Uncanny* and *Protest* (all Comma). In 2018 he directed his first feature film, *Possum*, based on his contribution to *The New Uncanny*.

Meave Haughey is a short story writer based in Birmingham. Recent stories have been published in Comma Press's ebook, *Forecast: New Writing from Birmingham*, Doestoevsky Wannabe's *Love Bites: Fiction Inspired by Pete Shelley and Buzzcocks* and in *Birmingham,* from the Dostoevsky Wannabe Cities series.

Adam Marek writes short stories about the futuristic and the fantastical colliding with everyday life. His two collections, *The Stone Thrower* and *Instruction Manual for Swallowing,* are published by Comma Press. His stories have appeared on BBC Radio 4, and in many magazines and anthologies, including *The Penguin Book of the British Short Story*. He is an Arts Foundation Short Story Fellow. He regularly teaches creative writing for Arvon, and occasionally works with SciFutures, using storytelling to help prototype the future. Visit Adam at www.adammarek.co.uk

Lucie McKnight Hardy's stories have featured in various publications, including *Best British Short Stories 2019, Black Static, The Lonely Crowd,* and as a limited edition chapbook from Nightjar Press. Her debut novel, *Water Shall Refuse Them* (Dead Ink Books, 2019) was shortlisted for the Mslexia Novel Competition and longlisted for the Caledonia Novel Award. *Dead Relatives*, her short story collection, will be published in late 2021, again by Dead Ink Books.

Mike Nelson is an installation artist who has twice been nominated for the Turner Prize (2001 and 2007), and in 2011 represented Britain at the Venice Biennale. Nelson's installations typically exist only for the time period of the exhibition they were made for. They are generally extended labyrinths, which the viewer is free to find their own way through, and where the locations of the exit and entrance are often difficult to determine. His *The Deliverance and the Patience* in a former brewery on the Giudecca was in the 2001 Venice Biennale. In September 2007, his exhibition *A Psychic Vacuum* was held in the old Essex Street Market, New York. He is represented by Matt's Gallery, London; 303 Gallery, New York; and Galleria Franco Noero, Turin.

Before **Christine Poulson** turned to writing fiction, she was an academic with a PhD in History of Art. Her Cassandra James mysteries are set in Cambridge. *Deep Water*, the first in a new series featuring medical researcher Katie Flanagan, appeared in 2016. The second, *Cold, Cold Heart*, set in Antarctica, came out in 2018, and the third, *An Air That Kills*, in 2019. Her short stories have been published in Comma Press anthologies, *Ellery Queen Mystery Magazine*, Crime Writers' Association anthologies, the *Mammoth Book of Best British Mysteries* and elsewhere. They have been short-listed for the Short Mystery Fiction Derringer, the Margery Allingham Prize, and the CWA Short Story Dagger.

Sarah Schofield's stories have been published in *Lemistry, Bio-Punk, Thought X, Beta Life, Spindles* and *Conradology* (all Comma Press) *Wall: Nine Stories from Edge Hill Writers,* (EHUP) *Best of British Short Stories 2020* (Salt) *Spilling Ink Flash Fiction Anthology, Back and Beyond* Arts Publication, Litfest's *The Language of Footprints, Synaesthesia Magazine, Lakeview International Journal, Woman's Weekly* and others. She has been shortlisted on the Bridport and the Guardian Travel Writing Competition and won the Orange New Voices Prize, Writer's Inc and The Calderdale Fiction Prize. An excerpt from her story 'The Bactogarden' featured on BBC Radio 4's Open Book. Sarah is an Associate Tutor of Creative Writing at

Edge Hill University and runs writing courses and workshops in a variety of community settings. Her debut short story collection is due out in 2021 with Comma Press.

Paul Theroux is an American travel writer and novelist, whose latest travel book is *On the Plain of Snakes - A Mexican Journey* (2019). He is the author of 27 novels – including *The Mosquito Coast* (1981), which won the 1981 James Tait Black Memorial Prize and was adapted for the 1986 movie of the same name, and *Doctor Slaughter* (1984), which was filmed as *Half Moon Street* (1986) – as well as six separate collections of short stories, most recently *Mr Bones: Twenty Stories (2014).*

Lara Williams is the author of the short story collection *Treats*, which was shortlisted for the Republic of Consciousness Prize, the Edinburgh First Book Award and the Saboteur Awards. Her debut novel *Supper Club* has been translated into five languages, won the *Guardian* 'Not the Booker' Prize and was listed as a Book of the Year 2019 by *TIME, Vogue* and other publications. She lives in Manchester and is a contributor to the *Guardian, Independent, Times Literary Supplement, Vice, Dazed* and others.

Gerard Woodward is a novelist, poet and short story writer, best known for his trilogy of novels concerning the troubled Jones family, *August* (shortlisted for the Whitbread Book Award), *I'll Go to Bed at Noon* (shortlisted for the 2004 Man-Booker Prize), and *A Curious Earth* (2008). He is the author of six collections of poetry and two collections of short fiction, *The Caravan Thieves* (2007) and *Legoland* (2016). His latest publication is the novel *The Paper Lovers.*

Special Thanks

We would like to thank Imogen Tyler for her enthusiasm, energy and input throughout the project, as well as for her original inspiration. We would also like to thank Dave and Eirinn Shrimpton, Ella McKenzie, C.D. Rose, John D. Rutter, Andy Murray, Andrew Chambers and Matt Bishop, all of whom helped in crucial ways. Payment for the opening story went to The Bernardine Bishop Appeal, which was set up in conjunction with the charity CLIC Sargent, helping children, young people and their families suffering the effects of cancer. To donate go to www.clicsargent.org.uk

The New Uncanny
Tales of Unease

Ra Page & Sarah Eyre (eds.)

WINNER OF THE SHIRLEY JACKSON AWARD

In 1919 Sigmund Freud published an essay that delved deep into the tradition of horror writing and claimed to understand one of its darkest tricks. Like a mad scientist, he performed literary vivisection on a still-breathing body of work, exploring its inner anatomy, and pulling out mysterious organs for classification. His aim: to present to the world a complete theory of 'das unheimliche', the uncanny.

In the spirit of this great experiment, 14 leading authors have here been challenged to write fresh fictional interpretations of what the uncanny might mean in the 21st century, to update Freud's famous checklist of what gives us the creeps, and to give the hulking canon of uncanny fiction a shot in the arm, a shock to the neck-bolts....

'Delightful and disturbing' – *Independent on Sunday*

'A masterclass in understated creepiness' – *Time Out*

ISBN: 978-1-90558-318-8
£9.99